Ronnie Knight and Peter ....id sixties in London's West End, though their paths were to cross many times during the next thirty years, as they both mixed with the wealthy, the famous and the infamous. Ronnie Knight, previously married to Barbara Windsor, is currently serving a seven year sentence and both men have clashed with the law throughout their respective careers. *Signed Confession* is their debut thriller, inspired by an actual event that one of them was heavily involved with.

Signed Confession

RONNIE KNIGHT & PETER PITTS

POCKET BOOKS

LONDON · SYDNEY · NEW YORK · TOKYO · SINGAPORE · TORONTO

First published in Great Britain by Pocket Books, 1996
An imprint of Simon & Schuster Ltd
A Viacom Company

Simon & Schuster Ltd
West Garden Place
Kendal Street
London W2 2AQ

Simon & Schuster of Australia Pty Ltd
Sydney

A CIP catalogue record for this book is available
from the British Library

ISBN 0-671-85569-7

Typeset in Sabon 11/13pt by
Palimpsest Book Production Limited, Polmont, Stirlingshire
Printed and bound in Great Britain by
Caledonian International Book Manufacturing Ltd, Glasgow

We would like to thank the following people for their help and encouragement in the writing and successful publication of this book:

Helen Simpson, Joan Deitch, Helen Donlon and – lastly but by no means least – Jim Lumley, a true friend.

I

Phillip Ross dipped the clutch, dropped down to third gear and swung the Range Rover right-handed into Kennington Lane. At nearly three in the morning, even a Saturday morning, there was virtually no traffic and he was able to accelerate hard away. He glanced affectionately at the beautiful young woman stretched out in the fully reclined passenger seat. Her eyes were closed and she was half asleep.

Light from the streetlamps gleamed on her long fair hair, which was fanned out over the leather upholstery and across her shoulders. One corner of her mouth lifted in a half-smile, as though she was aware of his attention. Then her smile widened and her eyes opened, sea-green and sparkling.

She looked at Phillip for a second. 'I could feel you staring at me,' she said.

Phillip smiled and returned his full attention to the road. 'Sorry,' he said lightly. 'You looked so at peace and contented, and so very pretty. I couldn't take my eyes off you.'

'Keep your eyes on the road,' she said, with mock sternness. 'It's been a wonderful evening. The last thing we want is to have an accident.'

'Yes, ma'am.' Phillip snapped a crisp salute, glanced at her again and said, 'We'll soon be back at the club.'

'Oh great.' Julie sat upright and adjusted the seat. She smoothed the grey satin of her skirt down over her knees, and brushed her hair back from her face. 'I do hope Gary managed OK tonight without the big cheese around to peer over his shoulder and offer good advice all the time,' she said mischievously.

Gary Thompson was not only Julie's brother but Phillip's best friend. He was also the manager of Phillip's newly opened nightclub, the Starlight Club, and the reason it had taken Phillip so long to ask Julie for a date.

Gary was fiercely protective of his sister, and had been since her teens, when every young buck in their home town of Dover had taken an interest in the beautiful teenager and started to hang around her, trying to persuade her to accompany them to the back of the bicycle sheds or into the bushes of the local park. He'd told them in no uncertain terms that they'd answer to him if they treated her with anything less than respect. If they touched her, he'd beat them to pulp. His reputation as a fearless and ferocious fighter, plus a couple of good

2

hidings handed out to young studs who ignored his warnings, had had the desired effect. Not until she was eighteen and had been going out with Mark, her first steady boyfriend, for several months did Julie decide that her relationship with Mark was serious enough for them to sleep together.

Even so, Phillip recalled, Gary was furious when he and Phillip came back on leave from an army posting in Germany and he found out. He'd raged that he'd kill the bastard who'd seduced his sister, and it had taken Phillip some time to calm him down and make him see sense.

'Julie's not a child any more, mate,' he said. 'She's a young woman now, and she has a mind and a life of her own. She'll decide what she wants to do and who she wants to do it with.' He'd smiled wrily to himself. His words applied to himself as much as to Gary: he'd fancied Julie from the moment he'd set eyes on her, and over the years had come to care a great deal about her. But she'd chosen Mark, not him, and he had to swallow his frustration and jealousy.

Besides, Gary had said many times, 'I don't want Julie to marry a bloody soldier and end up on an army base or in an army house, waiting months for her husband to come home, worrying whether he'll come back alive or in a fucking coffin.'

Phillip reckoned that until he was a civilian again he had no right to show his feelings for her. But, when Julie and Mark broke up, he determined to seize his chance, and resigned from the army. No one else was going to steal a march on him this time; he'd fight like hell for her if he had to.

Being no fool, Gary had read the situation accurately, and was secretly delighted. It came as no surprise to him when, on learning of their plans for the nightclub, Julie had volunteered to take six months' leave from her job as a supply teacher to help them get the club ready.

'I'll do anything,' she said eagerly. 'I can do all the paperwork, I can paint, choose wallpaper and furnishings, help interview staff – anything.'

It had taken all Phillips's savings, his gratuity from the army and a massive bank loan to buy the lease, and fit the club out to a suitably high standard. He, Gary and Julie had worked like dray-horses, doing almost everything themselves to keep costs down, putting in long, long hours seven days a week.

But it had worked. The net profits, after all overheads, were a little over a thousand pounds the week the Starlight opened; thirteen hundred the next week. Now in its third week, the club was looking good – Phillip mentally crossed his fingers – and new applications for membership were coming in by the bagful every day.

There had been good attendances in the early part of the week. But Friday and Saturday were the vital nights. The Starlight had to be full to keep up its profitability, so, although Phillip was sorry his first real date with Julie was nearly over, part of him itched to know how things had gone and what the

4

night's takings were. There'd be plenty of time for other dates, and anyway he knew she'd understand. He suspected that she was equally eager to see Gary and learn how he'd got on. The club meant just about as much to her as it did to them.

Gary stowed the night's takings in a canvas cash bag, folded the top over and tossed the bag on to the counter of the reception kiosk. He grinned to himself. Better than last Friday by three hundred pounds, he thought happily. That should please Phil, and stop him worrying so bloody much.

He glanced at his watch and shrugged. Phillip and Julie had promised to be back at the Starlight by three a.m., and they should show at any minute.

Just time for a last check around, he thought, as he stepped out of the kiosk into the dimly lit, mirrored entrance foyer. He smiled as he recalled having to push Phillip and his sister through the doors of the club, with assurances that he could hold the place together without their help for just one evening. Gary knew that Phillip badly needed a break. He'd taken virtually no time off during all the months of hard grind getting the club ready to open.

As he turned, Gary caught sight of himself in one of the mirrors. He was in good shape. The loose-fitting trousers and baggy jumper made him look short and fat, as though he'd be a pushover for anyone who wanted a fight. He grinned knowingly. At five foot eight he weighed two hundred and thirty pounds, eight ounces of which was fat. Gary Thompson was built like a Sherman tank. Layer upon layer of muscle – built up over a period of twelve years' hard physical training in the British Army, including a two-year tour of duty in the SAS, where he had met Phillip Ross and forged a lifelong friendship – made Gary look almost square.

His bulldog face creased into a smile, as he thought back to the main reason why Phillip had been reluctant to leave him alone to run the club. The first Friday night, just before two a.m., four hard-faced men had arrived, then, with smiling faces, had demanded the night's takings for protection services. They'd explained that they would be around every Friday to collect, and assured Phillip he'd have no trouble – 'like having the place burnt to the ground' – if he paid up.

Phillip had listened patiently, nodded and smiled in understanding in all the right places. Then, still smiling, he'd informed them politely that he didn't need their services and suggested they leave the premises to try elsewhere.

The main spokesman for the four men, who happened to be three inches taller than Phillip's six feet, took Phillip's quiet, unaggressive manner wrongly. He made the mistake of adding emphasis to his request by screwing up Phillip's lapel in a big, hairy fist, then dragging him so close that their noses almost touched. The thug's smile was a vicious snarl, which immediately turned to a mixture of surprise and excruciating pain as Phillip jabbed a karate knife-hand deep into his solar plexus, his fingers lancing up under the breastbone into a major nerve centre.

The man dropped like a felled tree. But not before Phillip had caught him on the way down with a short, straight left jab to his jaw, with a sickening snapping and crunching as bone and teeth crumbled under the impact.

The remaining three men launched themselves into an attack, which was swiftly subdued by the combined efforts of Phillip's and Gary's flying fists and feet. It was all over in less than twenty seconds. The four men were carried outside and laid in a neat row in a dark corner of the car park, to come back to consciousness in their own time.

The men had gone by three-fifteen a.m., when Phillip and Gary locked up for the night. They debated informing the police, but Phillip concluded it was best not to bring them into the affair, in case it should be held against the club in the future. It had been touch and go getting the liquor licence in the first place. Only Phillip's excellent army record, and the fact that he had been awarded the DCM while serving with the SAS during the Falklands War, had persuaded the court to grant him a late-night drinking licence.

He and Gary had laughed about the incident. It had, in a way, been a breath of fresh air in the safe, dull life of civvy street.

Their deep comradeship had been cemented on a lonely hilltop in the Falklands, in June 1982. They had shared the same hole in the ground for days on end, in the storms and gales of the bleak and desolate land. Then, on 11 June, they had attacked no fewer than five machine-gun posts of the Argentine army, giving each other covering fire as they advanced from one scrap of cover to the next. That day Phillip received the scar that marred his lean face. A piece of flying shrapnel had opened his face just below the left eye, in a two-inch gash, deep to the bone. His body had been peppered with tiny fragments of lead and stone from the ricochet of a long burst of machine-gun fire as he hugged into the ground. Only Gary's unrelenting charge and accurate fire had caused the enemy to turn their attention from Phillip to himself. Gary had drawn the fire that would within seconds have driven his mate into the open, to be cut to ribbons, to die on a rocky, windswept slope far from home.

Gary smiled grimly at the memory, then turned to make one last round of the club's dimly lit interior. He finished his routine checks and looked at his watch. Two-fifty-five. Phillip and Julie would be back at any time. He crossed to the kiosk and picked up the night's takings. The doorbell rang, breaking the silence. With a broad smile he grabbed his jacket, strode over to the door and swung it open.

It wasn't his kid sister's big green eyes or Phillip's blue ones that met and froze the smile on his face.

Gary found himself looking into two big round black holes. They were the business end of a sawn-off twelve-bore shotgun.

His face turned to stone as he looked up to stare into cold grey eyes that held as much expression as those of a dead fish. The flesh around the eyes was grey and bloodless. The thin lips hardly moved as the gunman growled, 'Back up, sonny.'

Gary backed slowly away as the gunman advanced. A second man slipped silently into the foyer, closed the door and slipped the bolt. In the dim light, Gary quickly appraised the two men. They were both in their late forties, not thick young toughs like the four previous visitors. These men had the cold, calm attitude of professionals, men with a serious job to do. No talk. No threats of violence. Killers.

Gary recognized the signs. He had come across the breed in the army. Men who killed without a second thought, and enjoyed it.

Like Phillip, he had killed a number of men in action. The enemy. It had been their duty. But they'd never discussed it when reminiscing about their army days. Neither of them ever mentioned the men they'd killed.

The second man stepped forward. He held a plastic carrier bag in his left hand. His right was in the pocket of a long dark overcoat. He was five foot nine, had dark, swarthy southern-European features and dark-brown eyes.

9

'Where is Ross?' he demanded in a south-of-the-Thames accent.

Gary met his gaze for a moment, then answered quietly, 'He's not here. He took a night off.'

The two invaders exchanged questioning glances. Then the gunman said, 'You opened the door like you was expecting someone.' He paused and a knowing smile spread his lips thinly. 'I think you was expecting Ross.'

'I was expecting a cab,' Gary lied quickly. He glanced at the clock. Three a.m. precisely. Dread swept over him with the knowledge that Phillip and Julie would be ringing the doorbell at any moment. He prayed that they'd be late, give him time to disarm the two men and beat the shit out of them.

He glanced at the shotgun. It was held steady, pointing straight at his belly. The distance was six feet. He dismissed the idea of jumping the man at this time. He looked up into the cold grey eyes and saw a spark of amusement in them, as the gunman read his mind. The grey lips parted in a hiss of encouragement: 'Go on, sonny, fucking well try it.'

Gary ignored the challenge. He turned his attention to the dark, swarthy one. 'Mr Ross will not be back tonight. So if there is anything I can do for you gentleman, say so.' He shrugged. 'Or come back some other time.'

Brown Eyes studied Gary for a moment. 'We'll

wait for the cab,' he said. 'In the meantime you can toss that bag over here.'

The brown eyes dropped to the canvas bag of cash, still tightly gripped in Gary's left hand. Gary glanced at the shotgun. It moved a threatening two inches nearer, to back up the demand. He tossed the bag casually high, to block the man's view, as he looked back to the fish eyes. They did not so much as blink. They were fixed on him like two glass marbles.

Brown Eyes inspected the contents of the bag in silence, then dropped it into the plastic carrier bag. He looked directly at Gary as he nodded towards the swing doors that led into the clubroom. 'Anyone in there?' he asked.

Gary shook his head. 'I'm here on my own.'

'Let's take a look.' He smiled thinly. 'Get the fuck in there.'

Fish Eyes motioned towards the doors with the shotgun. 'After you, soldier boy, and no fuck-ing tricks.'

A sinking feeling dragged at Gary, and he raged inwardly as he turned and walked slowly towards the clubroom, cursing himself. Christ on a bicycle! he thought. How could I be so fucking stupid? All that goddamned training, a life of caution, and I let myself get caught with my sodding pants down.

He wasn't afraid for himself or Phillip, just for Julie, the kid sister he'd adored and protected all his life. Soon she'd come prancing happily through the door, to be confronted by the two killers behind him, and he had let it happen so easily.

They hadn't come just to rob – they already had the money. That left only one reason Gary could think of: they'd come to kill Phillip and himself. And they'd leave no witnesses. They'd kill Julie too. No way was he going to let that happen. He had to find a way to distract them, for just a few seconds . . .

'Was it your mates we hammered and threw out of here a couple of weeks ago?' he asked.

'Big mistake,' said Fish Eyes harshly. 'You should have paid up.'

Gary's anger surged up. He fought to keep calm, think straight. If he couldn't come up with some kind of diversion before Phillip and Julie got back, he decided, he'd use the doorbell as his cue. The moment it rang, drawing the two killers' attention for a split second, he'd jump Fish Eyes. That was the only way he could warn Phillip. And Gary resolved he'd do it – and die if necessary. With luck he might throw Fish Eyes off balance, surprise him for the split seconds necessary to break his neck.

'Who Dares Wins' flashed through his mind, and he thought bitterly of the long, slim, double-edged throwing knife that he'd carried and used to good effect on several reconnaissance missions and that now lay under his pillow at home. If only he'd brought it with him. If only.

'Sit down.' Fish Eyes motioned with the shotgun to a low chair beside a glass-topped coffee table. Gary complied reluctantly. He'd sooner have been on his feet for the assault.

As he sat, he allowed his hands to fall either side of the chair. His right hand brushed against a wine glass. His fingers wrapped around it and turned it so that the slim stem fitted between his middle and index fingers. He lay back, letting his arms stretch out behind him, giving the appearance of total relaxation. In fact, he'd arched himself like a bow. He breathed slowly and deeply to charge his blood with oxygen as he steeled himself for the attack.

Brown Eyes looked around the club and said, 'Nice place.'

Gary watched him remove from the carrier bag two glass bottles of pinkish fluid and place them on the bar. From each bottle protruded a cork, through which a cotton wick protruded and hung limply down the neck.

Gary studied the two petrol bombs for a moment, then asked, 'You going to burn the place?'

Brown Eyes looked at Gary and smiled. 'Full marks, soldier boy. Go to the top of the class.'

Fish Eyes grinned broadly, showing for the first time a row of brown-stained teeth. 'And you, sonny, are going to have a first-class seat.'

Gary feigned alarm. 'Are you going to kill us?' His voice was filled with hopelessness, like that of a man who had given up.

Fish Eyes liked the effect, and for the first time

allowed his attention to wander. He turned his head to smile at Brown Eyes.

As he looked back to Gary the wine glass hit him just below the left eye. It broke on impact and sliced to the bone. A jet of crimson spurted in a long arc. He howled loudly in surprise and pain, as he stepped back a pace to regain his balance and bring the shotgun to bear on Gary. But by now Gary was airborne, flying like a human cannon-ball. The room was filled by a flash and a deafening explosion as Fish Eyes jerked frantically at the triggers of the gun.

Gary felt the impact in his left shoulder. It turned him in mid-air, like a blow from a sledge-hammer. But there was no pain, just an empty feeling as though part of him was missing. He hit Fish Eyes full in the chest, sending him reeling backwards to crash on to a low coffee table, which disintegrated under their combined weight, as the twelve-bore roared deafeningly again, discharging its deadly load of heavy, 00-size lead pellets harmlessly into the ceiling and showering the two struggling men with white plaster-dust.

His left arm dangling uselessly at his side, Gary pounded at Fish Eyes with his right fist. He felt the satisfying crunch of bone and cartilage as he drove his fist in jack-hammer blows into the man's face and throat until he went limp.

Gary leapt to his feet and turned to Brown Eyes, his legs propelling him like pistons towards the enemy. Life went into slow motion before his eyes as he saw the danger. His legs turned to lead. His feet felt as though they were running through treacle, sucking at him, holding him back as he drove towards Brown Eyes. The petrol bomb seemed suspended in mid-air. He realized he couldn't catch it before it crashed against the wall beside him.

He heard the impact of breaking glass as the bottle disintegrated in a glistening burst of flying liquid and shards of glass. The flash of ignition blinded him, searing his eyes with incredible pain as heat and flame exploded around him. The breath was sucked from his lungs as he surged forward through the wall of fire. His hair fizzed and crackled as it burst into a halo of orange flame. Still his legs drove him on through the fire towards the man his whole mind and every fibre of his body screamed at him to kill.

Brown Eyes stood his ground, his aim undeflected by the snarling, flame-engulfed form of Gary hurtling across the room. He calmly squeezed off one shot after another at the human fireball rocketing towards him.

Too late, Gary saw the pistol spit flame, heard the explosions, felt the heavy-calibre slugs thumping into his body. Within just a few feet of his quarry, his legs failed him as they turned to jelly, collapsing under his weight. He hit the floor with a dull thud, slid forward until he came to a halt, his face resting against Brown Eyes' polished black shoes. Paralysed, he coughed. He tasted blood. He felt the hard, cold steel of the pistol barrel touch the soft skin behind his right ear. His head exploded into a rainbow of brilliant colour, which turned instantly to total blackness.

Alex Gómez felt a pang of regret and admiration as he squeezed the trigger. He had killed many men and felt no remorse. It was just a job. But this man had died so bravely. His attack had been as ferocious, swift and courageous as that of a lion. He shrugged the feeling aside as he holstered the pistol, then hurled the second petrol bomb to the far end of the clubroom, adding fuel to the raging fire. He stepped backwards through the front door, away from the choking, blasting heat.

Less than an hour later, Gómez was climbing into bed beside his wife, who feigned sleep. She knew better than to enquire where he had been or what he had been doing. She also knew that during the next few weeks Alex would feed her small amounts of cash that would add up to a tidy sum. She would add them to their already substantial savings, which were far in excess of the profit they earned from the small, greasy café they ran in Streatham.

Gómez couldn't sleep. He tossed and turned as he thought about Albert Reed, the man who'd been sent to cover him. He grinned sourly in the darkness. He fucked up, he thought. Reed now lay in the burning ruin, alongside one of the men they had been sent to kill.

Reed meant nothing to Gómez. He was one of the Chalmers brothers' trusted henchmen, who Frank Chalmers had insisted accompany him to make sure things went according to plan. He wondered briefly what the Chalmerses would have to say about Reed's death. They wouldn't be pleased. Reed was a known associate. His body would connect them to the crime. He thought about the man Ross, who should have been at the club when they arrived, should be lying dead beside his buddy. How would Ross react? His best pal murdered, his business burnt out. Gómez had an uneasy feeling about that. 'They're just a pair of soldier boys,' Frank Chalmers had said. 'Make an example of them. Blow them away.'

Gómez felt a chill run down his spine and his skin goosed up as he saw in his mind's eye Gary Thompson pound the life out of Albert Reed, then turn and charge at him, left shoulder blown half away, hair and clothes alight as he leapt through a wall of fire. It had taken five nine-millimetre slugs to stop him.

Gómez shook his head and pulled a face as he decided that if the Chalmers brothers still wanted Ross killed they could find someone else to do the job. He wanted no further part in the affair.

Phillip braked and pulled into the kerb, allowing the fire engine to speed past, its blue lights flashing, headlights blazing, siren wailing. He watched as the driver expertly swung the big, cumbersome vehicle into a left-hand turn. A police Rover, speeding from the opposite direction, lights flashing, turned in behind the fire engine with a squeal of protest from its tyres.

The street they had entered was a mixture of terraced houses, factories, offices – and the Starlight Club. Phillip and Julie exchanged worried looks as Phillip accelerated. He summoned a smile and joked nervously, 'I hope Gary hasn't set fire to the club, just because we're fifteen minutes late.'

As Phillip flicked the Range Rover into a left-hand turn, he saw it. Behind the large sign that read 'The Starlight Club', the single-storey building was alight. Through a gaping hole in the roof, flames leapt fifty feet high, lighting up the whole area in a false dawn.

Julie gasped in horror and gripped Phillip's arm tightly, as she cried out, 'Gary!'

Phillip tried to smile reassuringly as he swerved the vehicle towards the side of the club's drive, locking the wheels in a controlled skid on loose gravel. 'Gary will be OK, Julie. It'd take more than a little fire to hurt your brother, I promise you.' But inside his head he screamed 'Bastards!' as he guessed who'd torched the club. He knew Gary would have put up a hell of a fight, no matter how many thugs he had faced, but he may have been heavily outnumbered, beaten up, injured.

And at the back of his mind, beneath his concern for his friend, was the nagging realization that he was broke, ruined. The Starlight was insured, but not for enough to cover the outstanding bank loan plus the top-up loan he'd needed as the costs rose. If the club was a total loss he'd be at least ten thousand pounds adrift. He was not only broke: he was in debt. And then there was all the work Gary and Julie had done, their loyalty and commitment. He squeezed Julie's hand and forced the realization to the back of his mind. Gary first; the rest would have to wait.

A large crowd had gathered, many in their dressing-gowns. They stood in groups behind the fire engines. One appliance was already in action, sending great streams of water in glistening arcs into the heart of the fire. The whole scene of uniformed men working quickly and efficiently, each knowing and doing his job, was in itself a spectacle. It was far too late to save the building. Their task now was to quench the fire and prevent it from spreading to the surrounding buildings.

With a resounding crash, a large section of the roof caved in, sending a fountain of sparks high into the dark sky, to fall down like a shower of red rain. Through a loud hailer, the fire chief urged the crowd to move further back, then called instructions to his men.

Phillip scanned the flame-lit faces of the spectators, searching for Gary. He expected to spot him at the front of the crowd. No luck. He turned to Julie and said gently, trying to keep his growing concern out of his voice, 'I can't see Gary. He must be in that group over there.' He pointed to a small crowd of onlookers between them and the fire, backlit and silhouetted by the flames. He took her hand and urged, 'Come on, let's go and find him.'

Hand in hand, they worked their way through the throng of people to the barrier the fire crew were hastily putting up. The local beat policeman was urging the crowd back. Every second that passed without their seeing Gary increased Phillip's alarm. Julie was ashen with anxiety, her eyes flicking from face to face in a silent but frantic search.

Phillip stopped and turned to face her, his black hair glinting auburn in the orange light of the flames behind him. He took her gently by the shoulders and said, 'Wait by the car. If Gary spots it he'll go to it. I don't want to have to search for both of you. I'm going to have a word with the chief fire officer.'

Julie managed a half-smile, and reluctantly nodded assent. She wanted to search with him, but she knew he was right. If Gary saw the Range Rover and went over to it, one of them must be there to meet him. Watching Phillip's tall figure stride purposefully towards the fire chief, she clenched her fists desperately, her nails almost drawing blood from the palms of her hands, and whispered aloud, 'Please find him . . . dear God . . . please find him.'

A policeman intercepted Phillip, then after a brief exchange of words pointed out the fire chief to him. Phillip and the chief talked for a minute, then Phillip stepped aside and the chief raised his bullhorn to his lips and turned to address the crowd.

Julie heard his words echo electronically above the roar and crackle of the fire. 'Gary Thompson, please come forward. I repeat, Gary Thompson, please come forward.'

Her hopes flared as she waited expectantly for her brother's familiar figure to step out of the crowd, but faded as the seconds ticked by and there was no sign of him. She looked back at Phillip. He was talking to the fire chief, who made notes on a clipboard. Then he turned and walked slowly back towards her.

The first streaks of light shot through the sky from the east, backlighting the cumulus clouds that towered twenty thousand feet into the sky in mingled white and grey. The crowds had dispersed as the flames died. A mere handful of die-hards remained. The blackened ruins of the Starlight Club smouldered and hissed in protest as the firemen damped down and raked over the glowing embers. Only the main walls still stood, cracked and broken by the intense heat. Small spirals of smoke wisped lazily into the air, to be dispersed by a slight breeze.

Phillip watched as the firemen stepped cautiously through the debris, poking around and searching with practised eyes. He glanced back to the Range Rover. Julie had elected to remain in the vehicle, dreading what might be discovered in the ashes. Her strained face showed white through the windscreen as she waited for a sign from him.

A young fireman clambered across the wet black sludge and debris towards Phillip and the fire chief, who stood watching the scene. The fireman's boots clanked loudly on the pavement as he approached. He stopped, wiped his soot- and sweat-stained forehead and said heavily, 'We've found a body, sir.'

The fire chief shook his head sadly, then, after exchanging a glance with Phillip, told the fireman, 'OK, get on with it. You know the drill. I'll be along shortly.' He turned to Phillip and asked, 'Are you sure Mr Thompson was alone?'

Phillip spread his hands helplessly. He was almost too shocked and grieved to speak. He cleared his throat and said huskily, 'He should have been on his own. But I don't really know. Perhaps one of the staff waited . . .' His voice trailed off.

The fire chief put an understanding hand on his shoulder and said, 'Go home now. There's little you can do here.' He shot a glance over Phillip's shoulder at the Range Rover. Julie was staring at them, her face pale and drawn. 'The young lady shouldn't be here any longer. It can be very distressing.'

Phillip nodded. 'You'll let me know instantly of any further developments? When the body's identified . . . ?'

'You'll be the first to know,' promised the fire chief. 'Now I have work to do. I'm sorry, Mr Ross, but I have to go. Go and get some rest. It will be some time – a matter of hours – before we know the identity of the body for certain. Goodbye, Mr Ross.' He turned and marched off.

Phillip stood staring into the ruin for a short time, then turned his back on it and trudged back to the Range Rover, trying to think of a way to break the bad news. It was all so unreal, like a nightmare he couldn't wake from. Anger built up inside him at the thought that the protection-racket thugs had done this to Gary and burnt his club because he'd refused to pay and instead had beaten them up. He forced the thought to the back of his mind.

Until I know for sure it wasn't an accident, he told himself, there's no point getting angry.

The flat felt quiet and empty. Phillip checked Gary's room, half hoping that he'd find him asleep in bed, and that it had all indeed been a nightmare. But the bed was still neatly made, army-fashion, the corners sharp and correct. He closed the door and returned to the lounge, where he found Julie slumped on the settee, crying. He sat beside her and put a comforting arm round her shoulders. She leant against him, seeking comfort, as she cried.

'He was always there for me,' she sobbed. 'He was too kind, too brave, to die. Surely it can't be true? He can't be dead.' She raised her head and looked imploringly at Phillip. 'Mum and Dad.

Oh dear God in heaven! How do I tell Mum and Dad?'

Phillip held her close and brushed a tear off her cheek. 'We'll tell them once we know for certain,' he said. 'Not yet, not until it's been proved beyond all reasonable doubt.'

At his insistence, Julie took a long, hot bath and retired to her room to get some rest. She tossed and turned for over two hours, her sorrow too heavy for sleep. Eventually she gave up and joined Phillip in the lounge.

He had made several phone calls, two of them to the number the fire chief had given him. But he had learnt nothing more.

A little after midday the doorbell rang. Phillip opened it to find two men in business suits. They introduced themselves as Detective Chief Inspector George Hill and Detective Sergeant John Thorpe. He invited them in and introduced them to Julie. They declined the offer of coffee.

The atmosphere was tense and subdued as the chief inspector got down to business. He was of medium height and heavily built. A collar of grey hair framed a shiny bald head. Piercing blue eyes were set in a fleshy, friendly face. His wide, generous mouth exposed a row of even white teeth when he smiled.

He stared directly at Phillip as he said quietly, 'I am very sorry to have to inform you that this has become a murder investigation, Mr Ross. We've found evidence of shooting, and the fire was started deliberately with an accelerant, petrol, we believe. But I can't expand on the details at the moment. We have to wait for the official reports from forensics.'

Julie gasped. Phillip clenched his fists, closed his eyes and shook his head grimly. He drew in a deep breath as he fought for composure, and braced himself for the news to come.

'We've recovered two bodies from the fire, both male,' continued the chief inspector.

Phillip glanced apprehensively at Julie and took her hand in his. She patted her eyes with a tissue, straightened herself to sit upright. Her face was pale and drawn but otherwise expressionless. Her big green eyes brimmed with tears.

'We believe we've identified one of the bodies from the contents of his wallet.' Hill referred briefly to a slim black notebook. 'Does the name Albert Reed mean anything to you, Mr Ross?'

Phillip shook his head. 'No.'

'Would you recognize Mr Thompson's wrist-watch?'

Phillip nodded and squeezed Julie's hand.

Hill gestured to the tall, thin, birdlike Sergeant Thorpe, who had remained watchful and silent throughout the interview. Thorpe leant forward and opened an attaché case that lay on the floor next to his chair. He removed a clear plastic bag, which had a card attached to one corner. A wristwatch was easily visible through the thin plastic. Even before

25

the sergeant put it down on the coffee table in front of him, Phillip recognized the heavy stainless-steel bracelet, blackened by fire, of the watch belonging to his long-time friend and best mate.

Julie recognized it too, and buried her face in her hands. Phillip reached out and picked up the plastic bag, turned it once, then dropped it back on the table. He looked directly into Hill's eyes as he said, 'That's Gary Thompson's wristwatch. I'd know it anywhere.'

Sergeant Thorpe replaced the watch and shut the case. He unwound his tall frame from the chair and stood up, speaking for the first time. 'In that case, Mr Ross, we'd like to take a look at Mr Thompson's personal belongings, if we may.'

Phillip stood up and, after a glance at Julie to see that she was OK, replied, 'Yes, of course. Follow me.'

He turned and led the two men to Gary's room, opened the door and stood aside for them to enter. 'Help yourselves, gentlemen. I'm going to get Miss Thompson to lie down and rest, but then if you need me I'll be in the lounge.'

Julie was crying silently. She looked up as Phillip came in and asked, 'Those men, the four who came to the club' – 'shouldn't we tell the policemen?'

Phillip put a finger to his lips and hushed her into silence. He led her into her bedroom, closed the door, and made her sit down on the bed.

'It's a fair bet they already know who's responsible,' he whispered. He glanced at the closed door. 'If they don't get the bastards I will.'

He took her by the shoulders and pushed gently until she was lying down. 'Don't say anything, anything at all. Leave it all to me.' He picked up the bedside phone. 'I'm going to call the doctor.' He explained the circumstances to the doctor's secretary and asked for a house call.

'The doctor's coming straight round,' he said as he put the receiver down. 'Stay here. I'd better get back to the cops.' He kissed her gently on the forehead and said quietly, 'I love you, Julie, and I loved Gary.' Then he turned on his heel and went abruptly out of the room, before his grief could get the better of him.

After about ten minutes, the two detectives emerged from Gary's room. Thorpe held a sheaf of documents. He raised them in display. 'I'd like to take these with me, Mr Ross. They're mainly army service records. I'll photocopy them and return them in a few days. They'll assist us in obtaining Mr Thompson's medical and dental records.'

Phillip nodded.

Hill asked more questions, while Thorpe made notes. He wanted details of their movements the previous evening. And did Phillip have any idea who could have wanted to kill Gary? Had there been any trouble at the club?

Phillip answered all the questions, but said nothing about the four thugs. He knew in his heart why

27

Gary was dead and who was responsible. His SAS anti-interrogation training enabled him to keep calm and impassive, giving away nothing of his seething anger and hatred for the men who'd killed his friend. Men, he'd already decided, who would pay, and pay in full, for what they'd done.

The doorbell rang, interrupting them. It was the doctor. Phillip showed him into Julie's room; she was still sobbing quietly. When he returned to the lounge, the two policemen were standing up, and looked ready to leave.

'One last question, Mr Ross.' Chief Inspector Hill searched Phillip's eyes. 'Have you had any dealings with the Chalmers brothers?'

Phillip raised an eyebrow questioningly. 'The Chalmers brothers?' He shook his head slowly. 'Never heard of them. Should I have done?'

Hill shrugged. 'Not necessarily. I thought I'd ask, because they have the nasty habit of demanding protection money from small businesses.' He paused and thought for a moment, as though deciding how far to go. 'They do get rough. And if that doesn't work they burn the man out of business.' He sniffed. 'They don't usually go as far as murder . . . except in exceptional circumstances.'

Phillip's voice took on a hard edge as he asked, 'What sort of special circumstances, Inspector?'

Hill pulled a face. 'Difficult to say really. Too much resistance . . . it could get personal, so the Chalmerses decide to make an example.'

'The dead man, the one found with Gary, was he one of the gang?' Phillip demanded.

The inspector dropped his gaze for a moment, then looked Phillip directly in the eye. 'Yes, Mr Ross, Albert Reed was a known associate of the Chalmers brothers. That's why I asked if you knew them.'

'Why don't you arrest them?' Phillip asked harshly. But he knew the answer even before he finished the question.

'We need evidence, Mr Ross. Witnesses.' Hill gestured helplessly. 'The Chalmerses will have twenty witnesses to prove they were miles away from the scene of the crime. They don't dirty their own hands any more. They just give the orders. They're feared and dangerous men. No one will give evidence against them.'

Phillip squeezed the bridge of his nose hard, forcing back his swelling anger. He asked quietly, 'Why are you telling me all this, Inspector?'

Hill took a deep breath before answering. He looked concerned. 'From what you've told me, you'd normally have been at the club at the time the killings took place. Because you and the young lady went out for the evening, you're still alive, Mr Ross. What I'm saying is that if it was the Chalmerses who sent the killers it was you they were after. Not your manager.'

Phillip nodded. 'I see,' he said.

'They would have killed both of you and then

Miss Thompson as well. This bunch don't leave witnesses.' The chief inspector rubbed his chin. 'I could provide protection if you request it, but only for a limited period. We haven't got the resources—'

Phillip cut sharply across him. 'That won't be necessary, Inspector.'

Hill cracked half a smile. 'No, Mr Ross, I didn't think it would. But I felt you were entitled to be forewarned.' He turned to the tall sergeant, who had been listening to the exchange between the two men. 'Let's be on our way, Sergeant.' As the two policemen went through the front door, Hill turned back to face Phillip. 'We'll be in touch, Mr Ross.' He handed him a visiting card. 'That's the number to call if you can think of anything else you want to tell me, or if I can be of assistance.'

Phillip thanked them and closed the door. He leant against it wearily as he gathered his thoughts.

The doctor appeared in the hallway. 'Ah, Mr Ross. Are you feeling all right?'

Phillip straightened, and smiled at the elderly man's concern. 'I'm OK, thank you, doctor. How's Miss Thompson?'

'She needs rest and quiet. She's suffered a great shock. She was obviously very close to her brother, and for him to suffer such an unexpected and violent death . . .' His voice trailed away, and he shook his head. 'It's very much worse to lose a loved one in such circumstances – murder – than from natural causes or in an accident. She's going to need a lot of care and support.'

Phillip nodded his understanding.

The doctor handed him two small bottles of pills. 'I've given Miss Thompson a sedative. I'd like you to take charge of those pills, Mr Ross. Give her two Valium every four hours, and one of the sleeping pills if necessary. I'll pop in tomorrow to see how she's doing.' He smiled warmly. 'And do give me a call before then if you think it necessary. Any time.'

Phillip thanked him, saw him out, then went back to Julie.

Chief Inspector George Hill and Sergeant John Thorpe sat in their unmarked Ford Granada outside the flat.

The chief broke the silence. 'What do you think of our friend Ross?'

'He took it very calmly, Guv.'

Hill nodded. 'He did, didn't he?'

'Should we put him under surveillance?'

The chief slowly shook his head. 'No . . .' He was silent for a moment, then asked, 'Did you see the photograph in Thompson's bedroom? The one of him and Ross in uniform?'

'Yes.'

'Did you notice what regiment they were serving in at the time it was taken?'

Thorpe looked a bit sheepish. 'Er . . . no, sir, I didn't.'

31

'It was the Twenty-second SAS, John. Thompson and Ross served together in the Special Air Services. And that was an SAS throwing knife under Thompson's pillow.' He turned and grinned at Thorpe. 'Our friend Ross would spot a surveillance team a bloody mile away.'

Thorpe started the engine. 'Now I understand why he didn't feel he needed the protection you offered him, Guv.' He made a clicking noise with his tongue. 'Still, Thompson came unstuck, didn't he?'

Hill smiled tightly. 'But he was caught unawares. Our friend Ross is forewarned. He knows what he's up against. The Chalmers gang won't catch Mr Ross napping, I can assure you of that, John.'

'Do you think he'll go after the Chalmers boys?'

The chief turned and looked hard into Thorpe's eyes. 'Don't quote me on this, but I sincerely hope he does. We'll sit back, give him a free hand. Ross could stir up the Chalmerses in a way that we couldn't. It may bring them out into the open, make them make mistakes.' He scratched the side of his chin, a malicious glint in his eyes as he added, 'Give us a chance to nail the bastards.'

Thorpe signalled and pulled out to join the traffic. 'I'll run a full check on Ross as soon as we get back to the office, sir. Find out if he's the type to take the law into his own hands.'

'He's angry now, and he doesn't know that we found a sawn-off shotgun at the scene of the fire.'

Hill stared vacantly out of the window, then said, 'We'll pay Ross another visit after we get the autopsy report. It'll be interesting to find out exactly how Thompson was killed.'

2

At precisely the same time as the two detectives drove away from Phillip's flat, a Rolls-Royce Silver Spirit glided silently to a halt outside a café in Streatham, south London. The door opened, and Frank Chalmers stepped out.

He looked left and right before crossing the pavement. Saturday shoppers still thronged the High Street, fifty yards away.

He removed his dark glasses as he entered the dim, dingy interior of the working men's café. He felt as uncomfortable as he looked out of place, wearing a six-hundred-pound Chester Barry suit and Gucci shoes. The café was empty except for two middle-aged men in overalls. They glanced up as he entered, downed the dregs of their tea and left.

Frank weighed fifteen stone. Everything about him was big, his nose, his ears, his belly and his feet. Everything, that is, except his height. Frank Chalmers was just five foot six. He drove big cars, smoked big cigars, lived in a big house and carried a big wad. But he was still only five foot six. And it griped him. It made him sour. It made him dangerous.

He walked to the counter and spoke to the small, mousy-looking woman behind it. 'I'll have a bacon sandwich, the bacon well done, and a tea, no sugar. And tell Alex there's someone here to see him.'

Alex Gómez appeared from the kitchen, wiping his hands on a soiled tea towel. He looked across and nodded acknowledgement to Chalmers. He tossed the tea towel on to the counter, crossed to the door, turned the sign to 'Closed' and locked the door. He drew two mugs of tea from the urn. His wife came out of the kitchen, carrying Chalmers's bacon sandwich.

'I'll take that. You go on upstairs,' Gómez ordered.

His wife turned and in silent obedience disappeared through the back door. She had been expecting the man with the big shiny car. He always turned up after Alex had been working late on his secret business. From now on she would expect the money to start appearing, a few hundred here, a few hundred there.

Gómez set the bacon sandwich and mugs of tea on the table in front of Chalmers and sat down. 'Hello, Frank,' he said flatly.

Chalmers grunted, pulled the sandwich nearer and lifted the top half. He inspected the contents, grimaced and slid the plate away in disgust.

'Hey, what's the matter with my food?' complained Gómez.

'It's sixty-per-cent fat, ten-per-cent grease and thirty-per-cent a mixture of gristle and meat. I wouldn't want to step in it, let alone eat it,' sneered Chalmers as he inspected the grease on his fingers. 'Got a serviette?'

'You kidding?' Gómez reached across, picked up the sandwich and took a large bite. Bacon grease squirted out and ran down his chin. He grinned as he chewed. 'You've been spoilt, Frank. Too much caviar and all that French shit.'

Chalmers grunted and turned his eyes away from Gómez's open mouth in distaste. He pulled an envelope from his inside jacket pocket, tossed it on to the table and said, 'There's your cash. Tell me about it.'

Gómez shot him a lopsided grin and wiped bacon fat from his chin, using the back of his hand. Chalmers always wanted to hear every gory detail of the deaths of the men he paid to have killed. He would listen, his eyes wide with excitement, as Gómez spelt it out. Usually Gómez would spice it up a bit – add things that hadn't happened – just to watch the expression on Chalmers's face.

'It was a bad one, Frank.' He picked up the envelope, tipped out the cash. There were two bundles of five thousand, in fifty-pound notes. He pocketed one bundle and threw the other back to Chalmers.

'What's this?' demanded Chalmers, astounded.

'I only got one of them, Frank. Ross was out.'

Chalmers said, 'But the radio . . . I heard on the radio that they found two bodies.'

Gómez looked hard at him for a moment. 'You heard from Albert?' he asked quietly.

Chalmers shook his head. 'He ain't checked in yet.'

'He ain't going to check in, Frank.'

Chalmers's mouth dropped open. He looked horror-stricken as the fact dawned on him. 'Albert?' he whispered.

'That's right, Frank. Albert got himself burnt in the fire. He's dead, Frank, dead.'

'How? What the fuck went wrong?' Chalmers demanded.

'The soldier boy was good, Frank, very good. Albert had him covered with that toy gun of his' – Gómez always referred to Reed's sawn-off shotgun as a toy-boy hitman's gun; it used to wind Reed up – 'but the soldier was fast, too fast for Reed. The guy must've had a death wish. He took a blast in the shoulder but kept on going.' Gómez paused for effect. Chalmers's eyes were wide and glazed as he listened. 'The soldier snapped Albert's neck like a carrot, Frank. It sounded like a branch of a tree breaking.'

Chalmers winced and rubbed the back of his own neck in sympathy. And shuddered.

Gómez grinned wickedly, pleased at the response.

'I tossed him a molotov cocktail, Frank, just to slow him down a bit. It didn't work. He just kept coming. The fucking petrol bomb burst almost in his face. His fucking hair was all alight. His clothes . . .' Gómez stared out of the window, remembering. 'I pumped five heavy-calibre slugs into the man to stop him, Frank. Five.' He held up his hand, fingers spread for emphasis.

Chalmers stared at Gómez as if in a trance, his eyes and mouth wide.

'He fell at my feet. He still wasn't dead.' Gómez shrugged. 'I put the gun to his head and blew his fucking brains out. That did the trick. That finished him, Frank.' He sat back and waited for a reaction.

Chalmers's forehead was beaded with sweat. He took a gulp of his tea. It dribbled down his chin and dripped on to the Formica table-top. He shook his head to clear it, rubbed his face hard with his left hand to bring himself back to reality. He took a deep breath as he regained his composure. 'You gotta kill the other one, Alex. You gotta kill him.'

Gómez pulled a face. 'I don't know about him, Frank. You said they was just two young soldier boys that thought they was tough . . .' He hesitated. 'I don't know that I want to do the other fella. I've got a funny feeling about him.'

Chalmers pushed the five thousand pounds across the table. 'In advance,' he said flatly.

Gómez shook his head. 'Sorry, Frank.' He pushed the cash back. 'This next joker, Ross or whatever you call him, could be just as tough.' He shrugged. 'Or even a bit tougher. It ain't worth the risk.'

Chalmers's anger got the better of him. 'You accepted the fucking contract,' he growled, 'so now fucking well finish it.' He slammed his hand down on the top of the Formica table.

Gómez's brown eyes turned dark and menacing as his pupils dilated with anger. 'Don't ever speak to me like that, Frank,' he said softly, icily. 'Not ever. Not for any reason at all.'

Chalmers knew he'd gone over the top. Even he couldn't risk talking like that to a cold-blooded killer like Gómez. He forced a half-smile, and said, 'Yeah, well, OK, I'll make it ten. Ten thousand to kill Ross. Five now, five when the job's done.' He sat back smugly, convinced that ten thousand in cash was enough to get anybody killed.

Gómez leant across the table, his eyes hard. 'Keep your fucking money, Frank. I've got a bad feeling about this guy. Get some of your own boys to do this one. I ain't interested.'

Chalmers rasped, 'What . . .? You ain't interested? I said ten thousand pounds, Alex. I could get the fucking Pope zotzed for that kind of money.'

Gómez shrugged. 'Then zotz the fucking Pope. I got no intention of going against this Ross fella.' He twisted one side of his face into a smile. 'Anyway, Ross ain't the fucking Pope.'

Chalmers leant back in his chair, exasperated. He stared hard at Gómez for a moment. He wanted to get mad, throw a few fucks into the man, threaten him. But . . . He didn't have the balls. He knew that Gómez was capable of killing his own mother, for the right price. And he'd suffer the same remorse as he would if he squashed a bug. No, he decided, he wouldn't threaten Gómez. He'd probably have to up the money. But not yet. He didn't want to sound desperate, the way that he felt inside. He, too, had a bad feeling about Ross.

Chalmers bent his head and rubbed his forehead, massaged it to ease away the tension, as he remembered the night four of his toughest men had limped and crawled back to the room over the Bethnal Green pub that he used as his headquarters. The men had been angry and humiliated. They looked as if a herd of bull elephants had stomped all over them. Two had needed hospital treatment. Frank had blown his top when he learnt from one of them, who had suffered a broken jaw and three broken teeth, that just two men, Phillip Ross and Gary Thompson, had pulverized the four of them in seconds, using only their bare hands.

He had screamed for revenge. 'They're dead! I'll show those two bastards. They're dead!'

The next day he had called on Gómez and fixed the contract. He omitted to inform him that the two ex-soldiers had beaten up four of his toughest men. After all, Gómez would be armed. He always shot his victims. He was too old for the fighting game. He did what he did just for the money. Purely business.

Frank had insisted that Albert Reed accompany Gómez. He knew Reed would enjoy keeping the men covered while Gómez shot them, but was not reliable enough to be entrusted with the job on his own – not enough bum. But OK as a back-up man. It should have been easy.

Now Reed was dead and one of the soldier boys was still alive. Frank wondered if Gómez would be sitting there now if Ross had also been at the Starlight when they had called. He doubted it.

His mind churned with anger and regret. I don't fucking need this, he thought. Albert, dead.

He'd known Albert Reed for over twenty years. Albert had been a man he could ask to do anything and know he'd keep a still tongue. Albert could keep a secret. Well, you certainly ain't going to say anything now, Albert, he thought – are you, my old son?

Gómez broke in. 'Do you think this guy Ross will come after you, Frank?'

The question took Chalmers by surprise. That thought hadn't crossed his mind. The bad feeling deepened into fear. 'What do you mean?' he rasped.

Gómez leant forward on his elbows. He was enjoying this. He forced a serious, concerned look on to his face. 'Well, Ross can't be too happy, Frank. His mate's dead and he's lost his business, burnt to a cinder . . .' He stopped, to let Chalmers work the rest out for himself.

Chalmers laughed nervously. 'One man! What the

fuck could he do to me and my gang? Don't be fucking stupid, Alex.'

'He could have a lot of friends, Frank,' persisted Gómez.

'I've got no choice but to kill the man, Alex. It's a matter of pride. I said the man was dead, in front of the whole fucking gang. Now I've gotta kill him. How would it look if I didn't? I'd lose face, lose respect. I'd be a fucking laughing-stock.'

Gómez pressed further. 'Well, you just look out for yourself, Frank. Make sure you keep a couple of the boys around. See they're tooled up. You never can tell.' At the expression on the fat face opposite, it was all he could do to keep a straight face. He really had Chalmers rattled.

Chalmers sneered. He was catching on to Gómez's game. He hitched his shoulders back. 'Ross don't even know my name. He don't know it was my gang that put the arm on him.'

'It won't take him long to find out. Albert was connected to you, a known associate. The police will know you were involved.'

'I don't give two fucks about the police. I've got twenty, thirty witnesses to prove I was at the Stirling Arms at a private party when the fire started.' He grinned smugly. 'There ain't a thing they can do about it.'

'That might help you in a court of law, Frank, but will Ross accept it? And just walk away?'

Chalmers glared at him, then said, 'I'll make it

fifteen grand, Alex. Fifteen grand to kill just one man. But you must do it fast. Kill him before he finds out about me.'

Gómez held up his hands, palms out. 'Hold on, Frank. Take it easy. These things can't be rushed. The police will be keeping an eye on Ross, and he can't be a complete prat. He must have guessed you went after him, that his life's on the line. He won't just swing the door open in welcome. He's gonna be ready next time, ready for anything.' He paused thoughtfully. 'Give me a couple of days to find out more about this guy. I want to check him out before I accept the contract.'

'OK, OK.' Chalmers sighed in exasperation. 'But for Chrissake don't leave it too long, Alex. I want that guy dead and buried. And I want it done soon.'

Gómez smiled sardonically to himself, thinking, as he watched Chalmers waddle to his car, There goes the tough Frank Chalmers, shitting himself over one guy. If only people knew what he's like when he's not surrounded by his strong-arm boys.

Chalmers's eyes darted about nervously. He checked the back of the Rolls before he opened the door and slid behind the wheel.

It took only until the next morning for Alex Gómez to find out more about Phillip Ross. The *South London Advertiser* gave the murder and arson headlines. An eager reporter had dug into the pasts of the two dead men. He wrote that Albert Reed was

44

a well-known villain with a long criminal record. The bit that interested Gómez most was about Gary Thompson and his army career with Ross.

Gómez left his wife in charge of the café and hurried to the nearest public phone booth. He dialled Chalmers's unlisted number. Frank Chalmers answered after two rings.

'Frank? It's Alex. Have you read the *Advertiser*? The local rag?'

'No.'

'Well send out for one and read the main story. Those two soldier boys served in the fucking SAS together. Ross won a fucking medal knocking out machine-gun posts in the Falklands. He's a fucking war hero, Frank. A real bad ass!' Gómez dropped the receiver back into its cradle with a grin of satisfaction. That'll make his fat bum squeak a bit, he thought. And the price ain't fifteen grand any more.

Chalmers was left holding the dead handset. He stared at it in astonishment, then slammed it down. 'Fuck you, you greedy bastard,' he yelled. Then he sat back in his chair and stared at the ceiling. 'I ain't paying that sort of money to kill one sodding man. We'll do it ourselves. I've got enough men. We can handle fucking Ross.'

Captain David Scott, of the Twenty-second Regiment, SAS, was dressed in civilian clothes. He finished reading the autopsy report on Gary Thompson, closed the folder and placed it gently on the desk. He looked at Chief Inspector George Hill for a moment, then glanced at the tall, skinny sergeant who sat next to him.

Scott's voice was polished, low and controlled as he spoke. 'It took quite a lot to kill him, Chief Inspector.'

Hill nodded. 'He must have been a tough man, Captain.'

'A tough man and a good man' – Scott paused for a moment – 'and above all an excellent soldier.' His eyes turned to Thorpe. 'I apologize, Sergeant, for sounding evasive on the phone, but our regiment has very strict codes regarding its members, either present or past.'

Thorpe nodded. 'I understand, Captain. It's good of you to have travelled down to talk to us.'

'No trouble at all, Sergeant. I'd travel a lot farther to help catch the men who killed Thompson.'

Hill cleared his throat. 'We were put in touch with you, Captain, as the man who would know Gary Thompson and Phillip Ross better than anyone else would.'

The captain stuck out his lower lip thoughtfully before replying. 'That may well be true, sir. We trained and fought together. We do tend to get pretty close to our men. We have to know them accurately. Lots of lives may depend on the confidence and knowledge we have in a soldier, before we send him off on a mission, sometimes alone, to carry out a task that involves great danger.' He nodded. 'Yes,

I'd say I got to know Thompson and Ross as well as most, if not better.'

'And how did they rate in your book, Captain?' asked Thorpe.

Scott smiled. 'To be accepted in the SAS a soldier must rate very highly indeed. To stay with the regiment he has to prove daily, by his actions and performance, that the choice was correct. In the cases of Thompson and Ross, both men excelled. They stood out above all others in all aspects of training and in action.'

Thorpe cut in. 'Have both men been under fire, Captain?'

Scott looked surprised at the question, but answered patiently, 'Of course, Sergeant. Both men served a two-year tour of duty with my regiment. They fought in the Falklands, among other places. Ross was awarded the DCM. Need I say more?'

Thorpe looked a little embarrassed. He cleared his throat. 'Er . . . no, sir.'

Hill saved Thorpe any further embarrassment by explaining, 'We do have to ask what may appear naive questions, Captain, to a man in your situation and position. What we're getting at is this: is Ross the type of man to take the law into his hands? Is he likely to go after the men responsible for his friend's murder?'

Scott rubbed his chin thoughtfully for a moment, then asked, 'What are the chances of you bringing the killers to justice?'

The chief inspector shifted uncomfortably in his seat and looked disgusted as he answered. 'Not good. You see, they've killed before and so far they've got away with it. They've always got a pack of witnesses to swear they were somewhere else at the time.' He shook his head, then, with a hard glint in his eye, went on, 'They're a ruthless gang of thugs. They'll lie in their teeth under oath. They rule by fear. So far no one has had the guts to stand against them. At least, those that have didn't live to regret it.'

The captain spoke with conviction. 'If that's the case, Chief Inspector, expect some corpses to turn up, or some of your suspects to disappear without trace.'

Hill looked sceptical. 'Do you honestly believe Ross is capable of taking on an entire gang of armed thugs?'

'If that's what he decides to do. This gang you speak of will stand as much chance as a bunch of rabbits locked in a tiger's cage.'

The chief inspector and the sergeant exchanged glances before Hill continued, 'You just said, Captain, "If that's what he decides to do." Why the "if"?'

The captain crossed his legs and leant back. 'It's not a case of "if", more a case of "when". When Ross finds out that the law is unlikely to take its course. When he knows, beyond all reasonable doubt, who was responsible. That's when he'll go into action. Not one minute before.'

'Would you like a cup of coffee, Captain?' asked Hill. On the captain's acceptance, he turned to Thorpe and said, 'Would you arrange that please, Sergeant.'

Thorpe nodded and left the room. He understood that the chief wanted to be left alone with the captain.

Hill watched the door close behind the sergeant, listened to the click of his heels fade into the distance. He then turned his full attention to the man facing him.

Scott listened intently while Hill outlined his theories, and described the link between the Chalmers gang and the dead man, Albert Reed. He finished by saying, 'So you see, Captain, we have a pretty good idea who was responsible for Thompson's murder, but no proof and not a hope in hell of getting any.'

The captain thought for a moment, then asked bluntly, 'What do you want from me? How can I help you?'

Hill smiled warmly, a conspiratorial gleam in his eye. 'I want you to tell me how Ross will react. What he's likely to do and how he's likely to do it.'

'That depends.' Scott reached out and picked up the autopsy report on Gary Thompson. 'Has Ross seen this?'

Hill shook his head.

'I get the distinct feeling, Chief Inspector, that you would very much like Ross to take action against this Chalmers gang. Am I correct?'

Hill nodded.

'To give you the chance to get the Chalmerses?'

Another nod.

'Of course, you wouldn't be after Ross, would you?'

A shake of the head.

'In fact, you wouldn't really try to get Ross, would you?'

Another shake of the head.

'Unless, of course, Ross left clues big enough to trip over.'

Hill allowed himself a chuckle. 'There are none so blind as those who don't wish to see, Captain.'

Scott nodded his understanding, and said, 'Once Ross has the full facts in front of him, he'll make his plans. I should think he'll go missing, create an alibi that'll make it impossible to locate or contact him. That'll give him time to reconnoitre the enemy, get to know their habitat, pick out targets and the killing ground. He'll be able to do as he wishes without fear of attack from his enemy.' He stopped as the door opened and Sergeant Thorpe appeared, carrying a tray of coffee.

Thorpe put the tray on the desk and said, 'Help yourself to sugar, Captain.' He looked enquiringly at Hill, who waved his hand at the chair Thorpe had recently vacated and said, 'Sit down, Sergeant. It won't hurt for you to listen in. We're only speaking hypothetically.'

The captain helped himself to sugar and stirred his

coffee. 'Once Ross is fully prepared,' he continued, 'he'll strike a devastating blow, and disappear into thin air having created fear, panic and havoc. Should he not kill all the men he set out to kill, he'll probably draw them out of their den into the open. To a place of his choosing.' He smiled. 'A bit like a game of cat and mouse, I should think.'

Both policemen asked further questions, which the captain answered candidly, for a further fifteen minutes. Then they thanked him and he left. The sergeant saw him to the main entrance of New Scotland Yard, then returned to the chief's office.

'Well, John, what did you make of all that?' asked Hill.

The sergeant pulled a face. 'It's like dealing with someone from another planet, Guv. He was starting to give me the creeps, the way he spoke of killing as though it was an everyday chore – about as exciting as making toast.'

'It probably is to him. They give medals for it in the army. The likes of us will never understand it. But I suppose there's a necessity for men like the captain and Phillip Ross while the world's full of terrorists and criminals. I dread to think what it would be like without them.' He picked up the autopsy report on Gary Thompson, plus a file on the Chalmers gang, slipped them into his briefcase and said, 'Let's pay our Mr Ross a visit.'

Phillip and Julie had driven down to Dover to

break the terrible news to her parents. She refused point-blank to tell them over the phone.

'They're going to need all the love and support I can give them – and you too, Phillip,' she said. 'You know how much they loved Gary, how they thought the sun shone in everything he said and did. I don't know if they'll be able to cope. It would be bad enough if he'd been killed in a car crash or something, but this . . .'

He glanced at her worriedly. She had already drawn heavily on her own reserves of strength and courage. Grief and strain had bleached her skin to grey and drawn dark shadows round her eyes; her hair was dull and lifeless. She was close to emotional exhaustion.

'What about getting one of their friends to come with us?' he asked. 'Someone their own age, who can imagine what it's like to lose a child?'

'Yes, perhaps – or, no, the vicar would be better. They're regular churchgoers and Mr Lorimer's a good friend. He'll know how to comfort them. Could we go to the vicarage first?'

'Of course,' said Phillip. 'Just give me directions when we get to Dover.'

The vicar's shock and distress when he heard the news were evident. He agreed at once to accompany them, and asked his wife to phone a few other church members and let them know, so that the Thompsons would have all the support they needed.

When they reached the Thompsons' house, Phillip

waited in the car while Julie and Mr Lorimer went in to break the news. Finally, Julie came to the door and beckoned him in.

'How are they taking it?' he asked.

'They're just sort of dazed and numb. They can't believe it yet. Mr Lorimer's being marvellous, of course. They'd like to see you, too, and ask you about what happened, if you can face it.'

'Of course I can.' He looked closely at her. It was clear that she'd put her own grief aside and was devoting all her strength and warmth to comforting her parents. He'd never admired her more. If she could do that, the least he could do was talk to her parents and try to ease her burden a little.

The interview was as painful as he'd feared, and Phillip was profoundly relieved when it was over and he was able to retreat upstairs to Gary's old room, where he was to spend the night. He slept badly. Flames flickered through his dreams, and time and again he heard Gary yelling to him, 'Get these bastards off my back, Phil!'

The next morning he drove back to London straight after breakfast, leaving the family to support each other in their grief. They were better off without outsiders, even close friends, for the moment.

He'd been home for only about ten minutes when the doorbell rang. He was glad of the interruption: the flat felt eerily empty and desolate. He peered through the newly fitted peephole and saw Hill and Thorpe standing on the landing.

He ushered them into the lounge, told them to make themselves comfortable and went to make a pot of tea.

'Have you got any further with your investigation, Chief Inspector?' he asked as he set the tray down.

'Not half as far as I'd like to have done, Mr Ross. But we have ascertained how Mr Thompson died.' Hill opened his briefcase, removed two files and pushed the briefcase to the side of his chair. 'This is not going to be very pleasant, I'm afraid. Do you want to know all the details or—'

'All of it,' snapped Phillip.

'Very well, sir. Read this.' Hill handed him the report. While Phillip read, Hill summarized. 'We found only one weapon, a sawn-off twelve-bore shotgun. It was near the body of Albert Reed. The spent cartridges in the chamber bore Reed's fingerprints, and his pockets contained several more rounds of the same make of ammunition.' He took a sip of his tea. 'The sawn-off, I must assume, belonged to Reed, and it was he who shot Mr Thompson in the shoulder. By the way, you may interested to hear that Albert Reed died from a broken neck.' He paused and ran a hand over his bald head. 'Forensics have identified the murder weapon, from marks caused by the firing pin and ejector mechanism on the six brass casings found close to where Mr Thompson fell. It's a nine-millimetre Walther P38. We didn't find the pistol, so we must assume that the killer took it away with him.'

Phillip grimaced. 'So there were at least two thugs involved. Possibly more.'

The three men sat in silence for a moment. The two policemen watched Phillip for a reaction. They saw none.

'When will the body be released for burial, Chief Inspector?' Phillip sounded cold and calm.

Hill glanced at Thorpe. 'I see no reason why the body shouldn't be released at once.'

'It would help the relatives. Gary's parents are suffering deeply. It'll be better for them once he's had a decent burial.'

'What are your plans, Mr Ross?' asked Thorpe.

'I have no immediate plans, Sergeant.' Phillip chose his words carefully. 'I've got a lot of odds and ends to tie up. Insurance claims, my bank, Gary's funeral ... Then I intend to take a long holiday. Get away from all this grief.' He looked blandly at the sergeant. 'I'll probably go camping on the Continent. Alone. I like to be alone at times, give myself a chance to plan out the future.'

'We may need to contact you, Mr Ross,' pressed the sergeant.

Phillip smiled. 'The places that I'm likely to go aren't renowned for communications, Sergeant. I'll leave you a phone number, one that I'll call every few days. If anything crops up, leave a message and I'll contact you.'

'Fair enough, sir. I suppose that will have to do.' Thorpe looked knowingly at Hill, who quickly disengaged his eyes and opened the second folder. He removed a sheet of photographs and placed it on the table in front of Phillip. 'Have you seen any of these men before, Mr Ross?'

Phillip looked them over. There were twelve full-face photos, with a profile shot beside each one. He recognized four of them: the men that he and Gary had beaten up and thrown out of the Starlight not so long ago. He shook his head and looked up.

'No, Mr Hill. I don't recall having met any of these men. Who are they?'

The chief leant forward and pointed as he spoke. 'The first two are Frank Chalmers and his brother, Robin.' His finger slid down the page. 'That's Albert Reed, the man found with Mr Thompson. The rest of them are all long-time members of the gang. They work their manor regularly.' He straightened and looked piercingly at Phillip.

'Is that the whole gang?' Phillip sounded unconcerned.

'I have some more pictures, of men associated with the gang' – Hill cocked his head at the folder – 'but I see no reason to show them to you if you don't recognize these. The others are just messenger boys and hangers-on.' He replaced the sheet of photographs in the folder, which he put down beside his chair and pushed almost out of sight. He picked up his teacup, looked at Thorpe and said, 'Let's be on our way then.' He drained the cup, threw the other folder into his open briefcase and snapped the case shut.

Phillip saw the two men out, then returned to the lounge. He was clearing away the used crockery when he spotted the folder lying beside the chair Hill had sat in. His first reaction was to pick it up and rush after the policemen. He'd taken three steps towards the door before he realized that it was the folder containing details and information on the Chalmers gang. He stopped and, with a wry grin of appreciation for Hill's tactics, opened the folder. The sheet of photographs stared back at him.

He hurried to the window. Hill and Thorpe were getting into their car. Phillip figured that the chief inspector would not 'discover' the folder was missing until he got back to his office. He decided to return it himself, perhaps stopping on the way at a photocopying machine.

It was two and a half hours later when Phillip asked for Detective Chief Inspector George Hill at the reception desk at New Scotland Yard. The chief himself came to reception to see him. He feigned surprise, and said he hadn't even realized he had forgotten the folder. He thanked Phillip profusely and apologized for troubling him.

Phillip returned to his flat, jubilant at the colossal amount of information he now had at hand about the whole Chalmers gang: names and addresses, pictures, their criminal records, haunts, associates, even phone numbers. It would save him weeks of work and give him an untold advantage.

He worked his way through the file until two

a.m., making notes and marking the information he thought would prove most useful. Finally, he closed the file and hid it behind a row of books above his desk. He leant back, relaxed and rubbed his tired eyes. 'Right, you bastards,' he said aloud, 'you've got it coming.'

Dover cemetery is set high on a hill overlooking the town. The sun was shining brightly, giving prominence to the sharp contrast between the white faces of the female relatives and the black hats and scarves that framed them. The service over, the mourners had split into small groups and were talking quietly.

Phillip excused himself to Gary's parents and to Julie, then crossed to a group of six fresh-looking young men. They greeted him with solemn smiles and warm handshakes. They had all served with Gary and him, and they were all still in the service. They chatted for several minutes, expressing their anger at what had happened to their friend. Phillip had phoned the relevant details through to one of them, Peter Russell, who had informed the whole regiment. Captain David Scott joined them from another group. After several minutes he excused himself to the soldiers and asked Phillip for a quiet word.

Once out of earshot, the captain said, 'It's a sad day, Phillip.' He hesitated for a moment, as though searching for the right words, then said conspiratorially, 'Strictly off the record, I've spoken to Chief

Inspector Hill. He wants you to get the bastards who killed Gary. Obviously, he can't officially condone it, but I'm of the firm belief that he won't do anything to cramp your style.'

Phillip smiled to himself. It confirmed his opinion of Hill as a thoroughly fly operator.

By now the captain was speaking out of the corner of his mouth. 'Don't leave any obvious clues and he won't have to follow them up. He'll know who's responsible if anything nasty happens to the Chalmers brothers, but unless you do something bloody silly it'll only be a hunch, one that he's unlikely to follow up.' He put a hand on Phillip's shoulder. 'I know what you must do, Phillip. Good luck, and keep in touch.' They shook hands, then the captain strode back to the group of soldiers to say goodbye.

Phillip stood deep in thought, looking out over the town. He watched smoke rise lazily from a factory chimney. After a few minutes he became aware of someone standing close by. He looked round. It was Peter Russell.

'Mind if I join you for a while, Phil?'

Phillip smiled and shook his head. 'No, it's nice to be surrounded by friends at a time like this, Peter.' He gave a long, tired sigh. 'I don't think I'll ever get over Gary's death. I feel so bloody responsible. It should have been me, not Gary.'

'Don't be bloody silly, Phil. Nobody blames you. It's those fucking thugs, the Chalmers brothers and their bloody hoodlums. They murdered Gary. No one else.' He shoved an envelope into Phillip's hand. 'Here, take this. We had a collection. Not just our regiment. Money's flooding in from all over the place. Soldiers who never even met Gary are sending in donations. It's a fund to cover your expenses, Phil, and there's no shortage of volunteers to help you when you need it.'

'I need some weapons and equipment, the stuff that I asked for over the phone.'

Russell grinned. 'It's all taken care of.' He handed Phillip a bunch of keys. 'You know Simon Allcock's cottage at Biggin Hill?'

Phillip nodded. 'Yes, I've been there, at a party he threw soon after we got back from the Falklands.'

'Well, Simon has gone abroad for a few months, on an assignment. He's given us the full use of it. It's a good safe house, remote, no neighbours for miles. Plus there's the fact that he often lets it out when he's away. Your being there won't cause any suspicion.'

'The guns?' asked Phillip.

'We're working on that right now.' Russell glanced quickly around, to make sure there was still no one within earshot. 'By the time you get back from France the cottage'll be loaded with everything you're likely to need. We've started stockpiling arms and ammo, and we've managed to get you some Semtex, timers and detonators. Everything you wanted and a bloody sight more.'

'Is any of it traceable?'

Russell allowed himself a small chuckle. 'Only to the IRA. We nicked most of it out of the special operations bin. You could easily blame the whole thing on them if you wanted. It's all got their trademark. None of it's on official records as stores, so no one's going to miss it.' He took a large brown envelope out of his pocket and passsed it to Phillip. 'Passport, driving licence and credit cards. All to match your new identity.'

'Thanks, Peter. Thanks for everything.' Phillip felt his throat tightening.

'Not just me, old pal. All the boys have helped.' He glanced back to the five men who stood silently watching them. 'We'll get all the thanks we need when we read about it in the papers.' He gripped Phillip's outstretched hand, and clasped it with his left. 'Good luck, Phil, and good hunting.'

Phillip lost no time. Having returned to the Thompsons' house immediately after the funeral, slowly sipped the obligatory sherry and spoken to Gary's immediate family, he took his leave and drove home to London. He could feel the beginnings of excitement lifting his spirits, could almost savour the taste of revenge.

The next two days were spent sorting out his affairs. He attended meetings with his bank manager and insurance broker, both of whom were helpful and sympathetic: they wished him well, agreed it would be best for him to get away for a break, and hoped he would return rested. He booked an open return ticket, for himself and his Range Rover, from Dover to Calais, cleaned up the flat and packed his bags.

He took one last look around, opened the door to Gary's bedroom, went in and sat heavily on the bed. He picked up the photograph of Gary and himself: two smart, proud young men in the uniform of the SAS. A lump formed in his throat as the memories came flooding back. 'I'll get the bastards, Gary, I promise,' he whispered. 'So long as there's breath in my body, I'll get them.'

He gently replaced the photograph, pulled the curtains closed, and returned to the lounge. He dialled New Scotland Yard and asked for the chief inspector. He told him that he'd be away for about a month, gave him Gary's parents' phone number, and promised to ring every few days, or whenever he was near a phone, to check for messages. Hill asked when he was leaving the country. Phillip said he expected to leave from Dover that evening. Hill wished him a safe journey.

Phillip locked the flat and drove directly to see Julie at her parents' house. On arrival he had two hours to spare before check-in time at the Eastern Dock ferry terminal. He took time to have tea with the Thompsons, then he and Julie went for a stroll along the seafront. They walked arm in arm in silence, both deep in thought, but at ease, taking comfort from each other's presence. They sat on a bench and stared out to sea.

Julie was the first to speak. 'I want to help you, Phillip.' She sounded determined.

'What do you mean?'

'The gangsters, the Chalmers brothers, you're going after them, aren't you?'

'Don't be silly. The law will take care of them.' He turned his head away. Lying to Julie did not come easily.

'I know you, Phillip. Well enough to know that you won't let those animals get away with Gary's murder.' She tossed her head to flick back from her face the long strands of blonde hair that had lifted in the sea breeze. 'I know that this so-called holiday just isn't you. You couldn't possibly go away while those killers are free. You loved Gary too much.'

Phillip turned to face her, took her hands in his, and asked, 'What would you think of me if I killed them? I'd be no better than them.'

She raised her eyes to the sky, took a long breath and sighed. 'Oh my dear God! You could never be the same as them, Phillip. I know that you've killed in the army. They gave you a medal for it.' She looked at him pleadingly, her green eyes wide. 'This is no different. They're animals, scum. They're the enemy of the people – much more so than young soldiers from another country, who are just doing as they're told.'

Phillip nodded. 'I can't argue with that. But if I were to take action against them I wouldn't want you involved.'

'I *am* bloody involved. He was my brother,' she snapped. 'And I'm telling you that if you won't let me help you, then I'll have to act alone.'

Phillip was aghast. 'What are you talking about?' he demanded.

Julie stared at him defiantly. 'If you keep up that ridiculous story of going away for time to think, I'll damn' well take you at your word. And I'll go after the Chalmerses myself.'

'For Christ's sake, Julie,' Phillip said angrily, 'these men are bloody dangerous. They won't give a monkey's that you're a woman. If you're a threat to them they'll snuff you out like a candle.'

'It's your choice, then,' she retorted. 'Either you let me help, or you leave me to do it on my own.'

Phillip ran his hands through his hair, playing for time as he weighed his decision. 'OK, then. If you're that determined, you're in. But you must realize that if we're caught it means prison. For a very long time.'

'Gary's going to be dead for a very long time,' she said quietly.

Phillip's jaw hardened. 'Yes,' he said shortly, 'he is.'

He made Julie promise not to do anything on her own, then scribbled down the address of the cottage in Biggin Hill and told her to destroy the piece of paper once she had memorized it. She was not to breathe a word about it to anyone, under any circumstances. They arranged to meet at the cottage at seven the following evening.

Having seen Julie back to her parents' home and said his farewells, Phillip drove directly to the Eastern Dock ferry terminal and checked in for his short trip across the Channel.

Within minutes of Phillip's passing through Immigration, Chief Inspector George Hill was informed that one Phillip Ross had departed from the UK. Destination: Calais. The chief grinned to himself and thought, 'I wonder how the blighter's going to get back in, and when?'

3

The false passport that Peter Russell had supplied bore Phillip's photograph, but the holder was given as Anthony Robert Cole; occupation: sales manager. The photograph was one taken several years earlier to be used on a previous false passport supplied by the British government, for use on a special assignment. Phillip smiled as he thumbed through the pages. They bore many entry and exit stamps, mostly issued at Spanish resorts famous for their attraction to British tourists. The cover looked well worn, as one would expect of a passport issued eight years before.

At ten p.m. Phillip booked into a small hotel in Calais. At eight the following morning he set off for Paris. He arrived at a small garage not far from Charles de Gaulle airport at midday. The Range Rover was misfiring badly, and the rear box of the exhaust system was badly holed. It had taken him only a few minutes to advance the timing and bash a hole in the exhaust box.

The garage proprietor was apologetic as he explained that he would have to order a new rear exhaust box. When asked – by an anxious, irritated Englishman, who said he had to be in Nice by midnight to join a yacht for three or four weeks' sailing – how long it would take, he threw up his hands, shrugged mightily, and said, 'Ah, that is impossible in this vehicle, monsieur. You must hire another auto or fly. To fly is quicker and will be cheaper, especially if you are not going to require an auto when you arrive in Nice.' He pointed to a road sign. 'The airport is very close, monsieur. Just ten minutes by taxi.'

Phillip thanked him for the good advice, then, after profuse assurances that the Range Rover would be kept safely in a corner to await his return, unloaded his suitcase while the proprietor hurried off to phone for a taxi.

At mid-afternoon, one Anthony Robert Cole cleared Gatwick airport Immigration and Customs without a hitch. He caught a train to Bromley South, where he took a taxi to Biggin Hill. He paid off the driver at a junction a mile and a half from the cottage, and walked from there.

While he waited for Julie to arrive, Phillip sorted through the supply of food, armaments and electronic equipment. Peter Russell had been as good as his word. There were enough weapons and equipment to start a small war: six pistols, all nine-millimetre Brownings – Phillip's favoured handgun

– a Savage pump-action twelve-bore shotgun, ten pounds of Semtex plastic explosive, detonators, a variety of digital electronic and radio-controlled timers, a two-inch mortar and a three-inch, complete with shells. He whistled with delight as he unearthed a cased Mannlicher hunting rifle with telescopic sight from the bottom of the case. The next case contained two crossbows, one full-size, the other half-size, plus barbed hunting bolts; and a box of assorted listening devices that resembled normal household items like two-way electric sockets and lightbulbs, along with a ten-channel crystal receiver.

With some amusement, Phillip sorted through a disguise box containing make-up, wigs, false moustaches, glasses, assorted coats and hats, and so on. They'd certainly come in useful because the members of the gang who knew what he looked like would undoubtedly have described him to the others.

His amusement lasted only a few minutes. He picked up one of the Brownings and thought sombrely of what he'd read in the autopsy report. Gary's shoulder had been blown apart by a shotgun blast, and there were five bullet wounds in his body and one in his head. His lungs had been seared by smoke and fire: he'd been alive when the fire was started.

That's how you're going to die, Chalmers, Phillip thought savagely, you and the other bastard who was at the club that night. And you're going to know who's killing you. And why.

He dropped the pistol back into the case and went

out to the garage to inspect the car. It was a black 325i BMW. He checked the fuel and oil: full. Turned the ignition key: the engine burst into life. Satisfied, he was returning to the cottage when Julie's silver Volkswagen Golf crunched up the gravel driveway.

She was in a much lighter mood, excited and a bit flustered. Phillip helped her in with her suitcase, then switched on the kettle. He made them both coffee and took it into the sitting-room. He found her looking at his false passport.

She jumped as he came in. 'Christ, Phillip, this is a bit James Bond or *Day of the Jackal*, isn't it?'

He smiled wryly. 'It does go on, believe me. But reading about it or watching it on TV isn't quite the same.' His voice hardened. 'This is for real. It'll be a case of kill or be killed.'

He was silent for a moment, then said quietly but firmly, 'Phillip Ross is in France on holiday. When we are completely alone call me Phillip, but in *any* company, with *any* people we may meet, call me Tony. My name is now Anthony Robert Cole. I'm a salesman. I sell cutting tools to the engineering industry.' He smiled. 'It's so bloody boring that nobody will follow it up.'

Julie entered into the spirit of things. 'What about me? What am I?'

'You're just a housewife. Cackle on about the price of cabbages or something. That should dry up the conversation, stop people prying too deeply.' He tried to keep a straight face as he added, 'Besides, that's what you're going to be.'

'Don't bet on it, sonny,' she snapped.

'Now hear this,' said Phillip. 'I only agreed to let you join me to keep you out of trouble and to do the odd job or errand. You can cook, clean and take messages.' His voice softened as he switched on the bullshit. 'That may not be exciting or glamorous, but it's a very important job.'

'Important job,' she echoed sarcastically. She dropped on to the settee and folded her arms, her eyes alight with anger. 'If you think for one bloody minute that I'm here simply to cook, scrub and take phone messages' – she tossed her head and her chin jutted mutinously – 'you're very much mistaken.'

Phillip stared at her in alarm. His mind raced as he tried to find the right words. 'Julie,' he said, 'we've already lost Gary. I'm not losing you as well. I love you, you know that. I won't let you put yourself in danger. We're not dealing with a bunch of priests. These men will kill you without a second thought if they think you're a danger to them. To do what I'm going to do will take training and skills that you simply haven't got, and there isn't time for you to learn. I don't doubt your courage for one minute, nor your determination, but it's not on.' He looked down at her, and said, quietly but with steel in his voice, 'Unless you agree to follow my instructions, I'll take you back to your parents' house and get my SAS mates to guard you.'

'Protective custody, you mean.' Julie glared at him, unimpressed. 'Very well,' she conceded, 'I'll do exactly as I'm told—' Phillip gave a small sigh of relief '—until I decide otherwise.'

He was about to embark on a lecture when she asked, 'Where's my bedroom? I'd like to get unpacked.'

Phillip nodded at a door on their right. 'Through there.' He decided to let the other matter rest for a while.

'Where are you sleeping?' she asked.

'You're sitting on my bed.' He glanced unhappily at the settee. It was at least a foot shorter than himself.

'Very well.' Julie rose, picked up her suitcase and walked over to the bedroom. She turned at the door. 'I'm hungry. Do I start work at once, and cook for you tonight, sir?' she asked sweetly.

Phillip said glumly, 'No, I'll pop out and get a curry or something.'

'I'll come with you. I'd like to choose my own food – if sir will graciously give his permission, that is.'

He didn't answer, just nodded.

'I'll get ready then.' She closed the bedroom door sharply behind her.

The bathroom was *en suite* and the only one in the small cottage. Phillip could hear her turn on the bath taps. He felt thoroughly miserable as he heard her splashing happily in the bath. He tried to console himself by picturing her naked. It didn't work. It made him feel randy, but rejected and thoroughly frustrated. He wished he'd left her out of it. He could do without the sexual distraction if it was to be without gratification.

When Julie came back into the sitting-room, Phillip glanced up at her, then looked quickly away. She not only looked beautiful, she looked bloody sexy, and as hot as a pancake. He squeezed his eyes with thumb and forefinger to hide his feelings, a mixture of longing, anger and frustration.

'Have you got a headache?' she asked innocently.

She was dressed in a pastel-green shift dress and matching ankle-strap high heels. Her blonde hair was groomed tightly back into a French pleat. She swung round to show off long, shapely legs in perfectly straight-seamed stockings. The sheer material of the dress clung to every contour of her lithe body. 'Do you like it?' she asked gleefully.

Phillip studied her for a moment, then nodded. 'Yes, I like it. But we're trying to keep a low profile, so change into some old jeans and a baggy sweater – unless you want me to choose your food.'

Julie looked annoyed and crestfallen. She was about to object, but, accepting that Phillip was right, turned and went back into the bedroom to change.

They found an Indian restaurant, the Raj, on the main road leading into the centre of Biggin Hill. It looked so inviting that they decided to stay and eat on the premises. They chose a corner table, where no one could overhear their conversation, and in a low voice Phillip outlined his plan. Julie was surprised when he told her he intended to make his first move against the Chalmers brothers the following morning.

They arrived back at the cottage relaxed and well satisfied after good food and good wine. Phillip said he wanted to go to bed and get a good night's sleep, be fresh for the task ahead. He explained that the bathroom off Julie's bedroom was the only one, and that they would have to share it, and suggested she use it first.

When he came out of the bathroom in his turn, a towel wrapped round his waist, Julie was already in bed, the duvet pulled up protectively under her chin. He smiled, and was about to wish her good night when she said, 'It's silly and unfair for you to sleep on that little settee when there's plenty of room in here.' She patted the bed beside her. 'Come on, jump in.'

Phillip was taken aback. 'I've got nothing on . . .'

Julie grinned mischievously. 'Neither have I.' She giggled nervously.

He loosened the towel and let it drop to the floor as he walked slowly over to the bed. He slid in beside her. Their bodies touched. He eased close, felt the length of her warm, slender body press closer. They turned and embraced, holding each other tightly as they engaged in a gentle, tongue-thrusting kiss of mingled longing and raw lust.

Phillip pulled away and threw back the duvet to expose her body. He traced a path with his fingertips across her breasts. Her nipples hardened and swelled as he brushed them lightly. Julie moaned softly, and she trembled as his hand slid down her body, stroking her gently. His lips, hot and passionate, closed on her breast.

'Now, Phillip, I want you now,' she said huskily. 'I've waited so long.'

'So've I, my darling. I've waited years for this.' He tensed and exhaled a long breath as Julie's hand caressed him, travelling slowly down his chest, across the taut muscles of his stomach to his groin. She took him in both hands, her breath catching in her throat as she felt his size. Her legs parted and she arched and pushed forward as his hand found her secret place and his fingers slipped into her hot wetness, gently exploring her.

Julie's head whirled, and she moaned with delight. She craved for him to enter her and bring her to orgasm. She clutched frantically at him, her nails digging into his back. 'Please, darling, now. I love you and I want you, oh God, I want you so much.'

Phillip rolled on top of her, the tip of his cock nuzzling between her labia. He rubbed it against her, entered her slightly. She was silky with juice, hot and tight around him. Teasingly, he withdrew and she clawed at his buttocks, thrusting herself up at him, trying to force him back inside her. She could hardly breathe.

His firm, gentle thrust, when it came, seemed to go on for ever as he plunged deep into her, until his pelvic bone ground against hers. She'd never been filled like this before. No man had ever reached the place Phillip touched deep inside her. She felt as if she'd never made love before, as if she'd been truly a virgin until now. He thrust again and again, harder now, more demandingly, deep within her. They moved together, building the rhythm of orgasm. As she reached her climax and cried out for joy, she heard Phillip's shout of fulfilment, felt him jerk inside her.

Afterwards, there was no need for words. They lay, panting and exhausted, holding each other close in their happiness, kissing gently now and then, until they drifted quietly into a deep sleep.

At eleven thirty the following morning, in his office above the Stirling Arms in Bethnal Green, Frank Chalmers answered the red telephone on his desk. It was his unlisted number, the one he gave only to people close to him.

His reaction to the voice and the name given on this sacred line of communication was so violent that he almost tipped his desk over as he jumped up, white-faced and shaking. The three men he'd been instructing on their day's work were so startled that they too jumped to their feet, concerned and uncertain.

'If this is a fucking joke, I'm not laughing,' Chalmers bellowed into the mouthpiece.

Phillip Ross replied, 'This is no joke, shithead. Now shut up and listen.'

Chalmers sank slowly back into his chair, almost too shocked to speak. His mind whirled with astonishment and anger as he listened to the demands Phillip coolly made to him.

'Yeah, yeah,' he said, 'I understand.'

He dropped the handset into its cradle. His hands fell to the desk. He looked at his three men and said, disbelievingly, 'That was Ross. The man must be fucking mad.' He jumped up again, and started pacing the office, laughing nervously. 'The fucking man wants fifty grand. Compensation for loss of profit, would you believe. He wants me to pay him fifty bleeding grand and tell him the name of my hitman.' His men listened in stunned silence.

'Can you believe this guy?' he shouted. 'He fucking well threatened me. Me, Frank Chalmers! Who the fuck does he think he is?' His face was red with rage. He looked ready to blow a fuse.

His three henchmen, Mickey Steele, Bobby Wilks and Kenny Martin, glanced at one another. They had all met Phillip Ross. It had been a bad experience.

Mickey Steele ran his fingers through his mop of wavy blond hair, then rubbed his jaw. His forefinger slipped inside his mouth and gently probed the section of gum that had once housed three teeth.

His pale-blue eyes glittered angrily. 'I want to meet that bastard again,' he growled.

Chalmers glared at him. 'Well, you're going to get your chance. But don't fuck up like you did last time.'

'He took me by surprise. I didn't know what I was up against. But I do now.' Steele's voice was full of hatred.

Chalmers ignored him and snapped an order to Kenny Martin. 'I want you to get over to Dalston and pick up the guns.' He looked from man to man. 'From now on you'll all be carrying. If you get caught, I'll pay the fines. If you get bird, you're on full wages plus a bonus when you get out.' His eyes narrowed. 'There's a ten-grand bonus for the man that kills Ross.'

All three suddenly looked very interested. Greed overcame misgivings. As Bobby Wilks put it, 'Ross ain't bullet-proof, is he?'

'What's the next move, Frank?' asked Steele.

'Ross is going to phone again, tonight at nine-thirty. To tell me where he wants to pick up the cash.' He grinned wolfishly. 'That's when we kill him.'

Phillip Ross telephoned, as promised, at nine-thirty. He instructed Frank Chalmers to drive in his Rolls-Royce, alone, to an abandoned warehouse in Docklands. In his oiliest voice, Chalmers assured Ross that he had the fifty grand, and thanked him for the chance to put things right.

His fat belly shaking with suppressed laughter, Chalmers told his boys, 'The fucking wally fell for it. He thinks Frank Chalmers is going to pay him fifty grand.'

His men grinned broadly as Chalmers fell about laughing. 'It's a pity Robin ain't here to hear all this,' he gasped.

Robin Chalmers was away on holiday at his favourite resort, Puerto Banus near Marbella in Southern Spain. He was on the Chalmerses' 140-foot motor yacht, the *Helena*, named after their late mother. Robin spent at least six months of the year on the yacht. Frank didn't like boats and moaned about the expense, but Robin shrugged it off. 'We can afford it, Frank. I've gotta have some fun.'

Frank loved his younger brother, who could do no wrong in his eyes. He would say, 'OK, OK. You play. I do all the work.' But he didn't really mind. Robin had never been cut out for the rough stuff. Frank knew he didn't like it, and had made sure over the years that Robin was well out of the way when violence was on the cards. The yacht had always been a convenient place to send his kid brother to get him out of harm's way. Frank Chalmers got all the kicks he needed from the respect he received from the population of east and south London, where he was known as 'The Man'. Frank Chalmers, the gang boss. A man it was dangerous to upset, a man who could have you killed.

'Check your pistols,' he ordered. 'We've got one

hour till we meet Ross. We don't want to keep him waiting. Bobby and Kenny, you leave now. Find a place to hide. You know the place where the meet's going to be. I've gotta park directly in front of the bollards in the road leading to the old paint factory and derelict warehouse, get out and walk forwards one hundred paces, then stop. So work it out and be in a position to gun the bastard down.' He turned to Steele. 'You get to ride in the Roller, Mickey. In the boot. Ross told me to come alone, so you mustn't be seen. You should be able to slip out unnoticed and cover me from behind.'

Steele didn't like it, but he nodded assent.

Chalmers grinned and chuckled fatly. 'Fucking Ross couldn't have picked a better place for a meet – for us. After all, that's where we all played as kids.' He took a map from a drawer in his desk and beckoned the three men closer. 'That's the exact place,' he said smugly, pointing. 'Bobby, I want you to hide in the warehouse here.' He stabbed a finger at the map, and waited for Wilks's nod of understanding. 'Kenny,' he said pointing to the map, 'that's the old paint factory.'

'Yeah, I know it.'

'Ross ain't likely to shoot me till he's had a word, to get the hitman's name, and I've handed him the dosh, is he now? So can you two get in position without going down the entrance road? Ross is probably there already, waiting for me to pitch up.'

Martin laughed. 'We can get in both of them

places from different alleys and overhead walkways. No problem, Frank, no problem at all. Ross won't see us.'

Chalmers's expression turned mean and pinched. 'The minute he shows his poxy face, we all start shooting. I don't give a flying fuck who or what he is. Once four of us start shooting at him from different directions, he's fucking well had it.'

He handed out three walky-talkies. 'They're set on the same channel. I'll be carrying one too, so we'll be able to keep in touch. They've got a range of five miles. I'll call you from outside the area to see you're in position.' He looked at each of them in turn. 'Any questions?'

The men looked at one another. Mickey Steel said, 'What if Ross brings some of his mates along?'

'We'll kill them as well,' Chalmers said viciously. 'When Ross sees me arrive on my own, and go tipsying down to meet him with a briefcase in my hand, he'll show himself. And if he's got any mates there they'll back him up.'

'What if they've got guns?' asked Martin.

'Guns? He ain't in the fucking army now, Kenny. We're the gangsters, we're the ones that can get tooled up. We're the bleeding army, ain't we?' He studied the faces around him. 'Any more little doubts?'

The men shook their heads.

'Well, let's get to it. Let's get the bastard.'

He sounded more confident than he felt. He

watched silently as Martin and Wilks set off. He pressed his arm against the revolver snug in its holster under his armpit. It made him feel tough, invincible.

One man against four, he thought. We must win! Ross will give in.

Frank Chalmers braked the Rolls to a halt about a quarter of a mile from his destination. He picked up the walky-talky that lay on the passenger seat. 'This is the Man. Do you receive? Over.'

Bobby Wilks's voice crackled back. 'This is Bobby. I receive. Over.'

'Have you spotted the target? Over.'

'No, not yet. Over.'

'Keep your fucking eyes open.' A short pause. 'Over.'

'He can't be here yet.' It was Kenny Martin. He sounded nervous.

'Where are you, Kenny?' Chalmers was concerned.

'About a hundred yards from where you're going to park, Frank. I'm inside the warehouse. I haven't heard a thing. Over.'

Chalmers thought for a moment. 'Where are you, Bobby?'

'Across the road from Kenny,' said Wilks. 'If Ross shows we'll have him in a crossfire.'

'I'm coming in,' said Chalmers, his voice full of confidence. 'Did you hear all that, Mickey?'

Mickey's voice from the boot was muffled; he sounded bored. 'Yeah, I heard.'

Chalmers let off the brake and accelerated. The Rolls, its headlamps blazing, swept through Docklands and soon reached the spot Phillip Ross had specified. It screeched to a halt as its wheels locked and rubber burnt from the casings in puffs of black smoke.

Frank Chalmers jumped out, hands outstretched, his left holding a black briefcase, his right as though ready to make a quick draw from a non-existent hip holster. He turned his head from side to side, scanning the dark, empty windows. They seemed to stare back at him.

He started to walk and count. At seventy-five he began to feel decidedly nervous. He was exposed and vulnerable. He asked himself, 'Why am I here? What the fuck am I doing here?'

His right hand crept towards his left armpit. He forced it back to his side. He wanted a shit! There was no way he could make the next twenty paces without a crap. He forced the cheeks of his bum together, tightly. It didn't help much. With each step his bowels threatened to open up and dump their smelly load.

He almost lost count of his paces. But the number one hundred echoed in his brain.

He stopped, relieved that he had not disgraced himself.

'Ross, this is Frank Chalmers,' he bellowed. His

voice echoed around the empty streets, bouncing off the walls of the buildings. 'Come out where I can see you.'

His taunt met only silence.

His eyes flickered from side to side. As his false confidence slipped away, sweat beaded his top lip and forehead.

He gritted his teeth, fighting to control his almost insane desire to turn and run for his life.

He lost control of his bowels as he farted. His underpants filled with a hot, wet, mush. 'Come out and face me, you cunt,' he screamed at the top of his voice.

The blast knocked him forwards off his feet. As he flew through the air, he heard a massive explosion. His whole world went into slow motion as his Rolls-Royce became a fireball. As the shell of the car lifted high into the air, Chalmers thudded down on to the ground. He screamed, 'Mickey! Mickey!'

When Phillip pressed the button, he was unsure whether any of the gang were still in the Rolls. What he did know was that two of them were in hiding at the very spot where he had told Chalmers to stop and wait for him. But Chalmers's actions, and those of the two men who ran from cover when the car exploded, confirmed his suspicion that there had indeed been a fourth man in the car. From his rooftop vantage-point, he watched the gang rant and rave at their unseen enemy, and had difficulty restraining his laughter. If he had intended to kill them all, it would have been child's play.

Chalmers's scream of 'Mickey! Mickey!' told Phillip the dead man's identity. He pulled from his inside jacket pocket the sheet of photographs of the Chalmers gang and drew a big black cross over the face of Mickey Steele.

Phillip peered over the parapet. The three men were now standing round the bomb crater. It was a neat round hole, about ten feet in diameter and four feet deep. Smoke rose lazily from it, to be dispersed in the slight breeze. Twenty feet away, the twisted wreckage of the Rolls-Royce blazed furiously, sending up a thick pall of black smoke. There was no sign of Mickey Steele.

Frank Chalmers had parked in exactly the correct position, right on top of the Semtex explosive and remote-controlled detonator that Phillip had spent part of the afternoon burying. He noted that all three men held firearms in their right hands. They were all fidgeting in fear, their eyes darting from place to place.

Chalmers yelled in anger and anguish, 'I'll kill you for this, you bastard! I'll kill you!'

The three waved their guns as they spun round, trying to cover themselves while they beat a hasty retreat.

Emergency sirens wailed in the distance. Phillip smiled with satisfaction. He'd achieved his object, shown he was capable of killing them – had killed one of them. They'd be wary now, afraid of a man who could kill without being seen.

Chalmers'll take me seriously now, he thought. In fact, now would be a good time to turn up the heat and demand more cash. Hit hard and get the hell out.'

Still smiling, he slipped silently away, into the deepening shadows.

Hill and Thorpe arrived at the Stirling Arms just after midnight. After hammering on the door, they were admitted and shown upstairs to the room Frank and Robin Chalmers used as an office. The chief entered the smoke-filled room first, with Thorpe close behind him.

Frank Chalmers called out, 'Come in, Mr Hill. Nice to see you.' He ignored the sergeant.

Hill's eyes swept the faces in the room. He knew them all. There were nine of the gang present. He wanted them all behind bars.

'Is this business or pleasure, Mr Hill?' Chalmers tried to sound jovial.

Hill ignored the question. He was brusque. 'It's about your car, Chalmers, so cut the crap and answer a few questions.'

Chalmers flushed in anger, and said unpleasantly, 'Which car is that, Mr Hill? I have several.'

'Your Roller. Do you know its present whereabouts?'

Chalmers shrugged. 'I ain't got a clue, Mr Hill.

I lent it to Mickey Steele. He wanted to impress a bird.'

A few of his men sniggered.

Hill grinned maliciously. 'Well he did a good trick. If it's him, we found his right leg a hundred yards from his left arm. We're still searching for the rest of him.'

'Is my car all right, Mr Hill?' Chalmers's voice cracked as he tried to sound nonchalant.

The chief chuckled. 'All right? If you're into modern art, it's fine.' His tone hardened. 'One of your friends blew it up. And that fine, upstanding young man Mickey Steele was inside it at the time.'

He paused, to let it sink in, then realized that his news was no news to them. All the faces in the room were bland, with no pretence of horror or surprise.

'But you all knew this already, didn't you?' he growled. 'I assume that you've all been together in this room all evening?'

All the men nodded.

'Nobody left the room, except for the usual piss?'

All the men nodded.

'Good. That saves me a lot of time checking different alibis. I'll let you get on with it then.' He smiled sweetly at Frank Chalmers. 'The man who blew up your Roller was a real dab hand with explosives. An expert. It looks as though you've upset the wrong one this time, Chalmers.' He laughed out loud. 'And I was not the tiniest bit upset about it.'

Still smiling, Hill walked to the door, followed by Thorpe. As he opened the door, he turned back to Chalmers. Savouring the moment, he said, 'If you want police protection, give me a call.'

Chalmers could hear the two policemen laughing as they went down the stairs.

'And fuck you too!' he howled.

A long, tense silence engulfed the room for several minutes. Finally Kenny Martin dared to speak.

'Do you think we should tell Hill who done it?' he asked.

Chalmers turned on him furiously. 'You daft bastard! I take care of things like this myself. I'm not a fucking grass. Besides, I'd be a fucking laughing-stock. Can you fucking well imagine what people would say if Frank Chalmers ran to the Old Bill? Just because of a wanker like Ross? Don't make me laugh!' He grunted in derision, then thought deeply for a few moments.

Taking a deep breath, he said quietly, 'We've got to play this thing down or we'll have every up-and-coming tough in London making a play.' He looked round the room. 'Spread the word that Mickey fell foul of someone over a tart. And that's all there is to it.' He sniffed loudly. 'Tell 'em we buried the geezer. No one will know no different.'

'What exactly are we going to do about this geezer Ross?' asked Bobby Wilks, scowling. 'Mickey was my best mate.'

'You can take Bert.' Chalmers flashed a look at Bert Warren. He was big, sullen and tough-looking, with a fleshy face and a broken nose. His thinning black hair was swept straight back. Chalmers knew he could handle himself. 'Go and sus out Ross's flat. Don't go in. The minute he shows, phone me and I'll send some of the boys to back you up. We don't take any more chances with this bastard. We find him and bury him. I'll send two blokes to relieve you two in the morning. Don't leave till they get there.'

Wilks and Warren made for the door.

'As for the rest of you,' ordered Chalmers, 'I want you all to get tooled up. There's ten grand for the man that nails Ross.' He looked at Kenny Martin, his closest and most trusted friend. 'You and two others' – he pointed to the Hawkins brothers, John and Tony – 'will stay with me until this Ross bastard is nailed good and proper. It's me he's after. I'm the prize. So I'll need plenty of bodies around me.'

He picked out Nobby Grant and Terry White. 'You two, go and get some shut-eye. Make sure you relieve Wilks and Warren in the morning. Be there by eight.'

'I ain't heard what Ross looks like,' complained White, his pale moon-face creased in a scowl.

Chalmers looked at Martin. 'Tell him,' he snapped.

Martin frowned as he searched his memory. 'He's about six foot, broad, athletic-looking, He's got short black curly hair. Blue eyes. Oh, and a scar.'

He pointed to his left cheek. 'That's it.' He looked back at Chalmers for approval.

'So now you all know, those that haven't been punched out by him,' said Chalmers. All the men present knew that Ross and Thompson had made short work of Kenny Martin, Mickey Steele, Chris Goddard and Bobby Wilks, and they laughed.

'He won't get the same chance next time. They took us by surprise,' whined Martin.

More laughter filled the room.

Chalmers ignored Martin's discomfiture. 'OK, let's break it up. We all need a good night's sleep. I want as many men as possible back here in the morning. We're going to smoke this bastard out. And the sooner the better.'

4

Phillip was jubilant. He'd scored his first success against the Chalmers gang.

'One down, eleven to go,' he said aloud as he steered the BMW in the direction of Croydon. He spotted two phone kiosks at the top end of Surrey Street, Croydon's high street, swung into the kerb and braked to a halt. He dialled Frank Chalmers's unlisted number at his office above the Stirling Arms, and listened impatiently to the ringing tone.

Chalmers answered almost immediately: he must have been expecting a call from his wife. 'Hi, darling.' He sounded tense and tired.

'Hi, beautiful.'

Chalmers spat with fury. 'You bastard, Ross. That's two of my men dead because of you and your fucking club.'

'There'll be a lot more before I'm finished. Unless you do as I tell you.'

Chalmers was silent, searching for something to

say that would bring Ross into the open. It was all he could do to keep his mouth shut and not tell him exactly what he intended to do to him once he caught up with him. He choked back his hatred and anger, gritted his teeth and listened.

Phillip continued, 'You tried to set me up, and Steele's dead as a result. Now the price has gone up. I want a hundred thousand pounds and the name of the man who murdered my friend. I'll ring again tomorrow.'

Chalmers crashed the handset back into its cradle. 'Christ All-bleeding-mighty!' He glared at the three men who were supposed to protect him night and day. 'That cunt Ross has upped the ante to a hundred grand. He's ringing back tomorrow. Next time, when he tells us where to make the drop we've got to stall for time, not just bowl in like a bunch of fucking bimbos.'

Kenny Martin asked, 'How did Ross get your private number, Frank?'

Chalmers shrugged. 'I've been wondering about that, and I'm fucked if I know. Some bastard must have given it to him. I wonder what else he told him.' He slammed his fist on to the desk and leapt to his feet. 'We've got a fucking spy in the camp. We must have.'

His men looked at each other questioningly.

Chalmers nodded at the Hawkins brothers. 'You two, John and Tony, find out how Ross got this number. If I find out that some bastard has grassed me to Ross, I'll kill him personally. Slowly.'

There was a wary silence. Then Chalmers added, 'Now, we all need sleep. Tomorrow will take care of itself. I want you all to hit the sack. We'll meet up here in the morning.'

Chalmers felt nervous on the short drive home to Whitechapel. He studied his three hand-picked personal bodyguards, and wondered how they would stand up against a highly trained, well-armed SAS man like Ross. He reckoned that if Ross could get his hands on explosives and detonators, he'd likely have half an arsenal of firearms as well. His conclusion gave him no comfort.

Chalmers suffered a bad night. He was up and down, unable to sleep. He paced the darkened house. Occasionally – and very cautiously – he peered out of the front windows at the row of large Victorian terraced houses opposite, identical to his own. With their curtained and reflecting windows, and the cars parked in front of them, they could easily conceal a sniper. The view from the back windows was even more threatening, with its multitude of walls, fences, bushes and trees, plus the row of darkened houses, about two hundred feet away, that made up the block. A dead easy shot for an expert with a rifle.

Restlessly, he stalked from room to room, leaving the doors open. Only with difficulty could he resist the temptation to kick awake his three bodyguards, who lay open-mouthed, relaxed and snoring loudly. But he knew that a shout or a shot from the automatic pistol that he clutched, cocked and ready to fire, in his right hand would bring them instantly to his aid, and he had no wish to make a fool of himself by waking them without good reason.

He whiled away the silent hours by reflecting on his past life and achievements. Financially, he was a vast success. He was worth over six million pounds, most of it the proceeds of crime, which he'd laundered and invested in property. The houses he'd bought cheaply in run-down areas of London had doubled, tripled, then quadrupled in price as yuppies flooded in from the City. He had no financial need to continue a life of crime. But it was more than money. It had become an obsession with power, almost to the point of megalomania. This was the first time in Frank Chalmers's career that he'd felt threatened and afraid.

He tried to reason with himself: it was one man, just one man, that he and his gang were up against. He'd arm them all. Ten armed men would be more than enough. But the snakes of fear crawled relentlessly in his belly as he recalled what, over the years, he'd read in the papers and seen on TV about the exploits and skills of the SAS. He'd made an implacable enemy of one of the most highly trained, dangerous and deadly men in the world. He, Frank Chalmers, had ordered that man killed, murdered his closest friend and burnt him out of business.

He considered paying Ross the hundred grand he'd demanded and giving him Gómez. But, he told himself acidly, it wasn't simply a case of paying the man off and getting on with his own life. A man like Ross wouldn't stop at that. He wouldn't stop until Chalmers was dead. Or until he, Ross, was dead himself. It had become a fight to the bitter end, and Chalmers realized that fact with increasing dread. He wondered briefly why Ross hadn't fired when he, Martin and Wilks had run out into the open to the smoking bomb crater where he'd parked his Rolls with Mickey Steele hidden in the boot. They'd all been sitting ducks.

Was Ross so confident that he could pick them off, one by one, at his leisure? He concluded that, besides himself, Ross wanted Gary Thompson's murderer and the cash. Gómez was the key to it all. Until Ross got to Gómez, Chalmers would be relatively safe. He'd first try to lure Ross into the open with the cash. If that didn't work out, he'd bring Gómez into play, use Gómez as bait. His skin goosed up as he thought about it: If Ross gets Gómez he'll come after me next. He shook his head and chuckled softly, thinking, There's fucking ten of us. Ten to one ain't bad odds.

Dawn came slowly. Chalmers woke the whole house by making himself some coffee, clashing crockery together and slamming cupboard doors as he busied himself, resentful of the fact that the others could sleep soundly while he could not. He intended to spend the day at the office while he waited for Ross to call.

He'd keep the rendezvous with Ross, preferably sending someone else. Kill the man, if possible. But if that failed he'd go straight to his country estate. He'd be safer there. The house stood in its own grounds. Ross would be unlikely to know of its existence. He'd post armed guards around the clock, leave the dogs out. Ross wouldn't get near him there. He'd install a call-diverter on the phone line Ross used. Ross'd believe Chalmers was talking from Bethnal Green when he was actually in East Sussex.

Chalmers felt more relaxed on the way to the Stirling Arms. The belief that he was relatively safe as long as Ross had no knowledge of Gómez's identity eased his fear considerably.

It would not have improved his frame of mind had he known that, at that very moment, Phillip Ross was in East Sussex, reconnoitring the grounds of Chalmers's house, and intended to enter the house to familiarize himself with the layout and to plant listening devices.

Dressed in camouflage combat clothing and with a lightweight rucksack on his back, Phillip crouched behind a low bush as he surveyed the grounds and studied the big house. It had been built in 1910 by a wealthy stockbroker. Its walls were of red brick, its window mullions of York stone, and the roof was of clay tiles, with overhanging eaves. Neatly trimmed ivy grew thickly up the front, to the height of the eaves. The dossier on Chalmers said he used this place 'only for occasional weekends and discreet business meetings'. It also said, 'House occupied by a middle-aged couple, who act as gardener and housekeeper. Names: Edward Thomas Smithers and Ruth Edwina Smithers, née Collins. No criminal record for either. CAUTION: two Dobermann guard dogs kept on premises.'

He cocked his head and listened with puzzled interest to the crackle and boom of grenades and artillery fire that he could hear not far away. Then he remembered. There was an army exercise and firing range nearby. He'd even trained there himself a few years back.

He spotted the two dogs through his binoculars. They were busy wolfing down food in a twenty foot by ten foot pen surrounded by heavy chain-link fencing. He focused on the pen door: it was fastened shut by a heavy steel bolt. He swung the binoculars slightly to the right, towards the rear of the house. An attractive middle-aged woman was busy at the sink. She appeared to be either singing or talking. A man passed the open door to stand beside the women, put a mug down on the worktop next to the sink and began to pour dark liquid from a polished stainless-steel pot.

Phillip quickly scanned the windows of the big house for any signs of movement that would show that a third person, or even more, might be there.

He saw none, so made his way swiftly and silently to the opposite end of the house.

At once he saw his point of entry, an open ground-floor window, the net curtains fluttering in the gentle breeze. Shielding his eyes against the bright morning sun, Phillip checked the open ground he'd have to cover to reach the window. He noted a three-foot-deep flower bed separating the house from the lawn. It was carefully tended, and brimming with campanula, pansies, cottage pinks, and, at the back, the sweet-scented white nicotiana. Drawing a deep breath, Philip launched himself across the grass towards the house.

He was across the lawn in seconds, leapt on to the window-sill and cautiously pulled the net curtain aside, to reveal expanding gate security shutters. Phillip cursed silently as he studied the steel grille for signs of an alarm. He spotted it in the top left-hand corner: a magnetic contact switch. From his left breast pocket he took a black canvas tool-wrap, which he spread on the sill, and from the wrap he took a length of thin electrical wire with a crocodile clip at each end. He fixed the clips to the metal frame and leading edge of the shutter, then went to work on the lock – it was a brass mortice – with a small rechargeable electric drill. He sliced easily through the brass casing and tumblers, withdrew the drill and, with a twist of a screwdriver, popped the lock open. The well-oiled grille slid silently to one side. Phillip scanned the room for heat-detector sensors, but couldn't see any. He stepped silently inside, into the shadows of what was obviously the main sitting-room.

He took in the room in one glance – noted the Jacobean oak chest, the Georgian silver on the mantelpiece, the scent of beeswax furniture polish – as he crossed noiselessly to the closed door. He dropped to his left knee and bent his head until he could see clearly through the keyhole into the empty hall. A clock chimed in the distance, but no movement disturbed the still air.

Slowly, he opened the door, taking in every aspect and detail of the dark oak-panelled hall. Several tall, solid-looking doors stared silently back at him from the shadows. A wide, sweeping staircase invited him to climb to the first floor. Laughter wafted faintly through from the kitchen. Phillip located the door from which the sound emanated, and opened it a crack. In front of him was a long corridor. A door at the far end was slightly ajar. The sound of the gardener and his wife talking and laughing came from beyond it – Mr and Mrs Smithers, if his information was correct. Phillip noted three doors off to the left of the corridor. Silently he opened each one and checked what lay beyond. Two led to storerooms, the third to a steep flight of stone stairs down to a dusty, junk-filled cellar. No problems there. Phillip soft-footed back down the passage and into the hall.

He eased the door shut, checked the remaining

doors off the hall, and climbed to the first floor, his feet making no sound on the Wilton staircarpet. He combed the house thoroughly, checking every door and window; not even the roof space escaped inspection. As he went, he exchanged several lightbulbs and two-way sockets for duplicates from his kit-bag.

Finally, satisfied he would be able to move confidently about the house, even in the dark, he drifted silently back down to the hall. Again he opened the door to the servants' quarters. A telephone rang in the kitchen and was quickly answered. Phillip went soft-footed to the slightly open door and listened.

'Yes, sir . . . I understand, sir . . . How many, sir? . . . Very well, sir . . . Leave it to me, sir. We'll be ready . . . Look forward to seeing you, sir . . . Goodbye, sir.'

Phillip heard the handset click back into place. There was a short silence, then Mrs Smithers enquired, 'Who was that, then?'

'Mr Chalmers.' A chair scraped as Smithers changed position. 'He's coming here tonight. Told me to lay in enough supplies for at least six people. Said he didn't know how long they'd be staying. Could be some time, he said.' The gardener didn't sound very happy.

There was a sound of light footsteps crossing the room, a rustle of clothing. Mrs Smithers's voice was soft and cajoling. 'Don't be cross, love. We haven't seen Mr Chalmers for weeks now. After all, it's his house. He pays our wages and all the bills, so he's entitled to come whenever he wants.'

'Yes, I know that,' said Smithers sullenly, 'but I can't stand the fat little bastard, or his bleeding hangers-on. They're worse than he is, dishing out orders as if they owned the place. As though we work for them, not him.'

'Be nice to them, Ted,' coaxed his wife. 'They probably won't be here very long. Mr Chalmers is a town bird, you know that. He only has to be here a couple of days and he starts to fidget – he can't get back to town quick enough.'

'Yes, I know all that, but I still don't like the little bastard. Or his band of scum.'

There was a short silence, then Mrs Smithers said lightly, 'You go and get the car started while I make out a shopping list. You know Mr Chalmers likes things to be in order when he arrives.'

Phillip had heard enough. He turned and drifted silently back the way he had come.

The telephone call came at exactly five p.m. Chalmers's voice was harsh with strain, despite his attempts to sound casual. 'Hello, this is Frank Chalmers.'

The voice on the other end of the line was, by contrast, relaxed and calm. 'Have you got the hundred grand, Frank?'

Chalmers fingered the briefcase on his desk uneasily, as he rasped, 'Yeah, I've got it. It's right here.'

'What's the name of the man who killed Gary Thompson?' Now the voice was harder.

'I won't tell you over the phone, Ross. I'll only give you that name face to face.' Chalmers managed to sound determined.

There was a short, pregnant silence, then Phillip conceded, 'OK, Frank. First the money. I want you to send it to Gatwick Airport and I want Bobby Wilks to deliver it.'

Chalmers blanched and shot a glance at Wilks. Wilks's face screwed up in bewilderment as he started to ask, 'Wha—'

Chalmers silenced him with an impatient wave. 'But he can't tell you the name you want – he don't know it.'

'Never mind about that, Frank. I'm the one giving the orders. Now I want you to listen very carefully, Frank, as though your life depended on it. Wilks is to deliver the money unarmed and alone. He's to take it to the arrivals hall at Gatwick and wait near the information desk. He's to arrive at precisely midnight. I'll instruct him from there. If my instructions aren't followed to the letter, I'll come straight after you, Frank, and you'll be dead within forty-eight hours. I'll forget the killer, I'll forget the money, but you will be dead.' There was a click, and the line was cut.

Chalmers's hand shook as he replaced the handset. He stared long and hard at Wilks before he spoke. 'Ross wants you to deliver the cash, Bobby.'

Wilks shrugged.

'He asked for you by name.'

Wilks's face dropped. He ran both hands nervously through his curly dark hair.

'He insists that you go alone.' Chalmers looked round at his men and explained, 'Ross has threatened to kill two of you boys if I don't do as he says. I can't risk that. You all mean too much to me to risk any one of your lives for a poxy hundred grand. I love you all like brothers. You're like my own flesh and blood to me, worth more than all the money in the world. No' – he shook his head decisively – 'I can't risk that.'

Kenny Martin spoke first. 'I'll go with Bobby, and finish this prat once and for all.' He patted the bulge under his left armpit.

'No,' snapped Chalmers. He looked at Martin and the Hawkins brothers. 'You and John and Tony, you three stay with me. We're going to High Trees straight from here.'

Bert Warren, his face as sullen as ever, chipped in, 'I'll go, boss.'

Chalmers smiled gratefully at the big man. 'I knew I could rely on you, Bert.'

Chris Goddard, one of the four men who had gone to the Starlight Club on that first, fateful Friday night – he'd received a broken nose and two cracked ribs for his trouble – touched the bridge of his nose as he said, 'I owe Ross one, and apart from Bobby and Kenny I'm the only one who's seen him in the flesh. So it's best I go along with Bert.'

Chalmers nodded. 'Good, that's three of you, and you're all tooled up. But be bloody careful. Don't start a shoot-out at Gatwick. The airport filth carry guns and they'd shoot you on sight if you had a shooter in your hand and was just waving it about, let alone firing the fucking thing – that's why bleeding Ross chose the place, ain't it?' He thought for a moment, then asked Wilks, 'Are Nobby and Terry still watching Ross's flat?'

'Yes, Frank. They relieved me and Bert at eight this morning. They must be getting pretty pissed off by now.'

Chalmers turned to Goddard. 'Go and fetch them back here, Chris. I don't see any point in watching the place any longer. Ross ain't going back there now. He's holed up somewhere else.'

Goddard hauled himself out of his chair and strode to the door. 'Back in about an hour, Frank.'

'Wait a minute, Chris.' Chalmers checked the time by an elaborately gilded wall-clock over the fireplace of the big, smoke-filled room. 'It's nearly six o'clock. Bobby, I want Bert and Chris to get to the airport by ten. You know what he looks like Chris, so keep your eyes peeled. Ross is bound to get there well before twelve. If you spot him, point him out to Bert. Make sure you've got a knife. If you get the chance, stick it in his fucking back. Better still, fucking well slit his throat.'

'What if Ross just walks up to me and asks for the cash in the middle of the airport?' asked Wilks worriedly. 'I can't shoot him there, Frank. There's bound to be hordes of people about, and like you said the place is always swarming with tooled-up Old Bill.'

Chalmers snapped his fingers and said, 'Like I also said, that's why Ross chose the place. He knows we can't produce shooters, not in the main building. The filth would fall on us like a ton of shit.' He tilted his head back and stared at the ceiling, his mind working fast. A slow, ugly smile spread over his face. 'I know. If Ross just comes up and asks for the money, hand it over like a lamb. Do whatever he tells you. Then leave it to Bert and Chris to get it back and snuff Ross as he goes back to his car.'

Wilks frowned. 'I think we should take Nobby and Terry along. If there's four blokes covering Ross when he leaves with the cash, I'd feel a lot better, Frank.'

Chalmers's eyes dropped to his desk, to the black attaché case containing the hundred grand. He didn't have to consider long. 'Yeah, take Nobby and Terry along.' He looked slowly from Wilks to Warren to Goddard. 'There'll be five of you to get one man. If you kill him and get the money back to me, half of it's yours. That's ten grand each. So don't fuck up!'

Chalmers shuffled around in a desk drawer and came up with a blank piece of A4 paper. He started to draw a plan of the arrivals hall at Gatwick Airport, speaking as he sketched. The others gathered round the desk.

'Right,' he said, 'you've all been there loads of times. There are only three ways to get in or out of the airport. Road, rail and air. We can forget about Ross making a getaway by air, can't we, lads?'

Wilks looked worried. 'Why can we, Frank? If he did, we couldn't follow him through into the departure lounge. You have to go through a bleeding metal detector, and we're all carrying.'

'That,' said Chalmers smugly, 'is why he can't go through there either. Plus the fact that he'd be carrying a briefcase with a hundred thousand fucking quid' – he stabbed a forefinger at his chest – 'of my fucking money. He can't risk being questioned by the filth and the Customs about where he got that kind of money. They'd reckon it's drugs money and confiscate it, and none of us would ever see it again.' He shook his head emphatically. 'No, he won't try to get out that way. So that leaves us with road or rail.'

Bert Warren chipped in. 'He'd have to be fucking desperate to use the trains, boss. If they're not late they're on strike – or else it's the wrong kind of bleeding leaves on the track.'

Laughter eased the tension in the smoke-filled room.

Chalmers said, 'No, he won't use a train. If he did he couldn't get off when and where he liked.

We'd have him trapped. We could take him any time. No, he'll use a car. It's odds on.' He stabbed at the section of the sketch map that showed the car park. 'Nobby and Terry, you two guard the exit from the car park, and keep an eye on Bobby. Ross ain't seen either of you, so you needn't worry about being recognized. Chris, you try and keep out of sight. Ross has met you, and he'll recognize you if he clocks you.'

'And I'll recognize him too, the bastard,' growled Goddard.

Grant and White looked sideways at each other and grinned. They quickly straightened their faces as Goddard scowled at them and demanded, 'What are you two arseholes grinning about?'

'Nothing, Chris, nothing at all,' said Nobby Grant.

'Pack it in, you bleeding lot, and concentrate,' snapped Chalmers. 'This is serious. Chris, you stand here.' He indicated on his sketch map the area marked 'shops & bogs'. 'You can see Bobby from there, and make sure Ross don't try to sneak through to the departure lounge.'

Goddard nodded.

Chalmers turned his attention to Warren. 'Bert, Ross don't know you either, so stick close to Bobby. Between him and the exit.' He pointed out the area between the information desk and the wide walkway to the trains and car parks.

Warren shrugged and nodded.

'When it's done, go straight to High Trees. That's where I'll be.'

A very different-looking Phillip Ross was in position on the open rooftop level of number two car park at Gatwick Airport at eight that evening. His blue eyes, his blond wig and moustache, the light beige reversible raincoat and matching soft hat, plus the blue Scandinavian Airlines shoulder bag, gave him the look of a Swede or a Dane. His heavy horn-rimmed glasses and the binoculars slung round his neck suggested an aircraft spotter. The fact that he paid more attention to the entrance barrier of the short-term car park attracted no notice as he moved about.

In position on the first level of number one car park was Julie. It had taken her over an hour to persuade Phillip to let her accompany him and help him. What had decided him in the end was the realization that if he refused she'd probably go anyway, and then he'd have no idea of where she was, what she was up to and whether she was safe.

'All right,' he'd said reluctantly. 'But you must give me your word that you'll follow my orders to the letter. I must know – and I mean *know* – that you're where you should be, and not getting into difficulties you aren't trained to deal with. You're to keep a careful watch, and ring me on the mobile if there's anything at all to report. Nothing more than that. Understand?'

'Yes, sir,' Julie said meekly. Then a slow, triumphant grin spread over her face and she leapt up from the settee and karate-chopped an imaginary opponent. 'I'll be good, Phillip, honestly I will. I couldn't just have sat here biting my damned nails, thinking about Gary and worrying about you.' And she'd flung her arms round his neck and kissed him.

Now, Phillip pushed out of his mind the memory of that kiss and the lovemaking that had followed, and gave every ounce of his concentration to the job in hand. His alertness paid off at nine-fifty. A dark-blue Jaguar containing four men stopped at the barrier to collect a ticket from the automatic machine. Phillip recognized the driver, Chris Goddard, as one of the four men he and Gary had beaten up on their first encounter with the Chalmers gang. The man in the passenger seat, Phillip recalled from the photographs of the whole gang, was Albert Warren. He couldn't make out the faces of the two men in the back of the car. He watched as the barrier lifted and the Jaguar drove in, then swept into the entrance to number two car park and disappeared from view.

His mobile phone warbled.

'Phillip, they're here,' came Julie's voice, hushed and excited. 'They're in a—'

'I know,' he interrupted. 'I saw them too. Try to see where they park, and then meet me in the covered way that leads into the terminal.'

'Gotcha. On my way.' She was gone.

Phillip had parked his BMW in number three car park, close to the exit. Julie's Golf was in number one, so that they had two escape routes if needed. Quickly, he went to the covered way that led from all three car parks to the main terminal, and waited. A few minutes later Julie hurried up to him, flushed and out of breath.

'They're coming,' she panted. 'Four of them.'

'That's fine,' he said, and grinned at her. 'The girl done good. Now calm down and get your breath back. We act natural and wait.'

Almost at once, it seemed, the four men appeared. They walked in pairs, Goddard and Warren in the lead, Nobby Grant and Terry White the back-markers. Phillip felt a surge of hatred for them all as they passed, no more than ten feet away, giving him and Julie only a cursory glance.

He tucked Julie's arm through his, and whispered, 'Now we follow them.'

The four men walked through to the arrivals hall, looked around, consulted the overhead signs, then went up the escalator to Gatwick Village and straight into the pub. Three of them sat down at a corner table, while White went to the bar and ordered four pints of bitter.

Amateurs, Phillip thought, and smiled. He led Julie to a seat from which she could see into the pub, and told her, 'Stay here and watch them. If they leave, or move out of your sight, ring me and tell me who's gone in which direction. I'm going back to wait for Bobby Wilks.'

Julie's first impulse was to say that she didn't want to be left on her own, that she'd rather go with him, but she realized instantly that if she did he'd think she couldn't cope with the situation and would send her back to the cottage. She swallowed her nerves, and said calmly, 'OK, you can count on me.'

'See you later,' said Phillip. He had a pretty accurate idea of how she was feeling, so gave her a smile of encouragement before turning and setting off back to his vantage point in the car park. Once there, he leant against a pillar and waited patiently.

At eleven-forty-five Bobby Wilks drove up to the barrier in a black 500 SEL Mercedes saloon. The big car purred into number three car park. Phillip was waiting on level one as Wilks drove up the slope, searched all round that level, then, finding no vacant space, climbed to the next level. There he parked next to a small family hatchback, whose driver was unloading several suitcases, helped by his wife and hampered by a whining little boy aged about four. Wilks waited until the family had moved off, then got out of the Merc, locked it and strode off towards the exit, carrying a black attaché case.

He'd gone only a few yards when a dark saloon car purred into view, its driver searching for a suitable parking slot. As it passed, an Asian couple with four orderly children, obviously dressed in their best, emerged from one of the lifts and started to walk towards Phillip. They stopped, puzzled, looked round, then realized they were on the wrong level and turned back towards the lifts.

Phillip cursed silently. He couldn't tackle Wilks while there were so many people around. He'd have to wait for another opportunity. In the meantime, he'd make damned sure Wilks couldn't make a run for it.

As soon as the two families had disappeared from view, Phillip crossed to the Mercedes. He bent down to the near-side wheel and cut the air valve with a razor-sharp lock-knife. The valve stem hissed noisily as air escaped with considerable force. Satisfied that the car would be going nowhere, fast, he turned and followed Wilks.

His quarry was easy to spot: Wilks stood in front of the information desk, clutching the attaché case in his left hand. He looked a bit tense, like a businessman waiting impatiently for his driver.

Julie hurried over to Phillip the moment she spotted him. 'Thank God! I wondered what had happened when Wilks appeared and there was no sign of you,' she said.

Phillip put one hand under her chin, tilted her face up to his and kissed her cheek. 'I had to fix his car,' he said softly. 'Tell you about it later. Now, don't try to look round. Just make like we're whispering sweet nothings to each other, and tell me where they all are.'

'Goddard's over by the toilets – we can't see him from here. Grant and White are together, behind that group of Japanese by the exit to the car park, and Warren's this side of Wilks, with his back to us.'

'Good work, love.'

'Glad you brought me, then?'

'OK, OK, OK,' he said wrily. 'But you're not finished yet. I couldn't get to Wilks in the car park – there were too many people around – so we'll use Plan B.' He dug a notebook and biro out of his pocket, scribbled a note and handed it to her. 'Go to the information desk, and get a leaflet that gives the desk's phone number. Don't use your mobile – it probably wouldn't work in here anyway. Ring from one of those public phones over there, ask them to page Wilks and give him this message. Say it's urgent.'

Julie's eyes widened as she read the note. 'You clever bastard,' she whispered admiringly. 'Nice one. I like it.' With a conspiratorial wink, she turned and went over to the information desk. Phillip watched her pass Wilks without a glance, pick up a couple of leaflets at the desk and head for the public phones. She dialled, spoke briefly, hung up and walked calmly back to him.

Within a minute, the bell of the public-address system chimed out, and a young woman announced,

'Would Mr Bobby Wilks please come to the information desk. Mr Bobby Wilks to the information desk, please.' Her voice echoed loudly round the hall.

Wilks was obviously shaken by the sound of his name. He glanced quickly over at Goddard and Warren, then at Grant and White. All four men stood still, upright and alert.

Wilks shrugged, turned and walked hesitantly to the desk. He spoke to one of the uniformed staff, who smiled, nodded and passed him a piece of paper. Wilks thanked her and walked slowly away from the desk studying the message, which read:

> Meeting cancelled. Send the boys back to the Stirling Arms. I'm on my way to High Trees. Meet me there ASAP with cash.
>
> Frank Chalmers.

Wilks beckoned the four men to join him. They hurried over. Phillip and Julie watched, amused, as Wilks showed them the note. There followed a serious discussion. Arm in arm, Phillip and Julie wandered aimlessly by them, passing close enough to hear Wilks saying sternly and urgently, 'We'll do exactly what the boss says. Now get your arses back to the office and don't hang about. Something's wrong.'

Phillip and Julie followed slowly, allowing them to pull well ahead. They saw the men pay at the car park kiosk and collect a blue ticket, the cardboard key that would raise the automatic barrier and let the car out. Then the five split up, Wilks turning left to car park number three and the others turning right to number two.

Phillip turned to Julie. 'Good. They've fallen for it. You follow Goddard and co. Make sure they all stay together, follow them just a little way, until you're sure they're not turning round and coming back, then go straight to the cottage and wait for me to ring you. I'll take care of Wilks.'

As he watched her out of sight, he smiled grimly, musing on his strategy. One, create a diversion. Two, divide the enemy. Three, surprise – hit hard and fast. He reversed his coat, so that the dark-blue material now showed, took off his hat and then, satisfied that his appearance was sufficiently different to fool his targets, followed Wilks.

He watched from the opposite side of the car park from where Wilks had parked the Mercedes. The sound of cursing drifted across as Wilks kicked the flat tyre in anger and frustration. Suddenly the gangster stopped and swung round. His right hand whipped inside his jacket as the thought struck him that this might be a trap and he'd have to face the danger alone.

'Fuck it!' he swore. He wished he'd got the others to come with him to the car. He'd thought of it, but dismissed the idea when the meeting was cancelled. And anyway Ross hadn't shown. The others would have taken the piss out of him, accusing him of losing his bottle, of being a right little pansy boy. He cursed the fact that Chalmers hated mobile phones. 'The bleeding things ain't secure,' he'd said 'Remember Prince Charlie boy's chats with his crumpet splashed all over the papers? Any road, I'm not having you lot wandering about like a load of fucking sales reps, chatting up your birds or your bleeding bookies when you're supposed to be working.' And he'd never allowed his men to use them.

Wilks looked from side to side, his eyes searching out the many places, behind any car or pillar, from which a man could leap out and attack. Or snipe . . .

Nervously, he backed up between the Merc and the hatchback parked alongside. He drew his pistol, slipped off the safety catch and squatted down behind a concrete pillar. He was shaking like a leaf, from a mixture of fear and anger. His throat felt like sandpaper. Cold sweat oozed on his forehead and top lip, in his armpits, on the palms of his hands. The pistol started to slide in his damp grip.

A nightmarish fifteen minutes passed. But no long, slender knife slipped silently between his ribs, no bullet smacked into him between the eyes, and Wilks started to regain some composure. He even began to feel slightly ridiculous. Like all men, he'd known fear. But until he met Ross, felt those devastatingly fast, accurate karate kicks and punches, he'd been under the illusion he was unbeatable. He'd believed that no one man could beat him in a fight.

Ross and Thompson had proved him wrong. He now knew Ross could punch his lights out with the same ease that he himself could knock out a fifteen-year-old boy. He also now knew what real, paralysing terror was. He didn't like it.

Wilks straightened slowly from his crouching position and peered round the pillar and over the car roofs. The car park was gloomy, deserted save for one couple some sixty yards away, climbing into a Volvo estate car. Distant traffic noise was drowned by the roar of a large jet taking off. He listened while the roar faded rapidly in the distance, then, wiping his sweaty hands on his shirt-front and fumbling with his keys, moved cautiously to the driver's door of the Mercedes. He dropped the keys, cursed under his breath as he bent to retrieve them. Trying to ignore possible threats from the shadows around him, he concentrated on unlocking the car door, angry and humiliated that his nerves made so simple a task so difficult.

At last he managed it. He threw the attaché case on to the passenger seat, took another fast look around, half convinced that he'd panicked over a flat tyre, that he'd simply picked up a nail on the journey to the airport. He thrust his automatic back into its holster under his left armpit and opened the car boot.

Wilks sighed with relief as he pressed hard on the

spare tyre and found it fully inflated. When he had finished changing the wheel he smiled wryly as he put the flat tyre in the boot, tossed the jack in after it and bent to straighten the boot carpet. The smile froze into a rictus grin as the cold steel of a silencer gently touched the soft skin behind his left ear. Fear flooded back with a vengeance. His legs threatened to collapse beneath him. He wanted to be sick. He started to shake uncontrollably.

Phillip spoke with icy authority: 'Get into the boot.'

Panic nailed Wilks to the ground. He managed to stutter, 'D-d-don't kill me, Ross.'

The silencer pressed harder. 'Get in,' Phillip ordered again, the menace in his voice all the stronger for the lack of histrionics and threats.

Wilks scrambled frantically into the boot, curled into a foetal position on his left side, and stared in disbelief and terror at the tall, blond stranger who pointed a big automatic pistol, complete with silencer, steadily at him between the eyes. 'You're not Ross,' he said confusedly.

Phillip removed the thick horn-rimmed glasses, the rim of which had concealed the scar below his left eye. He grinned maliciously as he murmured, 'You'd better believe it, Wilks.'

Recognition flooded through Wilks as he looked into the icy blue eyes and saw the scar. He shook his head in despair. 'Oh my God,' he gasped, 'don't do it, Ross. Don't kill me.'

His plea was ignored. 'I want the name of the man who killed Gary Thompson,' demanded Phillip.

Wilks licked his dry lips. 'I can't tell you that, because I don't know it. All I know is that Chalmers, Frank Chalmers, ordered him killed. You was supposed to be killed as well, but they missed you.'

'Who is "they"?'

Wilks raised a hand defensively. 'I swear I don't know the hitman's name. All I know is that Bert Reed was sent as back-up and ended up dead.'

'Who'd know the killer's name?'

'Only Frank Chalmers. He never told anyone who he used. He always said it was a top professional. The only bloke to get to meet the hitman was Reed. We all tried to find out from him who the geezer was, but Reed wouldn't tell you the time of day if you asked him. He was a mean, cold bastard.'

Phillip lowered the pistol until it was pointing at Wilks's heart. 'I'm wasting my time,' he said quietly, and his finger tightened on the trigger.

Wilks raised his hands pathetically, to ward off the bullet, as he pleaded, 'No! No! Don't kill me, Ross. Please! I'll tell you anything.'

Phillip's voice was hard and contemptuous. 'You can't tell me anything, scumbag.'

He squeezed the trigger.

The soft-nosed bullet clipped Wilks's left thumb, then made a deep thud, accompanied by a sharp cough from the silencer, as it smashed through his breastbone. Distorting and tumbling, it ruptured his pulmonary artery and ripped open his heart and his left lung before coming to rest lodged in his spine.

Phillip said a crisp 'Good night' and slammed the boot shut on Wilks's staring eyes. He reached into the Mercedes, took the attaché case from the passenger seat and strode away across the car park. It was twenty-five minutes to one.

Phillip took exit six of the M25 to get on to the A25. He stopped at a phone box in Oxted – he would have been sourly amused to know that he and Chalmers were equally distrustful of mobile phones' security – and dialled a number from memory.

Peter Russell's voice was thick with sleep as he answered.

'I've got about two hundred pounds of totalled garbage to dispose of, Peter. Could you deal with it, please?'

There was a short silence while Russell came fully alert and checked the time. 'Where is it?' he asked.

Phillip give him the location and registration number of the Mercedes.

'No problem,' said Russell. 'Leave it to me. At this time and this distance, I'll have it cleared by . . . five. Will that be OK?'

'Yes, that'll be fine. I'll let the people concerned think the garbage is in my possession. That'll stop them hunting for it.'

'Do you need any cash? It's still flooding in.'

Phillip chuckled. 'No, Peter. They tried to buy

120

me off, so I took the money to finance the venture. Send what you've got to Gary's parents and tell them to go on a long holiday or something. It'll be good for them.'

'Good idea. I'll deliver it personally. How's the cottage? Are you making good use of it?'

'It's fine, thanks. You did a great job of furnishing it.'

Russell laughed. 'I thought you'd like it. If I missed anything, let me know.'

'It's perfect – more than I could have hoped for. I'd better go now. I'll be in touch.'

'Be lucky, friend,' said Russell quietly, and he rang off.

Phillip drove to Biggin Hill, where he stopped at another phone box. He knew Frank Chalmers would be at High Trees, but didn't want him to know that his country house was no secret or that Phillip knew he was hiding out there. He wanted Chalmers to feel safe and well hidden. Then he'd give him a very nasty surprise.

He dialled Chalmers's number at the Stirling Arms. He was taken aback for a moment when Chalmers answered the phone, but quickly realized he must be using a call-diverter.

'Thanks for the cash, Frank.' He heard Chalmers gasp. 'I've also got your friend Bobby Wilks. You can have him back when you give me the name I want.' He rang up, leaving Chalmers howling abuse down the empty line.

*　　*　　*

Julie waited anxiously for Phillip's return. She'd followed the four men to their car, watched them drive off down the ramp, then dashed back to her own car and driven furiously to catch them up. She'd followed them along the M23 until they turned off to join the M25, then, with a sigh of relief, continued towards Croydon and Biggin Hill.

When she heard a car coming up the drive, she quickly checked it was indeed Phillip and then ran out to greet him, relief and happiness that he was safe bubbling up inside her. He smiled and kissed her. She could tell at once that he'd been successful.

Phillip opened the boot of the BMW and took out Wilks's attaché case. He held it up, smiling, and said, 'Guess what I've got in here.'

When, as they sat in the lounge, he showed her the answer, Julie's eyes and mouth opened wide in amazement. She picked up a few of the bundles of notes. 'I've never *seen* so much money,' she said.

'Neither have I,' chuckled Phillip. 'The Chalmers gang have kindly supplied us with the means to finish them off and then get ourselves a good start in a new life.'

'Will you reopen the Starlight Club?' she asked hesitantly.

'No, I couldn't do that.' Phillip's voice was quiet and sad. 'I'd never be able to get Gary out of my mind, knowing he'd been murdered there.' He took her hand and kissed the palm. 'We'll decide what to do with our lives once the job's done.'

He stood up and crossed the lounge to the desk. From a drawer he took a sheet of paper on which were printed photographs of twelve men. He returned to Julie, drew a black cross over Bobby Wilks's face, and handed her the sheet.

'Ten to go,' he said harshly.

Julie looked at the three photos that had black crosses scored through them: Albert Reed, Mickey Steele and Bobby Wilks. Puzzled, she counted the remaining faces. 'But there are only nine pictures left.'

'The man who actually murdered Gary isn't shown there. The only person who seems to know who that man is is' – he prodded at Frank Chalmers's fat face, his own face bitter – 'that bastard. And I can't kill him until I learn who actually pulled the trigger.'

'But how can you possibly get Chalmers to tell you that?'

Phillip smiled viciously. 'I'll ask him one more time. I don't expect him to tell me. I think he'll try to use the information to draw me out into the open. I'll let him do that, kill a couple more of his gang and wind him up so that he thinks I've given up any hope of getting the killer's name and am going to kill him, Chalmers, anyway. To save his own neck,' he said contemptuously, 'to buy himself some time, he'll give me the name.'

'If Chalmers tells you who killed Gary, who will you go after first, the killer or Chalmers?'

'I get the killer first. Chalmers comes last on my list. I want him to be totally alone, with nowhere to hide, no gang to hide behind, no friends, nothing. I want him running scared. Then I shall kill him.'

Julie moved a little apart from him and said quietly, 'Phillip, you frighten me when you speak like that.'

'Do you want me to stop?'

She shook her head. 'No . . . no, you mustn't stop. Not until they're all dead. I can't rest until they're all dead. It's just . . . you won't get to enjoy it too much, will you? You won't find yourself hunting them down and seeing their fear become a pleasure as well as a duty?'

Phillip crooked a finger under her chin, raised her head until she was looking straight into his eyes, and cupped her cheek in his hand. 'I'm a soldier, Julie,' he said quietly. 'I know that danger and how to avoid it. I shan't let myself degenerate into a sadistic thug like them.'

They held each other's gaze for a long minute. Then Julie turned her head until she could kiss the hand against her face. Phillip brushed away some stray strands of long blonde hair, bent his head and kissed her gently. The kiss became passionate, and he felt a stirring in his loins, felt himself hardening. Julie gently stroked the inside of his thigh, sliding her hand up to the bulge in his trousers. She felt him jerk and swell at her touch, and smiled provocatively up at him. He cupped her breasts, caressing her nipples until they hardened in his hands. She felt herself growing hot and wet between the thighs. Her breath came short. She straddled Phillip's thigh, rubbing her crotch eagerly against him.

He pushed her down on to the settee and very slowly undressed her, biting her nipples gently, running his tongue teasingly over her throat and belly until she moaned with desire. He slipped a hand into her panties, then ripped them off, digging his fingers deep into her, until she cried out, quaking and gasping under him.

'My turn now,' said Julie, when she'd got her breath back. She pulled him up off the settee and ran her fingernails hard down his spine. She wouldn't let him touch her. She stripped him naked, biting his neck and chest as she did so, licking his nipples and tweaking the hairs on his chest, then knelt in front of him, cupping his balls in her hands and squeezing gently. She kissed his cock, then took it in her mouth, taking him in deeper and deeper. Phillip groaned with pleasure, caught her head in his hands and pressed his hips hard against her, forcing himself still deeper into her until he could stand no more. He tore himself out of her mouth, flung her down on the settee, wrenched her legs apart and entered her ferociously. Again and again he slammed into her, and she moaned helplessly under him, her head rolling from side to side in mingled pain and pleasure. He quickened his thrusts until he felt the first spasms of her climax, and with a triumphant shout allowed himself to come. Julie moaned and writhed beneath him, digging her nails into his back until she drew blood. Then they collapsed together, and lay exhausted, sweating and panting, their hearts pounding.

Frank Chalmers screamed threats and abuse down the empty line for several seconds before he realized Phillip had hung up. Gripping the handset so tightly that his knuckles whitened, he stared at it for a moment before slamming it back into its cradle. In mingled fury and tension he paced up and down the High Trees sitting-room, his heels clicking loudly on the polished parquet floor. 'That bastard Ross has got Bobby and my hundred grand as well,' he stormed.

Kenny Martin and the Hawkins brothers looked on glumly, afraid to speak in case this raving lunatic in the form of their boss should turn and vent his rage on them, blaming them for the disaster as he had done before. But nothing they could think of had ever been this bad. They'd never seen Chalmers in such a rage. They could do nothing but look on in silence while he paced and swore in frustration.

Chalmers stopped in his tracks and swung round to face them, alight with fury. 'OK, so fucking Ross has got my fucking dosh. He's got Bobby. Where are the other four bleeding clowns I sent to protect the dosh? And Bobby.' He shook his head in disbelief. 'I don't believe the incompetence. Five big, tough guys against one man, and not only does this one fucking man waltz off with my hard-earned cash, he takes one of my men as a fucking hostage. What the fuck are you three dummies going to do about it? Are you just going to sit there like a bunch of fucking bimbos or what?'

Martin shifted nervously in his chair. 'What do you want us to do, boss?'

'Get my fucking money back – and Bobby. And kill that fucking Ross.' His voice dropped low and became menacing. He spat out each word singly. 'That ... is ... what ... I ... want ... you ... to ... do.'

Kenny Martin rose from his chair. 'I'll go and look for Bobby.'

Chalmers was aghast. 'Hold it, Kenny, let me think about this.' Scratching his head thoughtfully, he went over and checked the curtains to make sure there were no chinks between them. 'For all we know Ross could be out there now.'

'Do you want me to take a butcher's, boss?' Martin was eager to placate Chalmers.

His proposal was dismissed with a wave of the hand. 'No. Ross doesn't even know about this place.' But Chalmers frowned worriedly, and told the Hawkins brothers, 'You boys go and take a look around. Make sure the dogs are loose and the floodlights are on. I want the lights left on all night.' The two men went out, checking their guns.

Chalmers called after them, 'Keep your eyes peeled. He just might be out there.' Then he slumped heavily into a chair. He looked at Martin and smiled weakly. 'I'm sorry, Ken.' He rubbed his sweaty forehead, examined his wet palm, dried it on his trouser leg. 'It's just that I'm so wound up. This bastard Ross is getting to me.' He curled his fingers into claws. 'If only I could get my hands on him.'

The phone bell made them both jump.

Chalmers snatched up the receiver. 'Hello,' he rasped.

'We're back at the office, boss. What do you want us to do?'

Chalmers recognized Bert Warren's deep voice. 'What the fuck are you doing there? And who's with you?' he demanded.

There was a stunned silence on the other end of the line.

Chalmers shouted, 'Bert, can you hear me?'

'Yes, boss, I can hear you. But I don't understand. You ordered us to come back here. I saw the message myself.'

Chalmers listened in rising fear and anger as Warren explained. He made Warren repeat what the note had said.

'Are you sure it said I was on my way to High Trees?'

128

'Yes, boss, positive.'

'I want you all here as fast as possible. Ross knows I'm here. So get here fucking quick and don't stop on the way for nothing. Got it?' Chalmers slammed the phone down and sank back into his chair. His voice was low and unsteady as he said, 'Get me another drink, Kenny. I need it.'

As he gulped the brandy he filled Martin in on the current situation and explained how it had all gone wrong.

Martin whistled when the tale of woe was finished, and said with some trepidation, 'This Ross is one smart bastard.' His eyes checked the drawn curtains again, and he reached instinctively for his gun. He checked it was loaded before returning it to its shoulder holster. He pulled a wry face as he said, 'None of us are much good with pistols, boss. We don't get the practice. Some of the boys have never even fired one.'

'You only have to point the fucking thing,' said Chalmers, horrified, 'and then pull the trigger.'

Martin shook his head. 'No, boss, there's a lot more to it than that if you want to hit what you're shooting at. Besides, Ross ain't going to stand still while we all take pot-shots at him. Plus the fact that he'll more than likely be shooting back. And an SAS man'll be a helluva lot better with a hand-gun than any of us.'

Chalmers's concern was evident as he asked, 'How much ammo have we got?'

Martin did some mental arithmetic. 'All the pistols have got full clips. Plus about a hundred rounds.'

'Phone Eddy the Gun. Now. Tell him we want two thousand rounds of ammo and we want it fast. Offer him a monkey as bonus if he can deliver it before eight tomorrow morning.'

'What if he can't deliver?'

'Then the minute Bert gets here, send him to Dalston to pick it up,' Chalmers said through gritted teeth. 'Tomorrow everyone practises. I want those stupid bastards to be able to hit what they're shooting at.'

Martin scratched his head thoughtfully. 'We could do with some shotguns. They're easier to use and the boys are more likely to hit a moving target with one of them than with a pistol.'

'Then buy some fucking shotguns. Eddy can supply them. Buy machine-guns, buy whatever you think we'll fucking well need to blow Ross to hell!'

Eddy ('the Gun') Richards arrived at High Trees at seven the next morning. It was a good and highly profitable order, and to earn the five-hundred-pound bonus he had worked all through the night collecting guns and ammunition from his stores in and around London. He supplemented his dole cheques by selling and renting firearms to the underworld. He would sell a gang a gun, or any number of guns, for use in an armed robbery and then buy them back at half-price provided the weapons hadn't been used. The criminals liked the arrangement because they didn't have to keep guns around them, but knew that a phone call to Eddy would get them tooled up within the hour.

It was most unusual for Eddy to deliver guns personally. His usual procedure was to plant a gun where the buyer could collect it after he had handed over the cash. The size of the order and Eddy's greed got the better of him on this occasion, plus the fact that Frank Chalmers was a good customer and could be trusted not to grass. But nevertheless he was glad to arrive at the tall iron gates of High Trees without having been stopped by the police at a road-block.

The wrought-iron gates were shut, secured by a stout padlock and chain.

Eddy climbed out of his Ford Transit – he normally drove a Volvo estate car, but reckoned on something a bit more ordinary when carrying this amount of gear – stretched his tall, lean frame, yawned, unconsciously patted his Bobby Charlton hairdo to make sure it was in place, and pressed the bell push.

A loud metallic voice from one of the gateposts made him jump, demanding, 'Who's there?'

He spoke into a perforated metal plate on the gatepost. 'It's me, Eddy Richards. Frank Chalmers is expecting me.'

'OK, be right down,' said the metal plate, which then buzzed and clicked into silence.

Two men appeared in the driveway. Eddy recognized them as the Hawkins brothers, and felt a lot better. He studied them as they approached: the family resemblance was unmistakable. Both men were just under six foot tall, with sharp, boyish features, framed by badly cut blond hair curling over their collars, and hazel eyes set too close together. People often mistook them for twins, but John, at thirty-four, was the elder by thirteen months.

Richards greeted them cheerfully. 'Hello, boys. Starting a war, are we?'

'Ask no questions, you'll get no lies,' said Tony sourly.

Richards shrugged and got back behind the wheel of the van. John Hawkins pulled open one of the heavy gates and told him, 'Follow the drive to the front of the house. Frank's waiting for you.' Richards nodded. The van's wheels spun in the gravel as he accelerated up the drive, muttering under his breath, 'And fuck you too.'

Many hands made light work of unloading the cases of ammunition and firearms. They were carried into the large sitting-room and set on the floor for Richards to open them and show off his wares. Besides the ammunition he had brought four pump-action twelve-bore shotguns, two sawn-off double-barrelled shotguns and a Uzi nine-millimetre sub-machine-pistol.

Chalmers looked over the firearms as his men handled and inspected them. 'How much is this little lot, Eddy?' he asked bluntly.

Richards knew exactly what he was going to charge, but he went through the old routine. He rubbed his chin, ummed and aahed, then said, 'The nine-mil ammo is a nicker a round, Frank. That's two grand. The shotguns . . . I can let you have them for a monkey each. The Uzi . . . well, I've gotta ask a grand for that, and it's cheap at the price. I could get a lot more for it.' He shot Chalmers an oily smile. 'But as you're a good customer . . . And I'll throw in the shotgun cartridges for free.' He rubbed his chin again, made a show of adding up on his fingers. 'That comes to—'

Chalmers cut across him. 'Six grand.' He glanced across to Martin. 'Pay him, Kenny.'

Richards raised a hand and mumbled, 'Er . . . I was promised a bonus, a monkey, if I delivered by eight this morning, Frank. I wouldn't mention it, but I did work all night to get this lot together.' This smile was even oilier than the last.

Chalmers looked pissed off as he spoke to Martin again. 'Give him another five hundred.' He gave Richards a hard-eyed stare and spoke very deliberately: 'Not one word, Eddy. Not one word to anyone that I bought this gear. Or you end up in a ditch, Eddy. Understand?'

Richards tried to look offended. 'No need for all

133

that, Frank. I've got a reputation to uphold, you know.'

'See that you do uphold it, Eddy. Just see that you do, that's all.' Chalmers walked to the door. 'Kenny will pay you. Just make sure that the boys know how to load those bleeding guns before you leave.' He went out and slammed the door.

Phillip arrived at High Trees in time to see Richards's van drive off. He made a note of the registration number, then moved to his chosen vantage point in a copse of trees on a hillock overlooking the house and grounds. He could see the roof jutting out behind a group of fir trees that towered above the house to a height of sixty or seventy feet and almost hid it.

From his vantage point he could see most of the open ground around High Trees. A wooded area lay to his left. Near the house the gravel drive curved round the fir trees, then continued in a straight line for about a hundred yards to the entrance gates, which the Hawkins brothers were closing and padlocking. Phillip watched them walk up the drive and disappear from view as they neared the house.

He turned his attention to his own position. It was protected at the rear by a large thornbush, which formed a loose horseshoe around him, preventing anyone from approaching or attacking behind him. His angle of vision was about a hundred and ten degrees, so, although he couldn't be approached unseen, his only way out was forwards. He quickly decided to correct this by cutting an escape way through the thornbush big enough for him to crawl through. Five minutes later his hands were bleeding from numerous scratches and he was devoutly hoping he'd never need to use that exit.

From his rucksack he produced the tools needed for digging in, plus a small ten-channel radio receiver, crystal-tuned to the frequencies transmitted by the various listening devices planted around the big house. By turning a dial, Phillip could tune in to each bug in turn. He fixed the receiver to his belt and fitted an earpiece. From the bug planted by the kitchen door came the rattle of crockery and cutlery, accompanied by Mrs Smithers's cheerful singing as she worked. The signal was crystal-clear. The tiny transmitters worked perfectly at up to a thousand yards, and Phillip was half that distance away. He flicked through the channels, picking up only silence until he tuned in to the sitting-room. Lots of metallic clicking, plus two or three separate conversations, met his ear.

To a man so familiar with weapons the metallic clicks were unmistakable. Men were checking their guns: slides being drawn back, to cock the gun, then allowed to slam back into place, pushing a cartridge into the breech, safety catches clicking on, magazines sliding and clacking into place, breeches being snapped shut. Phillip visualized the scene as he listened to the men advising each other on how to load and handle a particular weapon.

A voice boomed out above the chatter. 'I'll stick to this sawn-off. I can't miss with this.'

Phillip frowned at the next snippet: 'I fancy myself with the Uzi.' A pause, then a magazine was slammed home. 'This little tool could cut Ross in half with just a short burst.'

A cockney voice chipped in. 'If yer stuck it up 'is arse and 'ung on t'the fucking trigger.' Much laughter.

Frank Chalmers's voice cut across the laughter. 'Stop fucking about with those guns and get out in the grounds to practise. There's an army firing range a mile or so away, so the local busybodies won't come sticking their bleeding noses in when they hear you. I want you all to be able to hit what you're shooting at, even a moving target. Now move!'

Phillip cut branches from several shrubs and stuck them in the ground to form a screen between him and the house, then worked diligently at his dug-out, stopping occasionally to watch, through his binoculars, Chalmers's men shooting at tin cans and empty bottles. At first he was not impressed by their marksmanship: they seemed unable to hit a small target at twenty paces. But the sprays of dirt as the bullets hit the ground around the targets warned him not to be blasé, and, sure enough, before long a bottle exploded into shards of flying glass, then a tin can pinged into the air. They were out of practice – it took weeks to become proficient with a hand-gun, and then standards had to be kept up by regular practice – but it wouldn't take long for at least some of them to get their eye in and then they'd be dangerous.

He had two great advantages, though. First, it was painfully obvious that some of Chalmers's men had little experience with firearms. Second, and more importantly, they had never been under fire. As he carried on digging, he grinned wryly at the thought of things to come.

When he had dug a hole large enough to sit in, with just his head showing above the surface, he scattered the loose earth over a wide area and moved off in search of a shrub big enough to be raised and lowered over the dug-out, camouflaging it against even the closest search. A thickly leaved rhododendron provided what he was looking for. He cut through the stem and fashioned the bottom of the shrub into an umbrella shape so that he could pull it down over his head with the outer branches and leaves touching the ground, forming a thick screen. He left two sturdy branches attached to the same side of the lower trunk and shaped them into large spikes, so that he could hammer them into the side of the dug-out in two positions, one raised to give him a good all-round view, the other lowered to conceal him completely should anyone approach.

It was late afternoon by the time Phillip was completely satisfied. He had worked quickly but moved slowly and cautiously. Although he was wearing full camouflage clothing and blended in with the surrounding countryside, he knew that movement, even from a considerable distance, caught the eye. And if *he* could see *them* . . .

He decided to settle down, look and listen for a while longer. The gang had long ago got bored, given up their target practice and returned to the house. Only the occasional barking of the two Dobermanns, and the movement of men, armed and in pairs, patrolling the grounds, broke the stillness of the afternoon. Frank Chalmers had not put in an appearance all day, preferring the seclusion and deceptive safety of the house.

Phillip turned on the receiver and listened, switching from channel to channel in the hope of learning something new. He got nothing but the boring backchat of Chalmers's men.

Chalmers himself mostly remained silent. Only the occasional outburst about what he was going to do to that bastard Ross 'when I get hold of him', demands to know 'where the fuck is Bobby?' and 'what has Ross done with him?', and complaints that 'that bastard has got my hundred grand' indicated his presence.

Phillip too was getting bored listening to the gang's idle chatter, so to liven things up a bit, and turn the screws on Chalmers, he decided he would kill one or two more of them before returning to Biggin Hill and Julie.

He would let fate decide who was going to die and how. At midnight whoever was on guard would die.

He watched the setting sun, a blazing red ball, dip lazily to the horizon, then, as though somebody had cut the string holding it up, drop out of sight. Darkness fell around him. By eleven-thirty the moon had taken over. It was almost full, its watery reflection bleaching the landscape to bone-white. Phillip became a silent shadow as he slipped soundlessly down the hillside to High Trees with vengeance in his heart and a razor-sharp double-edged dagger in his hand.

5

Since the target practice that afternoon Frank Chalmers had insisted that Kenny Martin and the Hawkins brothers stay in the house, in the same room as himself, at all times. The remaining four men had been assigned in pairs to night sentry duty, on four-hour shifts.

Bert Warren and Chris Goddard were patrolling the grounds of High Trees as Phillip slipped over the perimeter wall and dropped silently to the ground. He paused for a moment, watching and listening, then cat-footed down through the shrubbery to the edge of the lawn and surveyed the house. All the ground-floor curtains were tightly closed; the surrounding area was harshly illuminated by flood-lights. Warren and Goddard appeared from the rear of the house, each armed with a pump-action shot-gun and holding a Dobermann on a short leash.

They stopped near the front door and lit cigarettes. The soft murmur of their voices drifted across to

Phillip. The dogs were at ease: they were upwind of Phillip and could catch no trace of his scent.

Phillip drew the half-size crossbow from his pack, quickly assembled it and fitted it with a small Night Lite infra-red scope. He watched as the guard changed, and checked his watch. Midnight.

Nobby Grant and Terry White had chosen the unlucky shift. They'd been told to do eight to midnight but had persuaded Warren and Goddard to swap, so that they could watch *The Asphalt Jungle* on TV. Warren never watched TV and Goddard said he'd already seen it twice, so they readily agreed to the change.

White was armed with the Uzi machine-pistol, Grant with a sawn-off twelve-bore shotgun. Both men also carried holstered pistols. They appeared still to be discussing the film as they ambled off on patrol round the house. Phillip studied them. They were both over six feet tall, but whereas White was lean and tough-looking, Grant was thickset and overweight – Phillip judged from the sizeable bulge above his trousers that he liked his beer. His bald head gleamed in the glare of the floodlights.

Oblivious of imminent danger, the two men chatted and laughed, even acting out scenes from *The Asphalt Jungle* that they had particularly enjoyed. The dogs' calm made them feel secure, and, besides, Warren and Goddard had said all was quiet. Neither of them really believed Ross would attack a house guarded by armed men and Dobermanns.

Phillip moved round to the thickly wooded area at the rear of the house, so as to be upwind of the dogs and let them pick up his scent. They duly obliged, and began to bark and strain at their leashes. Grant and White felt the first twinges of uncertainty. They let the dogs drag them to within twenty yards of the woods; by now the animals were going berserk. The two men peered uneasily into the darkness, but their night-sight was still impaired by the floodlights, and all they could see was an ominous black mass.

'It could be a cat or a badger or something,' whispered Grant hopefully.

'Could be.' White looked back to the house. 'Do you think we should call the others?'

'And make ourselves look a right couple of prats?' Grant produced a torch from his hip pocket and shone it into the woods, but the light merely bounced off the leaves and branches of the undergrowth.

'I'd sooner look a prat than come up against Ross in that fucking lot,' said White, straining to see something – anything – in the darkness.

'Ross ain't here. He's probably tucked up in bed with a tart miles away.' Grant's attempt to sound convincing fooled neither of them.

'I wish I were tucked up with a tart right now. Even the wife would be better than this bleeding lot,' said White wistfully. He looked back at the house and saw a curtain twitch. 'They're watching us, Nobby. We'd better do something.'

'Let the dogs loose,' said Grant. He bent and

slipped the leash from his dog, which leapt into the bushes with a snarl of delight. White followed suit. They stood, guns at the ready, and listened to the animals barking as they crashed through the undergrowth.

Phillip was also listening. Once the dogs had taken the bait, he had retreated quickly deep into the woods, circling and backtracking, confusing his trail. He climbed a tree at the edge of a small clearing, settled himself on a low branch, his back firmly against the trunk, his left foot braced against a small branch. He fitted a steel-barbed hunting bolt into the crossbow, and waited.

The dogs came howling through the undergrowth. They bounded straight past Phillip's tree, then stopped, picked up his scent and began following it, circling the clearing, drawing nearer and nearer to the tree.

The crossbow gave a low, dull twang. The bolt embedded itself just behind the leading Dobermann's right shoulder, piercing its heart. The dog was dead before it hit the ground. Its mate whined nervously, sniffing and pawing at the body.

Phillip reached quickly for another bolt. As he did so, without warning the branch under his left foot snapped. He lost his balance, flailed down through the branches and landed on his back with a thud that momentarily winded him. He rolled over and up on to one knee, turning to face the second Dobermann, and saw it already in mid-air, hurtling towards him. The moonlight gleamed amber in its eyes, and saliva sprayed out as it opened its jaws wide, ready to strike. Desperately, he jammed the butt of the crossbow into its snarling mouth. He heard wood splinter as the powerful jaws snapped shut, the vicious teeth sinking in deep, then the dog was on him, its weight flinging him back to the ground. The end of the crossbow caught him a dizzying blow on the side of the head. Steel glinted in the moonlight as, in one movement, Phillip drew his knife and plunged the long, double-edged blade into the dog's soft lower belly, ripping upwards to disembowel the animal. The dog screamed in mortal agony as its entrails tumbled out. Phillip silenced it with a powerful thrust of the knife directly behind its left shoulder-blade.

Phillip pushed the carcass off him and disentangled himself from the glistening intestines that had wrapped round his legs, smothering them in a sticky, foul-smelling mess from the ruptured tubes. Listening intently for any sign that the guards might be following the dogs, he pulled up handfuls of grass and wiped himself down. Once the mess was virtually gone and he was satisfied the smell was no longer strong enough to betray his presence, he made his way quickly back to the edge of the woods, where he squatted down in the cover of the undergrowth. He was no more than ten yards from White and Grant, and could see and hear them clearly.

'The fucking dogs have stopped barking.' White

sounded unhappy, and his pale moon-face wore a heavy frown.

'Perhaps they've caught what they were after and are eating it,' offered Grant hopefully.

The two men spent five minutes whistling and calling. Then Grant said, 'You go in and have a look round, Terry. I'll wait here and keep an eye open.'

'On a fucking bike! You ain't getting me in there on my own, I can tell you.'

Grant started laughing, a loud, deep belly-laugh.

'What's so fucking funny, Nobby?' demanded White.

Grant, calmer but still chuckling, said, 'The look on your bleeding face, Terry. You're always mouthing off about how tough you are, and here you are, armed to the teeth, got a fucking machine-gun in your hand, and you're afraid to go into the woods because it's dark.' He began to laugh again.

'I ain't afraid of what I can see, Nobby,' said White furiously. 'You've got the torch. You bloody well go in and I'll come with you to cover you.'

'Come on, then.' Grant started forward, broke the sawn-off shotgun to check it was still loaded, and snapped it shut. 'We can't stand here all bleeding night like a couple of pansies. And be bloody careful with that Uzi. I don't want you pointing the fucking thing at me.'

'Bollocks,' came the curt reply from a very nervous White.

The two big men's attempts to creep soundlessly

through the bushes sounded like two bull elephants uprooting a tree. Phillip repressed a laugh as he followed closely but silently behind them.

White cursed loudly as a branch flicked back off Grant's shoulder and caught him in the eye. 'This is fucking stupid,' he complained bitterly, rubbing his eye, and stopped to let Grant get a bit further ahead.

After several minutes of stomping about in the dark, the torch beam bouncing around in front of them, the two men stumbled across the clearing and spotted the dogs. Grant held the torch beam on them. The flight feathers of the crossbow bolt could be seen clearly.

'Fuck me,' breathed Grant. 'Ross is here!' He shone the torch around. 'He's got a fucking bow and arrow.'

White tried to speak, but only a choking noise came out. He pointed the Uzi into the darkness, his hand locked like a vice round the grip, and squeezed the trigger, spraying the bushes with nine-millimetre slugs and filling the air with thunder and brilliant, flickering light until the firing pin fell on an empty chamber with a small, metallic click. He fumbled frantically for his spare magazine.

Grant grabbed him by the shoulder and shook him violently, shouting, 'Pack it in, Terry! Get a fucking grip on yourself.'

White turned and gasped, 'Help me, Nobby,' then

147

crumpled slack-mouthed to the ground, his eyes wide. A tufted bolt protruded from his back.

For a big man, Nobby Grant moved with surprising speed. He fled through the brush like a charging rhinoceros, but he tripped and crashed headlong into a snarl of brambles, dropping the torch and the shotgun as he shot his arms out to break his fall. He was groping around on his hands and knees, searching desperately for the gun, when he saw a man standing quietly ten feet away, watching him. He was dressed in combat gear, his face blackened. In his left hand, held loosely at his side, was a small crossbow.

Grant froze. He stared speechlessly. Finally he drew in a deep breath and said softly and resignedly, 'OK, Ross, get it over with.'

There was a brief silence.

'You can die like a dog on your hands and knees,' said Philip harshly, 'or you can stand up. You've got a pistol in your holster. So go for it.'

Grant swallowed hard and nodded. He felt sick and almost paralysed, but he somehow scrambled to his feet, never taking his eyes off Phillip, who stood watching, cool and relaxed.

Grant straightened his shoulders, took a deep breath and braced himself. I might get lucky, he thought. And at least I'll die like a man. And he grabbed for his pistol. It was half out of its holster when he saw a flash of light and something hit him a crushing blow in the throat. His body went numb.

He couldn't breathe. The pistol slipped from his hand. He reached feebly with heavy arms towards his throat. He heard a soft gurgling. His mouth filled with blood, warm and salty. Everything was blurred and hazy . . . he was falling, felt the thud as his back hit the ground. The stars whirled and dazzled above him, then he floated into unending blackness.

Phillip walked over and retrieved Gary's throwing knife from Grant's throat. He wiped it on the dead man's sleeve, returned it to its sheath, and disappeared silently into the shadows.

In the house Kenny Martin heard the dogs' barking above the din of the television. He jumped up and went to the window. Peering between the heavy silk curtains, he called out, 'Frank, the dogs are going bleeding mad out there.'

Chalmers tensed. 'Are Nobby and Terry sorting it out?'

'Yeah, they're heading for the woods.'

The Hawkins brothers exchanged meaningful looks. Tony pulled a face and muttered, 'Fuck that.'

Martin turned and said to John Hawkins, 'Turn the telly down a bit, will yer.' He looked out again and said, 'They've stopped at the edge of the woods. The dogs are going berserk.'

The Hawkinses joined him at the window. Tony grinned. 'Don't look as though they fancy going in.'

John laughed and said, 'Terry ain't too keen on the dark.'

Martin said irritably, 'Shut up, you two.' He peered out again. 'It could be a fox or something that set the dogs off.'

'Well, for Terry and Nobby's sake I hope it ain't Ross.' Tony Hawkins couldn't resist the jibe. He grinned at his brother. 'What's the betting they don't go in the woods?'

'Well, the dogs are loose and they just shot off like two rats up a pipe,' said Martin. He scratched his mop of ginger hair, his fleshy face creasing into a worried frown.

Frank Chalmers called out, 'What are Nobby and Terry doing?'

'Just standing there,' said Martin, 'looking into the trees.'

Tony Hawkins got bored and went back to his chair. 'They won't go in there, not if they've got any sodding sense they won't.'

Martin looked round and grinned. 'We'll I've got news for you, sonny. They've just gone in.'

Hawkins ran back to the window, laughing. 'I don't believe it. Well fuck a duck. I'd have bet a hundred quid they wouldn't do anything so fucking stupid.'

'Shut it, Tony,' ordered Martin.

Hawkins sneered, but sat sulkily down again. 'If Ross is there, I've got a grand that says we never see them again. Not alive, any road.'

The four men looked at each other. No one took the bet.

Chalmers glared at Hawkins. 'That's enough, Tony. You're giving us all the fucking creeps.'

'OK, Frank. It's just I'm glad it's them out there, not me.'

'If you don't shut it, I'll send you out to give them a hand.'

Hawkins scowled but obeyed.

A long crackle of machine-gun fire brought them all to their feet.

'Fuck me,' exclaimed John Hawkins. 'That sounded like a whole magazine.'

Martin said, 'Terry had the Uzi. I never heard the twelve-bore. Nobby hasn't fired yet.'

His face pale, Chalmers said, 'Tony, go and wake Bert and Chris. I want them down here. Now!'

As Hawkins reached the door it burst open and Warren and Goddard ran in.

'What the fuck's up, Frank?' asked Warren. 'We heard shooting.'

'Yeah, it's Terry and Nobby. The dogs must have sniffed something out, and they went into the woods after them,' said Chalmers. 'It could be nothing. Terry might have seen a ghost and panicked. We'll have to wait and see if they come out. Now for Chrissake turn the lights out and lock that fucking door.'

The leaden minutes dragged past in silence. Only

the occasional flare of a lighter and glow of a cigarette relieved the darkness.

Martin kept peering through the curtains. Finally he said, 'They've been in there for over half an hour. I'm beginning to think they won't be coming out.'

No one answered. A chair creaked as someone shifted uneasily in his seat.

'Frank, there are five of us,' Martin went on. 'Do you want us to go and see what's up?'

Chalmers nearly choked. 'What, and leave me here on my fucking jack? Not on your fucking life, Kenny. We're all staying right here in this room till they turn up.'

'Thank fuck for that. I don't fancy it out there tonight,' said Tony Hawkins. He giggled nervously. 'I'm breaking my neck for a piss, but I'm buggered if I'm going across that hall on my own. That bastard Ross might be sitting out there waiting for us. He's had time to get back here by now.'

'Shut the fuck up,' snarled Chalmers. 'I'm gonna kill that fucking cunt Ross when I get my hands on him. He's gonna die slowly for what he's done . . .' He choked with rage, unable to find words for how he felt.

'It's over an hour now, Frank,' said Martin. 'They definitely ain't coming back.'

John Hawkins swallowed hard. 'Ross is killing us one by one, Frank. He's done Mickey, blown him to kingdom come. He's got Bobby Wilks and I'd bet a pound to a pinch of shit Bobby's dead. Now Nobby and Terry. What with his mate killing Albert Reed, that's five of us dead – and we ain't even set eyes on the geezer. I don't like it, Frank, not one little bit I don't.'

'None of us like it,' snapped Chalmers. 'But we're all in this together, like it or not.'

Kenny Martin, his voice flat and toneless, said, 'Maybe you should give him the name of the hitman, Frank. The bloke that killed his mate.'

'No, not yet. That's not the answer.' Chalmers played for time to think. 'We need more men, trained men like Ross. Blokes that can fight him on his own terms.'

'What about Ron West?' suggested Goddard. 'He's a mercenary. He fought in that Angola war, and I've got his phone number.'

'He's too bloody old,' protested Warren.

'Yes, I know that, Bert, but he's got his own little team of ex-soldiers. He hires them out as bodyguards, sends them abroad and all over the place.'

'Kenny, get on the phone to this West geezer,' ordered Chalmers. 'I want five of his men here soonest. By the morning!'

'It's nearly two now, Frank,' said Martin doubtfully.

'Good, that means he'll likely be at home. Now, wake the bastard up. When he knows there's profit involved he won't mind, I promise you.'

West answered the phone with a gravelly 'This had better be important.'

'It's Kenny Martin, Ron. Frank Chalmers told me to phone.'

'Yeah? So what does he want?' West didn't sound impressed.

'He wants five of your best men out at his house in the country. East Sussex. They've got to be here as soon as possible, by morning at the latest. Can you fix it?'

Martin heard the creak of bedsprings as West sat up.

'Yeah, but I need to know a bit more about it. And it'll cost.'

'Don't worry about that, Ron. Frank'll be here and you can sort it out with him.'

'This sounds a bit serious, Kenny. Do my men need to be tooled up?'

'Yes, but don't worry about that. We've got enough guns here to start a war.'

'Stop bloody well telling me not to worry,' West snapped. 'I'm not the one who's worried: you are. So stop poncing about and tell me what fucking weapons you've got there.'

Martin reddened with anger at West's tone of voice. He was Frank Chalmers's right-hand man. He was used to being spoken to with respect, not scorned like some poxy schoolboy. But he bit back his anger and gave West a rundown of the arms and ammunition.

'It's getting more expensive by the minute.'

'Never mind that. Will you come?' demanded Martin.

'Give me the address. I'll be there with four men by seven o'clock at the latest. Just tell Chalmers to have my fee ready in the form of large amounts of cash. And I'll also want a deposit for each man, to go to his family if he gets killed. So I do mean large amounts, Kenny. Very large.'

Martin gave him the address of High Trees, told him what was required, and extracted a promise that the men would be good with firearms.

'They're the best available,' promised West. 'All ex-paras and commandos and all combat veterans. What's the gang we might have to fight and how many men have they got?'

'No gang, Ron,' said Martin sheepishly. 'Just one man.'

West laughed incredulously. 'Are you sure you want five of us?'

'That's what the boss has asked for.'

'Well he's paying,' chuckled West. 'I'll see you later.'

Martin told Chalmers what West had said. The others listened intently and began to relax slightly at the news that professional reinforcements were on the way. Tony Hawkins did a good imitation of the American cavalry's bugle call for 'Charge!'.

Chalmers gave his first smile for a long time. 'Now we'll see just how good Ross is.'

6

Philip awoke before dawn. Julie still slept soundly, snuggled up against him. He lay still, enjoying the soft, naked warmth of her body, the gentle movement of her skin against his as she breathed. He remembered the previous night, the sharp contrast between the violence at High Trees and, on his return, the warmth and excitement of making love to the beautiful woman beside him.

He kissed her gently on the forehead. She stirred, threw a long, slim leg across him and snuggled closer, her groin pushing against his thigh. Arousal flooded through him and he slid a hand down to her breasts and tweaked one of her nipples. She surfaced, laughing, stretched up to kiss him and said, 'Hey, wait till I'm awake, lover!'

'Why?'

'Because it's more fun that way.'

'Oh, I rather fancied doing what the prince would have done to the Sleeping Beauty if he hadn't been a wimp and stopped at a kiss.'

Julie chuckled. 'And so you shall one day, darling, but not right now. Right now it's time for a different fairy tale, the one about the princess who sat on the prince's lap.'

'I don't think I know that one.'

'I'll teach it to you,' she said, and rolled up and over to straddle his legs, pinning them between her thighs. She ran a fingernail slowly from the base of his throat down his chest and belly to his groin until he groaned with pleasure. She laughed deep in her throat, lifted herself up and forwards, and sank down hard, her breasts quivering as she moved on him, revelling in the effect she was having on him.

Phillip gazed at her through half-closed eyes, her pleasure feeding his own, the heat of her desire almost scorching him. She flung her head back, calling out his name, as she reached her climax. He seized her by the hips and thrust strongly up into her, feeling her contract and shudder around him. She called out again, once, twice, then, as he came uncontrollably inside her, fell forward to rest her head on his shoulder while he drove up into her once more, then held her tightly against him as if he'd never let her go.

When he'd got his breath back and his heartbeat had returned to something like normal, Phillip said, 'I didn't know they made fairy tales like that. Are there many of them?'

Julie smiled drowsily. 'A few. But if we run out,

we'll just have to make up some more, won't we?'

'I'm not sure my imagination's up to it. But we've got work to do today, so you'd better go back to sleep now, you gorgeous baggage.'

'Yes, sir,' said Julie, and did.

It was a long night for Frank Chalmers and his boys.

The euphoria that had filled them at the news that reinforcements, in the shape of Ron West and his mercenaries, would arrive by seven a.m. died away when they realized they still had over four hours to wait. Meanwhile, Ross was still out there, and might attack at any moment.

At six-thirty Kenny Martin, accompanied by the Hawkinses, ventured out into the hall, then slowly, carefully, reconnoitred the house. The sound of Ted and Ruth Smithers talking as they worked in the kitchen increased their feeling that normality was returning, and the thought of hot coffee and the smell of eggs and bacon cooking attracted them like flies.

They stacked the shotguns in a corner of the passage leading to the kitchen and went eagerly in. The Smitherses greeted them, staring openly at their unshaven, dishevelled state.

'Been up all night, have you?' asked Smithers.

'Yeah,' said Martin, 'playing cards.'

'I thought I heard shooting in the middle of the night' – Smithers glanced at his wife – 'but I paid it no mind.'

Martin smiled weakly. 'Yeah, a couple of the boys got a bit pissed and went out after a fox.'

'Did they kill it?' Smithers didn't believe a word, but felt it was none of his business. He didn't want to know the truth, not if it meant that he and his wife might lose their comfortable, undemanding, well-paid jobs.

'No, I don't think so. They're rotten shots.' Martin changed the subject firmly, and asked, 'Any chance of a bit of breakfast, Mrs Smithers?'

She smiled. 'Yes, coming up. Would you like a nice hot cup of coffee while you wait? It's on the stove and waiting for someone to drink it.'

The three men spoke in unison: 'Yes, please.'

During the long night Chalmers had said the Smitherses should be sent up to the London house, to get them out of the way. 'Tell them I want the house spring-cleaned and a bit of decorating done.'

Martin now passed on the order and told Smithers to get his tools together so that they could leave straight after breakfast. The Smitherses were plainly reluctant to leave their home.

'What about my garden and the grounds?' protested Ted.

'We'll take care of everything,' said Martin.

Smithers shook his head in dismay, but went obediently to the back door, muttering, 'I'll get my stuff together then.' Mrs Smithers wiped her hands on her apron and hurried upstairs to pack. Before long their car could be heard going down the drive, stopping while they opened and then closed the gates, and then fading in the direction of London.

The arrival of Ron West and his men was signalled soon afterwards by three long buzzes on the intercom from the gate. Martin glanced at his watch: six-fifty. He crossed to the kitchen control panel, pressed a button and asked, 'Who is it?'

He recognized West's gravelly voice. 'It's West. I'm expected.'

'Be right down,' said Martin. He turned to the Hawkins brothers. 'Get back to Frank and tell him they've arrived. I'll let them in.'

'What, all on your own?' sneered Tony Hawkins.

Martin gave him a long, measuring stare. 'Get on with it,' he snapped. He snatched the padlock key off its hook and went out.

The brothers gulped down their coffee and followed him into the hall. 'Brave man,' mocked Tony.

Two vehicles waited at the gates, a Range Rover and a beaten-up long-wheelbase Land Rover. Both were dark green. There were three men in the Range Rover and two in the Land Rover. As Martin reached the gates Ron West stepped out of the Range Rover. Martin recognized him at once. He didn't know him well, but had seen him around the Kingsland Road pubs in Hackney and had spoken to him now and then.

West smiled and said, 'Kenny Martin. We've met before, haven't we?'

Martin nodded. 'Yeah, once or twice, up in the Smoke.'

As Martin pulled the big gates open, he covertly studied West, who was taking a long, professional look around. He was a little over six feet, strongly built and fit-looking. Martin guessed him to be in his late forties, perhaps pushing fifty. His steel-grey hair was crew-cut, his face lined and craggy, with the deep tan that comes from spending a lot of time in the open air. His piercing blue eyes were sharp and intelligent; they missed nothing. He was dressed in army-style fatigues and ankle-length combat boots.

West stepped aside and waved the two vehicles through. He waited while Martin relocked the gates, then fell into step beside him as he walked up the drive towards the house.

'So what's it all about, Kenny? It must be serious for Chalmers to want five of us to babysit. I always heard he had quite a team of his own.'

'It's best if Frank fills you in on the details. He's in the house.'

West shrugged. 'As you like.' As they turned the bend and the house loomed up in front of them, he whistled and commented, 'Nice drum. Chalmers must be worth a few quid.'

Martin made no comment. When they reached the house, four men stood waiting, leaning casually against the Range Rover. They straightened as West stopped in front of them.

'Lads, this is Kenny Martin,' said West.

162

The four men eyed Martin and nodded; none of them spoke. Martin cracked a half-smile and nodded back and he looked them over. Two were about the same height as himself and West. One was a good three inches taller, six three, maybe six four. The fourth looked small by comparison, five eight or nine. They were all in their late twenties or early thirties, with close-cropped hair and tanned skin. When he looked into their eyes Martin felt a chill in the pit of his stomach. They all had the dead, flat look of men who had seen more than their share of pain and suffering, seen it and handed it out. Martin didn't doubt that they were ready to hand out more at their leader's word of command – or at the slightest provocation.

Martin was a hard case in his own right. All his life he had mixed with the toughs of London. He'd fought a lot of them and won. He was respected and feared by most. But these men showed by their attitude that they didn't give a toss for him or anyone else. He thought the small one might be the most dangerous.

West gave their names as he pointed them out. 'The tall one is known as Lofty.' He indicated the two six-footers: 'Luke and John. Can't forget them. Two good biblical names. And this is Digger. I hope you never find out why he's called that.' He grinned mirthlessly.

Martin ignored the comment and kept his face

blank. 'You'd better come and meet the boss,' he said.

West told his men to wait where they were, then followed him into the house.

Frank Chalmers lumbered to his feet as the two men entered the sitting-room. He shook hands with West, introduced him to Warren, Goddard and the Hawkins brothers, then told his four men to go and get their breakfast.

Chalmers and West sat down, facing each other across a large, polished, walnut coffee table, while Martin went to get them some coffee.

'OK, Mr Chalmers. I've got four men outside, ready for action. What's the problem?'

It took all Chalmers's self-control to sound unworried as he explained.

'A man. One man. He's out to kill me. I've got my own boys and they're good with their mitts, but this bloke is an ex-soldier and is good with explosives and . . . er . . . guns.' Under West's unwavering stare, he shifted awkwardly, aware that his mouth was dry and that cold sweat was beading his back. He slammed a clenched fist down on the table, and said venomously, 'I want the bastard dead. I don't want to lose any more of my boys.'

'Is that it?' asked West sharply.

Chalmers coughed. He raised his hands, palms up. 'He's already killed four of my men. At least I think he has. He blew one of them to smithereens. Three have disappeared and so far there's been no trace of them.' He went over to the window and pointed to the woods. West joined him and followed the direction of his pointing finger. 'Two of them went into those woods last night. We heard gunfire, and they haven't come back.'

'Have you been in there to look for them?'

Chalmers looked down at his feet. 'Er, no. I thought you and your boys'd want to do that.'

West grinned dryly. 'Could they just have fired a few rounds and pissed off?'

Chalmers shook his head vigorously. 'No. I've known them for years. They work for me. They ain't cowards – none of my men are fucking cowards. In the East End they're respected, known as hard cases. But they ain't bombproof or bulletproof, and the bastard sneaking about out there is a soldier. He's trained, like.'

West turned away from the window. 'We'd better discuss terms, Mr Chalmers. There's a risk that I could lose one or two of my men by the sound of it. We don't come cheap.'

Indeed they did not. The terms were a thousand pounds a week for each man and fifteen hundred for himself. A bounty on Ross's head of fifty thousand, to be shared between the surviving men. Minimum term was four weeks' pay for each man, even if Ross was killed that afternoon. All expenses were to be covered. And, finally, a banker's draught for a hundred grand for each man, made out to his next of kin, to be held in escrow by West's London solicitor. It would be handed over only in the event of the man's death or serious wounding. If the men were unharmed at the end of the contract, all the draughts would be returned.

Chalmers blanched as he listened, but was sourly aware that he had no choice but to agree. He handed over twenty-two thousand pounds in cash, with a promise that the bank draughts would be in the hands of West's solicitor that afternoon.

West told him to get all the available weapons together in the sitting-room, then, leaving Chalmers to ring his solicitor, went out to his men.

'Right, lads, let's get the wagons unloaded. We're staying.'

Chalmers's men watched, fascinated, as the mercenaries inspected the pistols and shotguns. They stripped them down to the last screw, cleaned and oiled them and fitted them back together in just minutes, having checked every screw, spring, firing-pin, barrel and sight.

Even Tony Hawkins was impressed. 'I think Ross could be in deep shit,' he muttered to his brother.

'These ain't men,' John muttered back. 'They're fucking robots.'

West addressed his men. 'Choose your weapons. There are, possibly, two dead men in those woods. He pointed through the window in the direction Grant and White had gone. 'A trained soldier may have ambushed and killed them. He may still be around. Proceed with caution. Cover every inch of ground. I want to know if they've been killed or if they left of their own accord. Get to it.'

Without a word his men picked up the weapons of their choice and went off. Frank Chalmers was impressed. Twenty-two grand – and worth every tanner, he thought. He could imagine the response he'd have got if he'd ordered his men into those woods: 'Not on your nelly'; 'On your bike'; 'Up yours'; 'Do fucking what? You must be fucking joking.'

He went over to the window and joined his men, who were watching with grudging admiration. The mercenaries avoided the open ground. Sticking to the boundary and the sparse cover provided, they moved one by one, covering each other, to the woods, then seemed to melt and disappear into the undergrowth.

Chalmers turned to his men and smiled with fat satisfaction. 'That's how it's done, lads. That's how it's done.' He went back to his chair and lowered himself ponderously into it. 'Get me a drink, Kenny, and make it a large one. That cunt Ross has just had his card marked.'

Phillip arrived back at his dug-out just in time to catch a glimpse of West's men crossing the lawn. He watched in calm indifference as the four men vanished into the woods, then settled down to watch and wait. 'Different ball game,' he thought.

Thirty minutes later the four men returned to the

house. He had known they would, had known what their report would be. He tuned the receiver to the bug planted in the sitting-room and waited.

He heard the men enter the room.

'Excuse me, sir,' said one of them. American.

A gravelly voice that he didn't recognize ordered, 'Make your report.'

'We've discovered the bodies of two men. Dead for approximately eight hours. One has a crossbow bolt in his back. The bolt entered the heart just right of the left shoulder-blade. The other has a knife wound to the throat. From the angle of entry and the severity of the wound, I assume that the weapon was thrown at the victim with some force – and accuracy, I might add. We also found two Dobermanns at the scene. One had been killed by a crossbow bolt, the other had been disembowelled and stabbed in the heart.'

'Is that all?'

'No, sir, not quite. There were signs of a fire-fight. We recovered these weapons.' Phillip heard a clanking and knocking as the guns were put down on a hard surface. 'The Uzi has been fired, a full clip. The two pistols and the sawn-off are unfired and still fully loaded. That's all, sir.'

'Any sign of the enemy?'

'No, sir. The ground was very trampled, mostly by the dead men. It's difficult to tell how many the enemy are. There might be two, but I'd guess it's the work of one highly skilled man.'

There was a long silence, then the gravelly voice

said, 'Right, get back out there and comb the whole estate. Keep in radio contact with me at all times. Get to know every inch of the ground. And pay special attention to that high ground overlooking the place. If I were watching the house, that's where I'd be.'

Phillip listened to all this with the respect of one professional for another. He'd have to leave his hiding place quickly or he'd certainly be found. He decided to move to another hillock nearby. From there he wouldn't be able to see the house, but he could still monitor the conversations inside, and he'd also be able to see if the new contingent found his dug-out.

He slid out of the dug-out and repositioned the rhododendron so that its branches brushed the ground. He sprinkled leaves and twigs around it so that it would be impossible to move the bush without disturbing them. Then, brushing out his tracks as he went, he snaked on elbows and knees to his next chosen vantage point, where he went to work on his camouflage. He made a grass mat by tying long cut grass into close-knit netting, turfing and shaping the grass to match the uneven texture of the surrounding terrain. Once it was finished to his satisfaction, he again checked his headphones.

He could still pick up the signals from the house, but they were much weaker and he lost the odd snippet of conversation. It was two hours before two of the mercenaries appeared, zigzagging one at a time across the hillside below his last position. They searched every possible place where a man might lie hidden, but missed the dug-out. They gave it a cursory glance in passing, but clearly dismissed it as a small bush that couldn't have concealed anything larger than a dog.

Slowly they worked their way across the high ground towards him. He cursed silently, pulled back the slide on his pistol and slipped off the safety catch. He snaked under the grass blanket, leaving only a small slit to look through, as the men, who had clearly decided to check out the next hill, moved towards him.

He lost sight of them for a few moments as they passed behind a thick stand of young trees. When they reappeared, they were only seventy-five metres away and heading directly for him. Not twenty metres from him, they came together and held a brief, low-voiced discussion. One pointed in his direction, and they both looked that way. Phillip could hear the odd snatch of their conversation: ' . . . see the house . . . too far . . .'

Phillip had tensed, ready to leap up and start shooting, when the men stopped again and looked around.

'This is far enough,' said one. 'There's nowhere out here to hide except those trees we've just checked. Not enough cover anywhere else.' He looked back towards the house. 'Too far away. We'd better get back. You take the left flank and we'll work it again as we go, just in case we've missed anything.'

A patch of grass a few metres away from them sagged slightly as they moved away. Phillip let out a long, slow breath and relaxed. He watched them until he was sure they were indeed going back to the house, then wriggled out from under his grass camouflage. By the time the two mercenaries had returned to report the hillside clear, he was back in his dug-out, sipping from his water-bottle, and maintaining a listening watch.

Frank Chalmers was almost his old cocky self again, his confidence restored by the security of having professional fighting men guarding him. He even ventured out for a breath of fresh air and a walk round the house. Ron West was at his side, armed with the Uzi machine-pistol.

Under the armed protection of Lofty and Digger, the American, his men had recovered the bodies of Nobby Grant and Terry White and loaded them into the boot of one of Chalmers's cars. They were to be disposed of in the flooded gravel pit where for twenty years Chalmers had dumped the bodies of his victims.

Alone in the sitting-room, Chalmers and West discussed the plan of operation and how West would protect Chalmers and kill Ross. Phillip listened with interest as West laid it out.

'Hopefully, Ross doesn't yet know about us. Or he may slink away and we'll have the job of finding him.' West eyed Chalmers warily as he went on, 'I want to use a couple of your men as decoys, to lure Ross into a trap. Will they cooperate?'

'They'll do exactly as they're told,' said Chalmers grimly.

'Good.' West got to his feet, crossed to the window and stared out, assessing the woods briefly. 'I'll keep my men out of sight. Two of them will stay under cover, guarding two of your men, who'll patrol the house as usual. Ross had it easy last night. He may come back tonight if he thinks he's got a soft target.'

Chalmers resented being called a soft target. He wanted to protest, to put up a tough front, but the stark reality of the situation stifled the words unuttered. He contented himself with clearing his throat and mumbling something unintelligible.

Unaware of Chalmers's rancour, West continued, 'I'll stay with you, Frank, at all times, night and day. My men will rest in the next room. But to an interloper I want everything to look the same as it was before we arrived. Ross will come tiptoeing in, and we'll be waiting.'

'Could you take him alive?'

'No problem. Dead or alive, it's all the same to me.'

Chalmers's face contorted into a vicious snarl and his voice was cruel. 'I want that bastard alive. I want to kill him slowly, with my bare hands. I'm going to rip his fucking eyes out and shove them up his arse. With a red-hot poker.'

In his dug-out, Phillip smiled sardonically. Careful, Frank, he thought; you might give me ideas. He planned his own strategy as he listened to Chalmers and West planning theirs. He would go in again hard, that very night. Surprise. Strike first, strike hard and fast. 'Who dares wins.'

The day dragged on. At last darkness fell slowly, like a hot, damp, heavy blanket. Night sounds filled the still air as the creatures of darkness awoke and announced their presence: an owl hooted, a toad burped, countless crickets shrilled their legs together, calling to their mates. Phillip slid silently out of his dug-out, startling a woodmouse, which scurried away through the undergrowth.

Low, heavy cloud obscured the moon, and Phillip moved cautiously through the thick darkness, navigating by his memory of the terrain and by intuition more than vision, which was limited to a few feet. Every few minutes he stopped to listen, to sniff the air and look around, straining to see through the blackness.

High Trees was again floodlit. The glare was reflected off the low cloud, and filled the damp air with an eerie glow. Phillip snaked soundlessly up and over the perimeter wall, landing coiled and ready to strike. He ducked into the cover of a clump of bushes and thought for a moment.

West's men had orders to protect Chalmers's men, who were patrolling the house, so they must be forward of his position, between him and the light. The plan was for the mercenaries to ambush Phillip when he attacked the patrolling guards, so he'd decided to attack the mercenaries while their attention was focused on the guards. Always do the unexpected, he thought. He'd worked out where they'd most likely have taken up their stations: between his current position and the blaze of the floodlights. He was careful not to look into the light, which would ruin his night vision. As it was, West's men would be staring into the lit area, watching the guards. Even if they turned to look at his approach line, he'd have several seconds' advantage before their night vision returned. But only several seconds. He'd have to move fast.

As he inched forwards, his sleeve brushed against the branch of a shrub, disturbing a sleeping blackbird, which chack-chack-chacked its alarm and flapped noisily away. The night creatures fell instantly silent. Phillip froze. It was fifteen minutes before the night sounds began again as the creatures accepted his presence, and he was once more able to move, cursing himself for the carelessness that could so easily have betrayed him. He slipped down on to his hands and knees and crawled forwards, stalking his prey.

Suddenly he sensed a presence. The light hair on the back of his neck bristled. Silent alarm bells rang in his head. He waited, motionless. Minutes passed . . . nothing. A false alarm? No, there was danger nearby. Wait, be patient. Look and listen. Then he heard it. A movement to his right, a rustle of clothing as a man shifted position.

A millimetre at a time, Phillip turned his head to the right. He half-closed his eyes so that no light could reflect off the whites and betray him, and studied the dark shapes of trees and undergrowth. In the faint reflected glow from the floodlights he thought he saw the shape of a man, not three metres away. Silently, watchfully, the man turned his head a fraction of an inch, just enough for Phillip to be sure of his target. He drew his knife and inched forward. His heart beat fast and loud in his chest. He kept his breathing light and controlled, soundless. Adrenalin pumped through his blood into his muscles, priming them until they screamed for the release of action.

Five feet . . . Lofty's attention was focused on two men parading up and down in front of the house. Suddenly he turned his head a full ninety degrees towards Phillip. Ten degrees more and he would have been staring directly at him. Lofty's instinct, honed by years of combat, warned him danger was close. He had heard nothing, seen nothing, smelt nothing, felt nothing, tasted nothing. None of his five senses registered anything concrete, but he knew: he turned his head and stared in the direction from which danger threatened.

Phillip coiled like a spring compressed almost to breaking-point, waiting for the moment of release, the right moment, the unspoken command. His eyes were unblinking, his body taut.

Slowly, Lofty turned his head and his attention back towards the house. Warren and Goddard were walking nervously along the front. They stopped, turned and walked back along their allotted course.

Then, suddenly, he cocked his head slightly to the right as he heard the whisper of steel. Too late. A razor-sharp knife cut almost soundlessly through the air and came to rest against his jugular. An iron fist clamped over his mouth, fingers choking off his involuntary gasp. The cold edge of steel pressed lovingly against his neck. From close to his left ear came a mocking murmur. 'Give in?'

Lofty put more conviction into his nod than into anything he had ever done in his life. He felt himself start to shake as he realized how easily he had been taken – he, one of West's top men. In his momentary distraction his hands twitched the barrel of his pump-action shotgun round towards Phillip. Instantly the knife stroked him in a swift caress, cutting effortlessly through his flesh to slide bitingly against the vertebrae of his neck. The shadow beside him let him slip noiselessly to the ground and, just as noiselessly, moved on.

Ron West had posted two guards in the woods, Lofty and Luke Richards. Richards was some fifty metres from his late colleague, also watching Warren and Goddard tramping up and down in front of the big house. He was bored stiff. Like the others, he'd taken the job merely for the money. It paid the bills, bought him some fun, and filled in the time between wars. He'd sold his skills all over Africa and in any other trouble spot where they were needed and could be afforded. He'd shaken his head incredulously on learning that he was to guard, in West's words, 'one fat little fucker'. Five of them – five – against one man, who'd been in the British Army and knew 'how to use a gun'.

His first inkling that the man known as Phillip Ross was more than just an ex-soldier who knew how to use a gun came at the precise instant when Phillip's knife pressed gently but insistently against his throat and a voice murmured in his ear, 'Give in?'

Luke Richards didn't make the same mistake as Lofty. He held his shotgun dead still and said hoarsely, through dry lips, 'Yeah, you got me beat.'

'Put the gun down. Slowly and quietly.'

With tender care, Richards bent forwards, reached to the ground and let go of the shotgun.

'Your friend is dead. If you want to join him, just nod.'

Richards held himself as rigid as the rock of Gibraltar.

'I take it you'd like to live? If so, nod.'

Richards swallowed hard, then nodded slowly and gently. The knife pressed a little harder against his neck, feeling as though it had drawn blood. He ignored it, a minor irritation.

'Stand up straight,' ordered Phillip.

Richards obeyed. The knife pressed harder still.

He ignored it. As he straightened, a hand gripped his hair and pulled his head back. The knife left his throat, to reappear between his thighs, pressed tight up against his crotch beside his right testicle.

'You know what happens if I cut you here?'

Richards tried to nod, but his head was held as if in a vice. 'Yes,' he managed to croak.

'I'll cut your femoral artery, among other things, and leave no room for a tourniquet. Do you understand?'

He managed a minuscule nod.

'Bend over and put your hands together between your legs.' Phillip released Richards's hair, grabbed his jacket and increased the pressure of the knife. Richards almost stood on tiptoe as he obeyed. Phillip slipped a thin wire noose over Richards's wrists, pulled it tightly through between his legs and looped it round his throat. He searched him and relieved him of an automatic pistol, an eight-inch hunting knife and a two-way radio, all of which he tossed to the ground.

With no further words, just a slight, encouraging tug on the wire, Phillip moved off, leading his prisoner, who was bent almost double, back towards the perimeter wall. When they reached it Phillip snipped the wire that bound Luke Richards's wrists to his throat. The wire had cut into his wrists as it tightened, drawing blood; his hands were wet and red. Phillip loosened the noose round his neck. It too had tightened and Richards's breathing was distressed. He gulped in air, his chest heaving. Phillip gave another tug on the wire, and together they went up and over the wall.

They walked in silence for five minutes, then Phillip said, 'Right, this'll do. Sit down.'

The two men sat facing each other in the darkness. Luke peered at his captor, but Phillip's face and hands were dark-camouflaged and all he could make out were the whites of his eyes and the occasional gleam of teeth. Even the outline of his body was broken and distorted by bunches of leaves.

Luke Richards was the first to speak. 'What regiment?' he asked quietly.

Phillip stared blandly back. 'It doesn't matter. What does matter, what matters very much, at this precise moment, is what I do with you.' He allowed his prisoner to register the threat, then rammed it home: 'I should kill you and be done with it.'

Richards was fully aware that he faced almost certain death. His mouth twisted into a lopsided smile and he nodded his understanding. His mouth was dry, his voice cracking with strain as he said, 'If there's another way, sir . . .? I'd be grateful if you'd consider it. I never expected to die on British soil. No, sir, I never expected this.'

'Listen carefully,' commanded Phillip. 'I'm going to ask you some questions. Your life depends on the truth and accuracy of your answers.'

Richards nodded.

'How many of you are there?'

'Five. At least there were five.'

'Who's in command? His name and rank?'

'Ron West. Sergeant. He's an ex-para.'

'The other two men. Names and experience.'

'John Jefferies, lance-corporal, Irish Guards, served in Northern Ireland. Digger Johnson, served in the US Marines, two years in Vietnam.'

'What's your opinion of Ron West?'

'He's OK. He looks after his men and stands by them. If he gives his word he won't break it. I'd go anywhere, any time, on his word. He's tough but he's fair – and he pays well.'

'Jefferies?'

'John's a bloody good bloke. You can rely on him to be right there beside you when the shooting starts.'

'Johnson?'

Richards hesitated. 'Digger . . . he's a bad bastard. If you'd had to be killed, Digger would've been the one to do it. Of course, in combat any one of us would kill rather than be killed. But in cold blood . . . it would've been Digger.'

'How many men has Chalmers got in the house?'

'Besides himself, five. But most of them haven't got much clue about firearms. All right for bashing up old ladies,' he said contemptuously, 'but no real bum.'

'If I let you go, what will you do?'

Richards strained to see Phillip's face in the darkness. He felt a first faint glimmer of hope, and put every ounce of sincerity at his command into his voice. 'I'd be obliged, Mr Ross. And I'd piss off out of here so fast you wouldn't see my arse for dust. I wouldn't come back – you have my word on it.'

Phillips said, 'I'll think on it.' Something about the way Richards spoke had reminded him vividly of Gary. He was sure Richards had told the truth. Had he told even one lie, he'd have been dead in an instant. He threw the end of the wire binding Richards's neck on to the ground between them. 'Shut your eyes. Let five minutes pass. If you can still open them after that time, I suggest you walk away. If you come back, I'll kill you without compunction.'

Luke Richards closed his eyes tighter than he'd ever done in his life. Almost pleadingly, he asked, 'Mr Ross, I must know. It was the Twenty-second SAS you served in, wasn't it?'

'Yes, it was the SAS.'

Richards smiled and nodded. 'It had to be. The only other blokes who could have done what you just did are the Gurkhas, and you're too tall to be one of them.' He relapsed into silence, steeling himself for a knife-thrust, as he said the Lord's Prayer, the only prayer he knew, over and over again. Ten minutes later he opened his eyes and waited for them to adjust to the night. He was alone. Phillip Ross had vanished as silently as he had appeared.

Richards loosened the wire noose round his neck. He used his teeth to unwind the wire from his wrists, then bandaged them with strips torn from his handkerchief. He got shakily to his feet, and shook his head to clear from it the nightmare of the past hour. He knew he was being watched, and took a moment to get his bearings. Then, praying to every god he'd ever heard of that he'd chosen the right direction, and thanking them all that he was still alive, he set off.

Phillip watched him go, hoping his decision to let him live was the right one. He knew that for his own safety he should have killed Richards. If Richards had walked in the wrong direction, he would have died without knowing anything about it. Phillip followed him for over two miles, until he was certain he intended to keep on going in the same direction. Something in the man's step as he put distance between himself and High Trees convinced Phillip Ross that he would not meet Luke Richards again.

7

Ron West's voice was full of anger and concern as he addressed the room full of men. 'I instructed them to return to the house at first light.' He turned to Warren and Goddard. 'Are you certain you heard nothing?'

The two men looked at each other and shook their heads. 'We never saw or heard a thing all night,' said Goddard.

West shook his head, unconvinced, and checked his watch for the umpteenth time as he tried yet again to raise his men on the radio.

Chalmers stuck his oar in: 'I hope I haven't paid out all that dough for a load of wankers.'

A dark look from West shut him up instantly. West turned to his two remaining men and said, 'Digger, John, get out there and find out what's happened.' They turned at once and went out.

Tony Hawkins grimaced at his brother. He didn't need to say a word.

It was an hour before John Jefferies and Digger Johnson returned, both grim-faced. Johnson reported, 'Lofty's dead. He's had his throat cut. Luke's gone. We found his weapons, and a trail of blood leading out of the grounds. Looks as though Ross has taken him prisoner.'

'Any sign of a struggle?' asked West.

Johnson shook his head. 'No, sir. It looks as though Ross caught them both napping.'

'No, not those two – they're professionals.'

Alarmed, Chalmers clambered out of his chair. 'One's out there with his fucking throat cut and the other one's gone missing, and that's all you can bleeding well say? "No, not those two – they're professionals"?' His mimicry of West was savage.

West turned on him. 'Shut it, you fat cunt. And sit down, or I'll kill you myself.'

All the men in the room tensed, expecting trouble. Jefferies and Johnson turned to face Chalmers. They still held their weapons, and looked ready to use them. Chalmers's men kept prudently quiet and stood very still.

Chalmers beat a hasty retreat. He gave a laugh that squeaked with nerves, and said, 'Hold on, hold on. We're all in this together, all of us against Ross. We ain't here to fight each other. That's exactly what the bastard wants.' He smiled sickly at West. 'Ron, I didn't mean to upset you, my son. Settle down and let's sort this thing out.'

West gave him a brief, unyielding look, then

agreed, 'Yes, we must sort this out.'

Johnson and Jefferies visibly relaxed: they let their gun barrels drop at least two inches. Tony and John Hawkins looked at each other in dismay.

'Now listen, Frank,' said West coldly, 'is there anything you haven't told me about this guy Ross? Anything at all?'

'No, not that I can think of.'

'Well think hard. You said he was in the army and was good with explosives and guns. What else do you know about him?'

Chalmers shrugged and looked to his men for support. Tony Hawkins came to his aid and put in, 'Ross was in the fucking SAS, would you believe.'

'Shit!' yelled West. He turned furiously on Chalmers. 'Why the fuck didn't you tell me that before? Right at the beginning, you stupid prick?'

Chalmers said sheepishly, 'I told you he was in the army and was good with—'

'He isn't just good, he's the best, the cream,' stormed West. 'He can slip through those woods quieter than a grass snake – and you'd have about as much chance of spotting him. Lofty and Luke were bloody good, but Ross would've been all over them and they wouldn't have got so much as a fucking sniff of him.'

'He can't be that good, can he?' Chalmers's face was pale as he looked at the glum faces round the room. 'The dogs sniffed him out, didn't they? We'll get more dogs – a hundred fucking dogs.'

West stared at Chalmers. His anger abated as he realized that the man just didn't begin to understand. He spoke softly, clearly and slowly, as though addressing an idiot child. 'Frank, the dogs didn't sniff Ross out. He deliberately let them know he was there. He sucked them into those woods like a couple of lemons, and your two goons followed, like little lambs to the slaughter.'

Chalmers's eyes widened. Sweat stood on his forehead and he wiped it furtively away with his sleeve. He tried to speak but failed.

John Hawkins asked, 'Why ain't he just come and killed us all? From what you say it'd have been a piece of piss, for him. Specially before you blokes arrived.'

'You're not dead because Ross hasn't bothered to kill you yet. He's been playing with you lot, like a cat with bunch of mice.'

Hawkins turned to Chalmers. 'Can't you buy him off, Frank? We'll all end up dead at this rate.'

Chalmers nodded. 'Yes, I'll pay anything to get rid of him.' He swallowed hard.'I'll pay him a million pounds. In cash.'

'I doubt very much that Ross is doing this for money.' West went over and sat down next to Chalmers. 'Now, I want you to tell me everything you know about Ross – and I do mean *everything*,' he said menacingly. 'Right from the beginning. How and where you first came across him, what's happened since then, who his friends are, what he eats for fucking breakfast. The lot.'

Chalmers blurted out the whole story: the demand for protection money, his four men getting beaten up and thrown out of the Starlight Club, the fire, the deaths of Gary Thompson and Bert Reed, the fact that he'd hired a professional killer, the blowing up of Mickey Steele in the Rolls-Royce, Bobby Wilks's disappearance along with a hundred grand in cash. When he'd finished, he looked sheepishly at West and said, 'You know the rest.'

'The man who got killed at the nightclub,' said West, 'was he a friend of Ross's?'

Chalmers looked as though he'd tasted rotting fish. 'Yeah, they was in the army together.'

'An old buddy from the SAS?'

Chalmers shrugged. 'I suppose so.'

'You don't half know how to pick 'em, Frank,' said West sardonically. 'It's a wonder the place isn't crawling with a whole platoon of bloody SAS, all queuing up to cut your throats.' He paused to think things through, then asked, 'This professional killer. Does Ross know who he is?'

Chalmers shook his head. 'No, no one knows, except me. Ross keeps demanding to know who the bloke is, but I ain't told him.'

'Very wise, Frank. If you had you'd be dead by now.' West smiled at Chalmers's men, who sat deadpan and unmoving. 'You'd all be dead,' he said cheerfully, and watched them absorb the impact of his words.

Bert Warren spoke for the first time in ages; he was a man of few words. 'If you gave Ross the name, Frank, and offered him lots of cash – like the million quid you just said – he might let us off the hook, mightn't he?'

Chalmers looked hopefully at West. 'What do you think?'

'I doubt it. I doubt it very much. It's you he wants, Frank, and when he gets you, you'll tell him that name. After a while you'll be only too pleased to tell him anything and everything he wants to know.'

Chalmers looked as if he was about to throw up. He wiped his plump, sweaty palms on his trousers and said, half angrily, half pleadingly, 'What am I going to do? What the fuck am I going to do, Ron?'

West stood up. 'The first thing we do,' he said briskly, 'is get organized. Are you still in, John?'

Jefferies nodded. 'If you're still in, guv, so am I.'

'Digger?'

'No pressing appointments, Ron,' said Johnson lightly. 'Besides, I wouldn't want to miss out on all the excitement.' He grinned like a tiger shark.

'Thanks, lads. What about your men, Frank? Can I rely on them? To the limit?'

Chalmers looked at his unhappy gang and nodded. 'They ain't going nowhere.' He managed a chuckle. 'They ain't got nowhere to go.'

West ignored the flippancy. 'There is a man I can think of. An ex-SAS man turned rogue, which I may say is something rarer than a dog with two dicks. If you're prepared to pay for his services I'll give him a call, see if he's available.'

'Get him,' said Chalmers without hesitation.

West consulted his notebook and dialled a number. He left a message with an answering service and hung up. 'Now we wait,' he said.

Less than five minutes later the phone rang. West picked it up. 'Ron West speaking.'

'What can I do for you, Ronald, my boy?' enquired a deep, cultured voice.

'Thanks for calling back, Carl. I've got this little problem.' Quickly, West ran through the relevant details, while Carl Meyer listened patiently.

After West had finished there was a short pause before Meyer said, 'Ex-Sass, you say. What's his name?'

West told him.

'Phillip Ross,' he mused. 'Rings a bell, but I don't know the chap. Look, give me a couple of hours and I'll ring back.'

'Thanks, Carl. I'll wait for your call.'

West hung up, and told Chalmers, 'I think he's going to check Ross out.'

Tony Hawkins put in, 'If he's got any bloody sense he'll leave it out, give this one a miss.' No one disagreed.

Meyer had asked for two hours, but in fact he was back on the phone in less than one. 'Look, Ron, I'm afraid I'm not in a position to help you on this one. I'm a bit booked up at the moment. But for old times' sake I'll give you some advice, the very best advice I can offer. Get the hell out of there. As soon as possible.'

'I can't do that, Carl. I'm committed.'

'Oh, I see. Well, in that case dig in and dig in deep. This Ross chappy is pretty hot stuff, top of the class in just about everything. Born athlete and a brain like a scalpel. He was unofficially offered a commission. Turned it down for personal reasons. Earned himself a DCM in that little fracas down in the Falklands. Not a man one would choose to go up against, at least not if one had any sense.'

'Thanks, Carl. I'll be seeing you.' West cut off Meyer's sceptical laugh by dropping the receiver into its cradle from a height of two feet. The crash as it landed made everyone jump. He turned to Chalmers. 'Like I said, Frank, you sure know how to pick 'em.' He told his audience what he'd learnt about Ross. They didn't look particularly happy about it.

Tony Hawkins leapt to his feet and shouted, 'Fuck me! It gets worse every poxy minute. Now we find out that Ross is really Superman in fucking disguise! I don't understand all this. We can clear any pub in the East End or south of the river by just walking in and looking in a bad mood. And one man – one fucking man! – has got us all shaking in our bleeding boots.' He glowered at Chalmers.

From the corner of the room, Kenny Martin said, 'Ross may be only one man, but he's already killed five, maybe six, of us. And he ain't even had his hair ruffled yet.' He crossed the room and confronted Chalmers. 'You're the boss, Frank. You're responsible. What do you want us to do? We need organizing or Ross is going to pick us off one at a time – or two at a time, like he's been doing.'

Chalmers couldn't meet Martin's eyes. He gestured limply to West. 'Take your orders from Ron. He's the expert. That's why I'm paying him to protect us.'

Martin turned to West. 'Well, Ron, what do you want us to do?'

'One thing's for sure. Ross'll come to us if we don't go to him. I reckon it's still our best bet to stake the place out and bushwhack him.' He looked consideringly at Martin for a moment. 'If we force him to move in on us, we've got much more chance of spotting him first. If we're moving about he'll see us and knock us off like ducks at a goddamn fairground' – he chuckled mirthlessly – 'and I doubt if we'd even see where the shots were coming from.'

'Now, I want two of you to get back out there and patrol round the house. Do not, I repeat, do not, on any account, start firing into the woods. My men will be in there. If you see anything, it won't be Ross. The last thing I need is you lot shooting at my men. Or at me, for that matter. John and Digger, get back out there and cover each other. You know now what you're up against. So be bloody careful.'

191

Tony Hawkins volunteered himself and his brother for this first stint of guard duty. He had quickly worked out that they could then spend most of the night tucked up safely in bed. West sent Chris Goddard and Bert Warren off to get some rest. He advised Kenny Martin to do the same, telling him he'd accompany him on guard duty.

Chalmers cancelled that out by insisting, 'I want you two to stick close to me. Like shit to a blanket.'

West shrugged and agreed. 'That's OK by me. It just means the other men will have to cover it.'

'Let them do twelve hours on and twelve hours off. It ain't hard work,' insisted Chalmers. 'There are four of them.'

A radio attached to West's belt bleeped and buzzed. He snatched it up, held it close to his mouth and said, 'Pass your message.'

Digger Johnson's voice crackled over the air. 'We're in position, sir. John's covering the house and I'm covering him.'

'Good. Report every thirty minutes, on the hour and half-hour. Out.' West returned the radio to his belt and checked his watch. 'We're going to have to send out for more equipment,' he said to Chalmers. 'I'm going to need electronic listening devices to set out in the grounds, and some anti-personnel mines. We're going to need every bit of advantage we can get to catch this slippery fish, also—' He broke off abruptly and stared round the room. 'Fuck me,' he said slowly. 'Ross could have this place bugged.'

In his hillside dug-out, a thousand yards away, Phillip grinned derisively.

'When did he find out about this place?' demanded West.

Chalmers flapped his pudgy hands as though he was warding off mosquitoes. 'I don't know,' he said sullenly. 'I don't fucking well know. Tell him, Kenny. Tell the man.'

'Search me,' said Martin, at a total loss.

'I need a bug-detector,' said West flatly. 'I'll have to sweep the whole sodding house.'

'Let's search the place,' offered Chalmers.

West snorted. 'Be a complete waste of time.' He went over to a standard lamp and peered at the bulb. 'I could be looking at a bug right now, and I wouldn't know it. It's not like the good old days, when all you had to worry about was a little black box with a bit of wire hanging down from it. It could be a light bulb, a wall socket' – he walked slowly round the room, pointing out the relevant fittings as he spoke – 'a light switch, a curtain ring. It could be built into the phone. It could even be a little black speck on the window-pane. No, the only way to find those little fuckers is with a sweeper.

'If Ross has got this place bugged – and we have to assume that he has – from now on we don't discuss anything of any relevance to our plans of defence. And we must drastically alter those. Come on, Frank, let's go for a little walk.'

'Is it safe?' asked Chalmers doubtfully.

'He could take you out with a good rifle, but he won't do that. Not until he gets the name of your hitman.' West had reached the door. He turned and said loudly, 'Isn't that right, Mr Ross?'

Phillip smiled grimly and nodded. 'That is indeed right, Mr West,' he said aloud.

After a little persuasion, West managed to get Chalmers to venture out into the grounds, though he insisted Martin come along for added protection. Once they were well clear of the house, West turned and pointed to the hill overlooking High Trees. 'Our friend Ross is up there now, watching us.'

Chalmers dodged rapidly behind West and peered up at the high ground. 'What the fuck are you playing at?' he demanded.

'Relax, Frank,' said West calmly. 'He's not going to shoot you. You're as safe as houses until he gets that name.'

'He might just change his fucking mind,' said Chalmers, still sheltering behind West. 'I'm going back behind the house. I'm not happy about this, not happy at all.'

The three men turned and walked out of Phillip's sight, Chalmers being careful to keep West and Martin between himself and the hill. Once they had the solid bulk of the house between them and Ross, Chalmers relaxed a bit.

'That was a fucking silly thing to do,' he growled at West. 'I'm paying you to protect me, not lead me out into the open like a poxy sitting duck.'

West smiled and said, 'Just proving a point.'

'Well, OK, but don't prove any more points. Telling me is quite enough. I'll take your bleeding word for it.'

Martin asked, 'Can't you and your boys go up there and get Ross?'

West grinned mockingly at him. 'Do you fancy it?'

'Well, no, but I ain't a professional. You blokes are, so couldn't you do it?'

'Ross is a professional too, Kenny, and he's had plenty of time to dig in and to set traps and warning devices. We'd trip over him before we found him.' He looked over towards the woods. 'Besides, we've already searched that high ground, and we didn't find a sign of him. That must tell you something.'

'Perhaps he wasn't there then,' put in Chalmers.

'He was there,' said West, 'he was there.' He turned back to Chalmers. 'Is there anywhere else we could go? Have you got any other properties?'

'I've got a house in London.' Chalmers described it.

West dismissed it out of hand when he heard that it was terraced and surrounded by other houses.

'I've got a boat, a big boat, in Spain. My brother's on it now. We could sail off anywhere.'

'Where is it?'

'Puerto Banus, near Marbella.'

'What length is it?'

'A hundred and forty feet.' Chalmers couldn't

resist boasting. 'It'll cruise at twenty-four knots and its range is about two thousand miles. It's got the lot – master cabin with *en suite* bathroom, fully equipped kitchen and everything, built-in cocktail bar, flying bridge, bleeding great diesels. It's a real diamond.'

'We'll keep it in mind,' said West, 'but for the moment I think we're better off here.' He looked searchingly at Chalmers. The man's fat face was puffy with tiredness, and he had a nervous tic at the corner of his right eye. His thinning hair was lank and greasy, and he bore the stubble of several days without shaving. West had difficulty hiding his dislike and contempt for him.

'Frank, your brother, is he a member of your gang?' he asked.

Chalmers looked puzzled. 'Well, yeah. But he spends most of his time playing around on the boat. He never gets involved in the rough stuff.'

'Why isn't he here, standing by you?'

Chalmers said flatly, 'No, no, I don't want Robin involved in this. It ain't his scene. He stays where he is.'

'If Ross knows about him, he *is* involved, Frank, whether you like it or not.'

'Why? Robin wasn't even here when it all started.'

'That doesn't mean a damn' thing, Frank, and I'll tell you why. My guess is that Ross has set out to kill your whole gang, wipe it off the face of the earth. He won't spare anyone at all, even if they had nothing to do with the murder of his mate. Just being a member of the gang will bring the death sentence.'

'Oh Christ,' muttered Chalmers. 'What did I ever do to deserve this?'

West debated telling him, but decided it wasn't worth the time and effort. He had more pressing matters to deal with.

'You must warn your brother, Frank. Give him the choice of staying where he is or getting back here under our protection.'

'Are you sure about this? You really mean to tell me Ross is likely to sod off down to Spain and bump my fucking brother off? Do you?'

'It's something you've got to take into consideration.' West paused to study Chalmers, who looked near breaking-point at this new threat: his eyes glittered wildly and his hands were shaking. 'Ross won't leave any loose ends. Specially not any that might – just might – shoot back at him.'

'No.' Chalmers was adamant. 'I ain't going to worry Robin. He's dead loyal. He'd come straight back and stand by me. He's safer where he is. Besides, Ross don't even know he exists.' He exerted every remaining ounce of self-control and pulled himself together. 'OK, Ron, how much will it cost me for you and your men to storm that hill and kill Ross? Now. Just name your price. I won't argue.'

'Money doesn't come into it, Frank,' said West with exaggerated patience. 'Like I keep telling you, Ross isn't just sitting up there with his dick in his hand. He'd pick us off like apples off a goddamn' tree. You haven't got enough money in the world to get us to go up there and commit suicide. It's hairy enough without taking half-arsed risks. At least we're in with a fighting chance at the moment.'

'Well I'm sure I'm bleeding glad to hear some good news at last,' said Chalmers sarcastically. 'Up to now all you've said is how fucking clever Ross is. You've made him out to be unbeatable, like fucking Rambo or something.'

West's eyes narrowed in cold anger. 'No one's unbeatable, Frank. You should know – Ross has proved it to you pretty goddamned clearly. What was it? Five of your men against him? And he creamed them. So don't take that tone with me. I don't like it and what I don't like I don't tolerate. End of subject.' He looked up at the woods again, and said more mildly, 'Ross will make a mistake some time. He must have an Achilles' heel somewhere. What we've got to do is find it.'

Martin broke his long silence. 'Perhaps he's got family or someone close to him we could grab and hold hostage. That would bring him out into the open.'

Chalmers's eyes glinted with malevolence and the beginnings of hope. 'That's it, that has to be the answer. Everybody's got someone close, someone they don't want to lose at any price. Yeah, yeah, that's it. Think about it. That bloke, Ross's mate, Thompson, he practically committed suicide to kill

Bert Reed. The fucker charged at Bert when Bert was pointing a sawn-off at him. Bert just about blew his arm off, but he snapped Bert's neck like a bleeding carrot. Then my hitman threw a molotov at him, started a big fire, and Thompson was burning – all his hair and clothes and that – and he just went for my man, belted through the flames like they weren't even there. Now my man's a pro hitman, right? He's standing there with a fucking big cannon in his hand, a nine-mil German job. He pumps five bullets into Thompson and only just stops him. He has to stick another bullet in Thompson's head to put his lights out.

'Now, what man in his right mind does that? Not on his own account, any road. I reckon he was protecting someone, someone better than close to him, right? Ross was due back at the club right about then. If he'd been out on the town, he was probably with a tart.' He grinned slyly. 'If you got your own nightclub full of crumpet, you ain't gonna go out on your fucking tod, are you. So Thompson was expecting two people back, Ross and the tart. And which one was he protecting? Ross or the tart?'

'Not Ross,' said West with certainty. 'Thompson would have waited till Ross arrived and there were two of them. Then he'd have made his move, with Ross backing him. Those two knew all the moves in unarmed combat. They'd have beaten your men, Frank. I reckon you're right, and Thompson threw his life away.'

Chalmers nodded vigorously. 'Yeah, and if it wasn't for Ross, then it's got to be for the tart, right?'

'It makes sense,' agreed West. 'Now all we have to do is find out who she is.'

'It's got to be family,' said Martin. 'He wouldn't have done it unless he really loved her.'

'Perhaps they both had the hots for the same bird,' suggested West.

'No, never in a million years,' said Chalmers. 'No one commits bleeding suicide for a lost cause. If Ross was screwing this tart, even if he loved her too Thompson would have waited and doubled his chances when his mate turned up. You don't die for another man's meat.'

Martin's face brightened. 'Thompson was buried at Dover. I read about it in the paper. The local rag down there's bound to have the whole story, tell us all about Thompson's family, I shouldn't wonder.'

'Good thinking, Kenny,' said Chalmers. 'Send the Hawkins boys to Dover. Instead of parading round this house like a couple of stuffed pricks, they can do something useful. Visit the parents. Make out they're old friends of the dear departed. Tell 'em to ask why Ross weren't there the night Thompson got done – and who he was with.' He grinned triumphantly at Martin. 'If he was out with a tart and we can find out who she was, we might've got him!'

'Why not grab Thompson's ma and pa?' suggested

Martin. 'I bet Ross wouldn't stand by and see us hurt them.'

'You can leave the old people out of this, Frank.' West's voice was cold and hard. 'There are some things I won't be party to. You touch them, and you can kiss goodbye to me and my men.'

Chalmers got the message. 'Yeah, yeah, OK, Ron. Kenny, you leave them alone, you hear? But that don't apply to brothers and sisters, do it? You find out if there are any more bleeding Thompson kids.'

'What if it's a sister?' asked Martin, glancing hesitantly at West. 'Do we grab her?'

Chalmers didn't hesitate. 'If there's a Thompson bird, I want her here. I want her like the dog wants the fucking rabbit.'

'He might have had more than one sister,' said Martin.

'Then bring the fucking lot of them back here,' ordered Chalmers. 'Even if Ross don't love 'em, I can't see him standing by while we have ourselves a bit of fun with his dead mate's sisters.' He laughed. 'We could have him walking in here with his hands in the air, begging us to kill him.'

8

John and Tony Hawkins sped through the open gates of High Trees, the wheels of the Jaguar spinning viciously in the gravel. They swung right and hammered down the road, burning rubber for the first thirty yards. Kenny Martin and Ron West dragged the gates closed, locked them and hurried back to the house.

Phillip watched the Hawkinses go. He reckoned they must be after the listening devices, sweeper and anti-personnel mines West had asked for. Once they got back, it would not be long before West had electronically swept and cleared the house. Even now it was clear that Chalmers and his men were heeding West's warning about talking of their plans in areas Phillip might have bugged. All he could pick up now was the odd clink of a cup or glass being set down on a hard surface, the occasional faint mutter or the sounds of people moving about. The advantage he had enjoyed in being able to eavesdrop on them was over.

He decided to call it a day. He would let them set their little traps and bugs, then he'd move a few about and set some more of his own. That should cause confusion in the ranks.

Meanwhile, Julie was due to visit her parents for the weekend, and Phillip badly wanted to spend some time with her before she left. He wasted no further thought on the Jaguar and its occupants. Time enough to deal with them when they got back.

The Hawkins brothers booked into a small hotel on the Dover–Folkestone road. They removed the local phone book from one of the booths in the foyer and took it up to their room. It contained a dismaying number of Thompsons.

'It'll take us a year to get through this poxy lot,' complained Tony.

'Let's run through the Gs first,' suggested John. 'Lots of people take the easy way out and name their sons after themselves. I'll do the odds and you do the evens.'

'You what?'

'I'll start with the first one, then you do the second, then I'll do the third, then you do the fourth, and so on,' explained John with weary patience. Tony might be his brother, but Jeez he was thick! 'Listen to what I say and do the same when it's your turn.'

He picked up the phone and dialled. 'Mrs

Thompson? I'm an old friend of your son, Gary. I've just heard the terrible news . . . Oh, sorry to trouble you. I must have the wrong number.' He hung up and handed the phone to Tony.

After several calls John struck lucky. 'You must be wanting Victor and Mary,' said the current Mrs Thompson, obviously eager to help. 'They had a son called Gary. He was killed recently, in a fire in London. Murdered, they say.'

John Hawkins quickly scanned the last block of Thompsons and found a V. Thompson. 'Do they live at number seventeen, Marstons Road?'

'That's them. They were at church last Sunday. Lovely people . . . such a shame.'

He thanked her and hung up. His brother had long since refused to do any more phoning, and was asleep in an armchair, his mouth half open as he snored gently. John kicked him on the ankle. 'Tony! Wake up, you prat. I've found them.'

Tony looked blearily up at him. 'What do we do now?'

'We go round there, dickhead,' snapped John. 'Go and get the Jag. Now.'

Mary Thompson opened the door. She looked pale and strained, but she managed a smile for the two young men who introduced themselves as old friends of Gary's.

'We've been abroad, Mrs Thompson,' explained John Hawkins, 'and only heard the news when we got back a few days ago. We thought we ought to come round and offer our condolences.'

'Come in, boys.' She ushered them into the lounge. 'It's so good of you to come all the way from London. I expect you could do with a cup of tea. Sit yourselves down. I'll just go and put the kettle on, and I'll give my husband a call.'

The lounge was small but welcoming. None of the furniture was new but it all looked comfortable, and everything was spotlessly clean. A faint smell of beeswax furniture polish mingled pleasantly with the scent from a vase of roses on the mantelpiece.

Next to the fireplace, on an oak sideboard, was an array of framed photographs. Some were sepia prints of people in Victorian dress: unsmiling, dark-suited men whose imposing side-whiskers bristled above stiff white shirt-fronts, and women in high-necked dark dresses with bustles and lace collars. Others were Edwardian, others still from the 1920s. The different generations of the Thompson family were there for all to see.

Tony Hawkins picked up a photo of a fresh-faced young man in British Army uniform. He nudged his brother, and read out the inscription: 'To Mum and Dad, from your loving son, Gary.'

'Put it back. This is the one we're after,' said John. He pointed to a full-length colour photo of a beautiful, long-legged blonde girl. She was dressed in a white skirt, open-necked red blouse and high-heeled red sandals.

Tony gave a long, low whistle. 'Fuck me, I'd like a good dig at that.'

'Shut up!' hissed his brother. 'Do you want the old woman to hear you?' He read the neat handwritten inscription: 'To the best Mum and Dad in the world, with lots of love and kisses, Julie.'

They both turned hastily as they heard steps in the hall, and moved away from the dresser. The elderly man who entered the room looked bowed by grief. His eyes, of the same green as his daughter's, were deeply shadowed, and there were lines of pain round his mouth.

He crossed to them, his hand held out in welcome, and said, 'My wife tells me you were friends of Gary's. I can't tell you how much it means to us that you should take the trouble to come all this way to see us. But sit down, sit down and make yourselves comfortable. Mary's bringing some tea and home-made cakes. You'll like them. She's the best cook this side of the border.'

He was right. The cakes were delicious, and the Hawkinses munched their way through the lot in the hour they spent there. John did most of the talking. He avoided answering questions like 'Where did you serve with Gary?' by referring to 'special assignments that I'm not allowed to talk about'. Victor Thompson nodded understandingly, and didn't pursue the matter.

John said, 'Gary often talked about his sister. Is she all right?'

Both the Thompsons smiled warmly. Mary said, 'Gary and Julie were very close. We started late in life and were blessed with two wonderful children.' She tried to fight back the tears that welled up in her eyes. Her husband put his arm round her and held her close.

'Julie's been staying with a friend up in London,' he said. 'It's a pity you didn't arrive tomorrow. She's coming home for the weekend.'

'Seen anything of Phillip Ross?' enquired John Hawkins casually.

'Not since the funeral. He went off to France for a bit of a break. He and Gary were great friends, you know. Phillip can't forgive himself for not being there the night Gary was killed.'

'Where was he, Mr Thompson? I'm sure he couldn't help not being around.'

'He was having a night out with Julie. They were actually on their way back to the club when it happened, but they got there just too late. When they arrived the fire had already started.' Victor Thompson gripped his wife's hand tightly. 'We can only thank God that they were spared. It was hard enough to bear when he took Gary. If he'd taken Phillip and Julie as well I think we'd have found it hard to keep our faith. I know the Good Lord moves in mysterious ways and must have had good reasons for taking our son, though it's hard to understand what they could have been. But we still have Julie, and Phillip's like a second son to us – in fact, we very much hope that one day he'll become our son-in-law – so in that at least God was good to us.'

The Hawkinses made suitable replies and soon afterwards, having learnt all they needed to know, made ready to leave.

'What did you say your names were?' enquired Victor Thompson, as he saw them to the front door.

'John and Tony King, Mr Thompson,' said John.

'I'll tell Julie you called. She'll be sorry to have missed you – I'm sure Gary would have mentioned you to her. Please drop in again if you're in the area. It's so good to meet people who knew our son. It makes things easier to bear.'

'Phew!' breathed Tony Hawkins, as they walked to their car. 'I started to feel a right heel, what with the old geezer being so nice, and her bringing out those cakes and that.'

'Forget it,' ordered his brother. 'That bastard Ross is out to kill us, cut our bleeding throats, and we've just found the way to stop him. It's looks like the Good Lord is putting in a bit of work on our side now, don't it?'

Tony grinned. 'And putting a choice piece of pussy our way.'

The two men were laughing as they climbed into the Jaguar and drove away.

Julie ran out of the bungalow to greet Phillip as he climbed out of the BMW. She threw her arms round his neck and hugged him. 'Oh, I'm so glad you're back, Phillip. I've been so worried. When you didn't come home last night, I was almost frantic.'

Phillip grinned at her and gave her a long kiss. 'Better now?' He picked her off the ground and swung her round in circles, kissed her again and returned her hug with interest. As he put her down, he said, 'Come inside, love, there are a couple of things we need to talk about.'

Once they were settled comfortably in the lounge, he said, 'Julie, there could come a time when I have to be away for a week or more. And I may not be able to phone you. But please don't worry. Nothing's going to happen to me, I promise you.'

'I know that, and I do understand, but I love you and I can't help worrying.' She tilted her head on one side and looked narrowly at him. 'Something's up isn't it? Tell me all about it.'

Phillip told her everything, starting with his arrival at his dug-out the previous morning to find what looked like an army exercise going on in the grounds of High Trees. He glossed over the ruthless way he'd despatched Grant and White, but did say they'd set the dogs on him. 'I had to kill them, Julie. I couldn't take the chance.'

Julie looked up from the salad she was preparing. 'Don't ever take a chance, darling. Those men were paid killers, there with orders to hunt you down. And they were part of the gang that murdered Gary. They're no loss to the world.'

He finished his story over the meal, frowning as he saw how troubled Julie looked.

'Shouldn't you get some of your friends to help you?' she asked. 'These mercenaries aren't like Chalmers's mob. I mean, they're real professionals, not just a bunch of thugs. They'll know a lot of the moves that you know, won't they? They might be able to anticipate what you'll do next.'

'Yes, I've got to be a bit more cautious now, darling, but I've still got a trick or two up my sleeve. I'll soon bring the odds down again. If they bring in too many men, I'll call for help. But at the moment, I promise you, I can handle it on my own.'

Julie changed tack. 'I know I told Mum and Dad I'd go home for the weekend, but I could postpone it. All it would take would be a phone call. Shall I do it? We could have a bit more time together, and . . . well . . . I could come with you to High Trees as look out or back up or something.'

Phillip looked at her in mingled exasperation and concern. 'You just don't understand, do you, love? It was reasonably safe for you to help out at Gatwick because there were lots of people around, and if all else failed we could have called in the airport police – they're armed and ready to deal with emergencies. But it's not going to be like that from now on. It's going to be a matter of moving around at speed in the dark and on unfamiliar ground. I've had the best training in the world at this sort of thing, better than West's men. Sure, they're all trained and experienced soldiers, but none of them's had the highly specialized, intensive training and retraining I've had. And you've not had even the basics. How d'you think you'd cope stuck all on your own on a hillside in the dark, with guns firing around you and grenades going off, and knowing that if you took one more step you might tread on an anti-personnel mine. Would you know what to do? Of course you wouldn't. I very much doubt it. And that's not all. Suppose Chalmers got hold of you? Could you escape? No, you couldn't. And Chalmers knows that I wouldn't let him harm anyone else on my account, so I'd have to come in after you and then we'd both die. He'd kill me, of course, but you'd be a witness, and he couldn't leave you alive. He'd kill you for sure – and probably let his boys gang-rape you first. Is that what you want?'

Julie was abashed by his vehemence. She shook her head and said in a small voice, 'No.'

'Don't look so woebegone, sweetheart. I've told you before and I tell you again: I don't doubt your courage – how could I? And I know damn' well you'll do everything I ask of you when I ask it, and do it damn' well. But the time isn't yet. So for now, go and visit your parents and look after them. They need you badly, and they're longing to see you again. Besides, I've got to get back to High Trees in the morning to see what they've been up to. I'll have to leave very early. I want to let them know I'm still around, keep them on their toes. Perhaps I'll wake them up with a good loud bang at about, oh, say, five o'clock.'

Julie laughed, a bit shakily. 'That won't win you any popularity awards. And it doesn't leave us much time. I'll make us a hot drink and we can drink it in bed.' She summoned up a come-hither smile.

Phillip came hither with alacrity. He traced the line of her eyebrows with one finger and kissed her on the tip of her nose. 'Sounds wonderful. But first there are one or two little toys I need to get out and get ready for the morning.'

'OK. I'll have a shower while you're sorting them out. You can join me if you like.'

'I'll be with you in' – he checked his watch – 'precisely five minutes.'

As Julie vanished into the bedroom, he opened the boxes they'd brought in. He picked out the Mannlicher hunting rifle, with its telescopic sight, the three-inch mortar and six mortar bombs. 'This little lot should liven things up a bit,' he said to himself as he stacked them up for the morning. He added a mobile phone plus a fully charged long-life battery to the pile, and then, asking loudly, 'Is the water hot enough? I'm in the mood for the hottest shower of my life,' followed Julie through to the bathroom.

All was quiet at High Trees. Frank Chalmers was asleep, snoring loudly, in the master bedroom; Ron West was dozing on a camp bed in the corner of the room. Kenny Martin was asleep in the next room, and Bert Warren and Chris Goddard were sitting on the floodlit rear porch, having just completed a full-circle patrol of the house. John Jefferies and Digger Johnson were in position in the woods. Johnson, deeper in, was guarding Jefferies and the various paths leading to their positions.

A mortar bomb landed in the centre of the lawn, with a deafening explosion that blew in all the windows at the front of the house and knocked out the floodlights. Chalmers was blown out of bed, screaming in panic. He was lucky: though ripped to tatters, the heavy velvet curtains caught most of the shattered glass from the windows, which otherwise would have sliced him like bacon. West rolled out of bed and crouched by one of the windows, Uzi cocked and at the ready. He shouted to Chalmers to get down on the floor.

The second mortar dropped into the woods. West judged that it had fallen close to his men, and grimaced at the thought of what it might have done to them. He reached for his radio and pressed the transmit button. 'John, Digger, come in. Over.'

There was a crackle of static, then Johnson's voice said, 'I'm worried about John. That mortar fell right by him. I can see him, and he's not moving. Over.'

'Right, I'm coming out the front. Cover me.' Bent double, West ran to the door.

A hand grabbed at his ankle. 'Where the fuck are you going?' squawked Chalmers.

West kicked him away. 'Get down to the cellar. Get everyone down there. The next bomb could drop through the fucking roof.' He raced out and down the stairs.

Chalmers bumped into Martin as he fled out on to the landing. He shoved him aside, almost knocking him over, and yelled, 'The bastard's bombing us! Get down in the fucking cellar!'

Goddard and Warren had bolted inside when they heard the first explosion, and were crouched in the hall, clutching their guns for dear life. Chalmers yelled at them to get down in the fucking cellar as he ran past at the best speed his fat legs could manage.

West raised Johnson on the radio and said, 'Digger? Now.' He sprinted out through the wrecked front door, zigzagged at top speed across the open ground and dived into the woods. Once in cover, he waited until his eyes had adjusted to the darkness before moving off stealthily towards his men's positions. He soon spotted Jefferies lying motionless, moaning softly, a few metres from the smoking bomb crater. West crawled over and inspected his wounds. The most serious was to his right leg. Splinters of white bone stuck out from the torn flesh above his knee, and blood was spurting from torn arteries and veins. West stripped off his belt and, using a dead branch ripped from a nearby bush, applied a rough tourniquet. As soon as the bleeding was under control, he hoisted Jefferies over his shoulder and set off back to the house. Digger Johnson watched from his hiding-place, moving not a muscle.

Once in the hall, West lowered Jefferies gently to the floor and checked his leg again in the light. He'd seen wounds like that before: the leg would have to come off.

He heard the faint whistle that signalled the arrival of another bomb, then another, and lay across the wounded man to protect him.

Same places, he thought. So Ross isn't aiming directly at the house. He snatched up his radio. 'Digger, are you OK? Over.'

Incredibly, Johnson was laughing when he answered. 'Yeah, it's getting to be good fun out here. I'm starting to feel right at home. Over.'

'Well keep your goddamn' head down. John's copped it in the leg and he's going to lose it. Stand by. Out.'

From the hillside, Phillip had seen the front windows blown in. He remembered that the master bedroom suite was at the front of the house, and was grinning as he dialled Chalmers's London number. The call-diverter put him through to High Trees.

West heard the phone in the sitting-room ringing and shouted for someone to answer it. A few moments later Kenny Martin ran into the hall. 'It's Ross. He wants to speak to you.'

West stood up and asked wryly, 'Did he ask for me by name?'

Martin nodded.

'That confirms the house is bugged. Keep an eye on John. I'll be back in a minute.' He went into the wrecked sitting-room.

Phillip, waiting impatiently, heard a gravelly voice say, 'West speaking.'

'This is Ross. I'm giving you and your men the chance to withdraw. If you don't take it, I'll find it necessary to kill you all.'

There was a long silence before West said, 'I'm sorry, Ross, But I've accepted the contract for one month. I won't go back on my word.'

'Very admirable, West. Foolish but admirable. There's one thing I want to say to you.'

'Go ahead. I'm listening.'

'If you bring in more men and escalate the situation, I'll call on my friends to help me. We'll go through that house like a dose of salts, and no one will survive, not one human being. Do you understand what I'm saying?'

'I understand. I've no intention of escalating.'

'Good,' said Phillip. 'I want to handle this on my own. Win or lose, I'll do it alone, provided you don't bring in more troops.'

'After what you've just told me, I probably couldn't recruit more men anyway. I'd have to tell them what they were up against. That's my way.'

'Good. Put Frank Chalmers on, will you?'

'OK, but it'll take a few minutes.' Phillip could

217

hear dry amusement in West's voice. 'He's down in the cellar.'

'I'll call back in ten minutes,' said Phillip curtly. He knew he'd spent about as long as was safe in one position and needed to shift to another vantage point.

'Wait, Ross,' said West urgently.

'Why?'

'I've got a seriously wounded man in here. Your mortar got him, and his right leg's hanging off. He's right out of it. Give me free passage to take him out of here. I'll dump him at a hospital. It's his only chance.'

'Who is it?'

'John Jefferies. He's a good man.'

Phillip remembered that Luke Richards had spoken highly of Jefferies. He turned it over in his mind, then said, 'OK. You take him out personally. I'll let you out and back in – if you decide to come back.'

'I've got to come back, Ross. I don't like it, but I've got to come back. I think you'll understand.'

Phillip did understand, but he ignored the remark. 'Is anyone else hurt?'

West grunted. 'A few minor cuts and bruises, but nothing so serious that a change of underpants won't cure it.'

'Right, you have ten minutes to get the wounded man out. When you come back, give three long blasts on the horn. I'll grant you safe passage. I'll hold my fire when you leave and when you come back.' He switched off the mobile phone and moved fast but silently to a new position. The first streaks of sunlight burst over the horizon.

After speaking to Phillip Ross, West went down to the cellar and banged on the door. 'It's me, Ron. I'm coming in.'

The three men in the cellar lowered their guns as West went in. He said to Chalmers, 'I've just spoken to Ross. That was him on the phone. He asked me to withdraw my men. I said I couldn't do that.'

'Thank fuck for that.' Chalmers was surly.

'John Jefferies is seriously wounded. His right leg's hanging off. Ross has given me safe passage to take him out, to get him to hospital.'

'It's a trick,' said Chalmers suspiciously. 'The minute you piss off out of here, Ross'll come in and get us. You can't go, you gotta stay here.'

West raised his right hand. It held the Uzi. 'I've got one of my men badly injured out there and he's going to die if I don't get him to hospital fast. So if anyone cares to try to stop me' – his smile was tight and mean – 'we can decide the issue here and now.'

Chalmers tried to put a good face on things. 'Well, if you feel like that about it, you'd better get going. Try not to be too long, that's all. I don't trust that bastard Ross not to blow us all up while you're away.'

West was already halfway up the stairs. 'I'll call Digger back to the house,' he shouted down. 'He'll guard you till I get back. Stay down here till after

I've left, or I might think you were trying to stop me. Oh, by the way, Ross is ringing back in a few minutes, Frank. He wants to talk to you.'

Martin was still hovering in the hall, uncertain what to do. West told him what was happening, then picked up his walky-talky. 'Digger, come in. Over.'

Johnson answered instantly. 'Digger here. Receiving you loud and clear. Over.'

'Listen, Digger, I'm taking John out. I've got to get him to hospital if he's to have any kind of a chance. Get the Range Rover out and bring it round to the front of the house.'

'Roger, wilco, yessir. Out,' said Johnson cheerfully.

West grinned and thought, 'Cool bastard. He doesn't give a fuck about anything.'

The Range Rover soon appeared and skidded to a halt outside the front door. Johnson jumped out. He went straight to Jefferies and inspected the wound, while West and Martin prepared to lift the injured man into the back of the vehicle. Johnson pulled a face and said, 'Ooh, nasty.'

West told him to go down to the gates and open them. 'Ross has granted me free passage. Then come back to the house and stay here. I'll be back as soon as I've dropped John off at a hospital door.'

Johnson gave him a mocking salute and loped off down the drive. Phillip watched through his binoculars as he heaved the gates open and the

Range Rover drove out. He could just make out Jefferies's huddled form on the back seat, covered by a blood-stained blanket.

Johnson calmly closed and locked the gates, then walked unhurriedly back up to the house. Phillip could easily have taken him out with the Mannlicher, but he had granted free passage, and Johnson knew very well that that covered the man who dealt with the gates.

As he went back into the house, Kenny Martin pounced on him. 'Do you think Ron'll come back?' Martin asked anxiously. 'Or will he reckon he should get out while the going's good?'

'Don't even think about it, my son,' said Johnson with his shark-grin. 'He's got to come back for me. I'd get all lonely without him.' He looked around. 'Where are the others?'

Martin looked fixedly at his feet. 'They're . . . er . . . in the cellar.'

Johnson roared with laughter. 'I don't believe this, I just don't fucking believe it.'

Bert Warren appeared from the back of the house, his craggy face about as expressive as a bulldog's. 'The boss wants to know what's going on up here.'

Johnson stopped laughing long enough to say, 'We was just having a little discussion about you three hiding in the cellar.'

Warren looked at Martin. His face still expressionless, he said, 'You fucking prat! Five minutes ago, you was down there with us.'

That set Johnson off again. 'Well,' he managed, 'it looks like I'm going to have to babysit all four of you.'

The phone in the sitting-room rang again. Warren turned his head towards the sound and said, 'That'll be Ross again, for Frank.' He went into the kitchen passage and yelled down the cellar steps, 'Frank, telephone!'

Johnson watched Chalmers, still puffing from his climb up the cellar stairs, walk heavily across the hall to the sitting-room, with Martin close on his heels. He smiled maliciously at Warren and said, 'If Ross don't like what Chalmers says, you can expect another couple of bombs to drop in.'

Both men moved fast to the back of the hall, went into the kitchen passage and pulled the hall door shut.

In the sitting-room, a subdued Frank Chalmers picked up the phone and said, 'Hello.'

'Things aren't going too well for you, Frank, are they?' said Phillip mockingly. 'Have you had enough yet? Are you ready to tell me who killed Gary Thompson?'

'Get stuffed, Ross.' Chalmers came suddenly to life and sounded defiant.

'You have twenty-four hours to give me that name. Then I'm coming in to finish the job. That isn't a threat, Frank, it's a plain statement of fact.'

Chalmers tried to buy some time. 'Ring me at six this evening. I'll give you my decision then.'

'OK, but some more of your men will be dead by then,' Phillip warned him.

'So fucking what?'

Was it possible, Phillip wondered with astonishment and bitter contempt, that Chalmers genuinely didn't care if more men died? He switched the mobile phone off without another word, loaded the mortar, and sent another shell crashing on to the lawn in front of the house. The front door, already badly damaged, disappeared in a whirl of splinters, and clods of grass and earth flew up all around.

Out in the kitchen, Johnson grinned his shark-grin at the noise. 'Whatever it was Frank said, Ross didn't like it.'

'Well, at least he hasn't had a direct hit on the house yet,' said Warren.

'He ain't fucking well aiming at the house,' said Johnson gleefully. 'You wait till he does, my son. He can drop one of those mortar bombs straight down whichever chimney he likes.'

Warren said, 'Oh fuck it! Oh bloody hell fire!' and bolted back to the cellar.

The dust from the last mortar shell settled round the house.

Meanwhile, in a small hotel on the Dover–Folkestone road, the Hawkins brothers slept peacefully on.

9

At eight-thirty the next morning the Hawkins brothers were on watch in their Jaguar, parked a little way down the road from the Thompsons' house. At nine o'clock Julie arrived. She parked her Volkswagen Golf outside the house, took her overnight bag out of the boot and slung it over her shoulder.

'Bingo!' said John. 'That's the bird.' He nudged Tony, who was reading the comic strips in the *Sun*, and pointed to Julie as she went into the house.

Tony dropped his paper and stared. 'Cor, what a piece of arse! She looks even better than her photo.' He leered across at his brother and said, 'You drive, mate. I'll sit in the back with her.'

'Not on your fucking nelly. You're driving, Tony. First we snatch her and get her back to Frank. Then, if he gives the go-ahead, you can do what you like with her. But until then you don't lay a finger on her, understand?'

Tony lay back in his seat, draped his newspaper over his face and began to daydream about what he'd do to Julie Thompson once he had her alone and helpless.

At ten-thirty Julie came out of the house, turned left and started down the road towards the corner shop.

John Hawkins whipped the newspaper off Tony's face. 'Wake up, you prat,' he said, 'there's the tart. Start up and pull alongside so I can grab her.' He pulled his automatic pistol from his shoulder holster and held it out of sight under the dashboard.

Julie was deep in thought, wondering how to persuade her parents to go away for a short break. They badly needed a rest from the constant, wearying, well-meant sympathy of their friends and neighbours. She only vaguely registered a car pulling up to the kerb just ahead of her, nothing unusual in a residential road.

Her arm was caught in a cruelly tight grip and a low, threatening voice said, 'Get in the car.' Before she could scream or begin to struggle, something crashed against the side of her head, stunning her. 'Get in the fucking car,' said the voice. Barely conscious, she was half dragged, half carried to the car. The back door was open. She was shoved roughly inside. Her attacker crammed in beside her and slammed the door, and the car sped off.

John Hawkins holstered his pistol and said, 'Piece of cake. The tart didn't know what hit her.'

His brother grinned. 'That's nothing,' he said. 'Wait till she finds out what's *going* to hit her,' and he rubbed his crotch vigorously.

Julie heard their voices faintly, as if from far away. She tried to speak but couldn't, tried to struggle but couldn't move. She was dizzy and felt sick with fear. Someone tied her hands behind her back, bound her ankles and gagged her with plastic tape. A cloth that stank of petrol was tied over her eyes. She was pushed down on to the floor of the car and covered with a blanket.

As the car raced along, Julie's head slowly cleared. She kept still, huddled under the blanket, hoping her kidnappers would think she'd fainted. She guessed it was Chalmers's men who had abducted her and wondered whether she was to be used to pressurize Phillip or whether the men would simply throw her out of the speeding car.

'Think, girl,' she told herself fiercely. 'You're afraid, but you're not going to let your fear beat you. There's got to be a way out of this, and you've got to find it. So bloody well *think*!' Clearly there was nothing she could do while she was bound and blindfolded and gagged. Once she could move and see and yell, though . . . She steeled herself to wait, and resolved to fight for her life with all her strength.

The car stopped and the man next to her got out, leaving the door open. She waited to see if he would drag the blanket off her, but he just walked a few paces away. The driver turned round. She heard the leather creak as he moved, leaning heavily on the back of the seat. A hand stroked her backside, lingering over the cleft between her buttocks. The man said, 'Won't be long, darling. We're nearly there,' and laughed coarsely. Julie forced herself to remain motionless and silent.

The car had obviously halted right beside a phone booth. Julie could hear the familiar sounds of coins being deposited and someone hitting the metal buttons. The man spoke to someone called Kenny and asked for someone to be standing by at the gates. 'We'll be there in about five minutes,' he said, 'and we're bringing Frank a little present from Dover. Nicely gift-wrapped, tell him.'

The back seat sank under the man's weight as he got back in, and the door slammed. The engine fired into life and the car lurched off again. Some time later – she could not be sure how long – she was thrown violently to the right as the car swerved suddenly to the left. The tyre noise changed from a swishing hum to a rasp as they hit gravel and the car fought for grip on the loose surface. It skidded to a halt and the men jumped out. The nearside rear door opened and she was dragged out and carried into a house – she could smell furniture polish and cigarette smoke.

She was dumped roughly down on what felt like a settee, and someone pulled the blanket off her and abruptly ripped away the blindfold. Bright light struck directly into her face, half blinding her, but she could see that she was in a large sitting-room. A shadow loomed. She stared up into the fat, grinning face of Frank Chalmers.

Secure in his dug-out, Phillip heard the car approaching. West had returned some time earlier, giving the agreed three long blasts on his horn, and Phillip had let him pass. He had seen no sign of the Hawkinses since their departure the previous day, so was not unduly surprised to see the Jaguar appear, with Tony Hawkins at the wheel. He watched through his binoculars as Warren and Goddard opened the gates. The Jaguar swung into the drive, scattering gravel, and accelerated up to the house, where they hauled out a large, blanket-wrapped bundle and lugged it indoors.

I wonder what that little load of goodies was, he thought. Let's see what's up.

He put the earpiece of the transceiver to his ear and tuned in to the sitting-room. The banging he had heard earlier, as Chalmers's men broke up furniture and used it to board up the windows, had stopped. He heard men moving around and the murmur of low-voiced conversations. A door slammed.

Chalmers's voice rang out suddenly, startling him. 'If you can hear me, Ross, give me a call on the blower. I've got a little surprise for you.'

The triumph in his voice set off alarm bells in Phillip's head. He checked his watch. Nearly noon. He wasn't due to ring Chalmers until six that evening, but he knew West had realized that the house was bugged and that he'd be keeping a listening watch. On the other hand, if he didn't respond to Chalmers's message they might think he had gone, and they might therefore give something away. He decided to ring at the agreed time and not before. Let them think he wasn't there or wasn't listening.

Chalmers spoke again. 'No more bombs, Ross. We've got the Thompson bird in here, and she's sitting right by the window. You chuck another bomb and she gets the full blast. That'd be a pity, wouldn't it? Pretty bird like her, all smashed to bits.'

Phillip fought down the rage that blurred his vision for a moment. Julie in the hands of vicious thugs like Tony Hawkins and Digger Johnson – icy fear mingled with his anger and his shoulders were rigid with tension. He took a deep breath and forced himself to relax, to regain control of his mind and emotions. As soon as the moment of fury had passed, he picked up his mobile phone and dialled Victor Thompson's number.

'Hello, Victor, it's Phillip. Is Julie there?'

'Well, yes, but she went down to the corner shop about' – a note of surprise crept into his voice – 'oh, an hour and a half ago. She should have been back long since. But she probably just dropped in to see a friend for a chat and a cup of coffee. Where are you? Are you phoning from France?'

'Yes,' said Phillip. He managed to keep his voice calm as they exchanged the usual courtesies. He promised to call back in half an hour, and rang off as soon as he decently could. He desperately needed to think.

If he called in the police, Chalmers might panic and start shooting in all directions. Julie would no doubt be used as a human shield – he forced the thought out of his mind. Besides, the local police probably weren't adequately equipped or sufficiently experienced to handle a situation like this. Chief Inspector Hill very definitely was, but it would take time for him to contact the local force, cut through the necessary red tape and get down to Sussex. Phillip knew he hadn't got that much time. If he called on his SAS pals, enough of them would be free to come and carry out a raid, but that too would take time to set up, and it would be risky.

His best – his only – option was to play along with Chalmers for the time being. Chalmers was unlikely to harm Julie until he got his hands on Phillip. Then, of course, they would both have to die: as he'd told Julie, Chalmers would leave no witnesses.

Half an hour passed. Phillip rang Victor Thompson again, and this time the older man's voice held not just surprise but the beginnings of concern. 'Julie still hasn't come back,' he said. 'I can't think where she can be. She only went to get some pâté for lunch, and even if she'd gone for a coffee or something with a friend she ought to be back by now.'

Phillip steeled himself and said in the coolest tone at his command, 'Victor, please keep calm and listen carefully to what I tell you. Julie's been kidnapped.' He overrode Victor's shocked, fearful questions, and went on, 'I'll get her back, I promise you, safe and sound. And soon.'

'The police,' asked Thompson shakily, 'shouldn't we call the police?'

'Not yet. It would be more dangerous for Julie if the police were involved at this stage. Please leave it to me, Victor. I love your daughter more than my life. I know what I'm doing, and I swear to you that I'll get her back safely.'

'Phillip, if Julie's hurt or . . . if she . . . It would kill Mary coming on top of Gary's death. What am I going to tell her when Julie doesn't come back?'

'Don't tell her unless you have to. I think I can get Julie back quickly. We'll think up something to tell Mary, and she needn't know anything about what's happened until Julie's safely home.'

'But what can I tell her? I've never lied to Mary, never deceived her in my life. I can't think, can't . . .' His voice faded into desperate silence.

Phillip thought rapidly. What the hell would be a plausible explanation for Julie's dashing off again within a few hours of arriving at her parents? It would have to be both simple and urgent.

'Is Mary there at the moment?'

'No. She went out early to put fresh flowers on Gary's grave and she isn't back yet.'

'Good. When she gets back, tell her that I rang from France, that I told Julie I'd remembered something – a document – that might be useful to the police hunting Gary's killers. Tell her I left the document in the flat, and as Julie's got a key I asked her to go and pick it up and take it to Chief Inspector Hill at Scotland Yard. You don't know what the document is, but Julie said Hill would probably want to talk to her about it, and that she might well not get back home until late, or perhaps not even until tomorrow, if he wasn't there and she had to wait. Have you got that? Can you tell it to Mary so she believes it?'

'Yes, I think so,' said Thompson hesitantly. 'A document in your flat . . . I don't know what . . . Julie's taking it to the police . . . not back till tomorrow.' His voice strengthened a little. 'Very well, Phillip, I'll leave everything in your hands and trust you to do what's needed. You know about these things. I'll pray for you and for Julie. And will you ring me again soon? Please do. It'll help me keep going.'

'I'll ring you tomorrow – you have my word on it. I should have some news by then. But if I haven't, don't start imagining the worst. These things can't be rushed.'

'God bless you, Phillip. I know you'll do everything humanly possible.'

Phillip said goodbye and rang off. He checked his watch: only five hours until he was due to phone Chalmers again. He knew now what he had to do: offer Chalmers a trade. But what would Chalmers accept? It was no use offering himself. As he'd told Julie, that would only get them both killed. Who or what did Chalmers care about? Of course! His brother. Little brother Robin. But he was in Spain, a thousand miles away.

He did some rapid mental arithmetic. It was possible. Just.

Julie recognized Chalmers instantly from the photos Phillip had shown her. She had been afraid before but now she felt the chill of terror trickle down her spine. Her hands were shaking. She was almost grateful for the plaster over her mouth: no matter how much she felt like screaming, she couldn't betray her fear to Chalmers and his thugs.

The air in the room was full of the stench of explosives, unpleasantly laced with stale tobacco smoke. Her stomach heaved but she fought down the nausea and tried to keep her mind clear. If she got the slightest chance to escape she must be alert and ready to take it.

There were men standing all around her, and she noted that they were all armed. The man who had driven the car tore her shoes roughly off her feet, cut the cord round her ankles, leering at her, stroking her legs and trying to peer up her skirt as he did so. She tried to kick him in the throat, but he dodged back and jeered at her.

She ignored him and looked round the room. It looked as if a bomb had, quite literally, hit it. All the lights were on. The windows had been roughly boarded up. The curtains hung in tatters and the carpet was strewn with shards of broken glass and porcelain.

She covertly studied the men surrounding her. The man who had forced her into the car and the man who had driven were also among those whose photos Phillip had shown her. Their hair was longer now, and their faces were more heavily lined, but she recognized them as the Hawkins brothers. Chalmers she already knew. She identified three other men: Chris Goddard and Albert Warren, sitting sullen and quiet in a corner, and Kenny Martin, who was whispering something to Chalmers.

One man she could not place. He was big, middle-aged and heavily built, with close-cropped greying hair. He wore military clothing and held a funny-looking gun in his right hand. Julie guessed him to be one of the mercenaries Phillip had spoken of.

A voice crackled from a radio on the mercenary's left hip. He grabbed the radio, muttered inaudibly into it and replaced it.

Chalmers turned and said loudly, 'If you can hear me, Ross . . .'

Julie's mind raced. They know the house is bugged, she thought. Phillip had told her he listened in. She wanted to cry out, to warn him to keep away, but the plaster over her mouth kept her silent.

There was no answer to Chalmers's challenge. He spoke again, more loudly, telling Phillip that they had her and that her safety depended on him. Still no answer. The longer he waited, the angrier Chalmers became.

'Take her down to the fucking cellar and lock her up,' he ordered the Hawkins brothers. 'It looks as if we'll have to wait till five o'clock.'

Tony Hawkins yanked Julie to her feet. 'I'll take her,' he said. He gripped her arm hard enough to make her wince and half led, half dragged her to the door, heedless of the way the broken glass cut her bare feet. He grinned at his brother; John shook his head and looked away.

The exchange between the brothers was not lost on Ron West. He turned to Chalmers and said, 'I want as many men as possible posted around the house and in the grounds. If Ross is listening he may come in and try to take the girl back.'

'What, in broad daylight?' Chalmers thought about it for a minute, then said hastily, 'Right, you lot, outside and spread out. Kenny, you and Ron stay with me.'

West called after the other three as they made for the door, 'Careful in the woods. Digger's out there.'

'Quiet,' hissed Chalmers. 'Ross might be listening.'

236

'It's nothing he doesn't already know. You wait here, Frank. I'd better go and check the men are in position.'

'OK, but don't be long.'

West made a tour of the house. He saw no sign of Tony Hawkins, so made his way down to the cellar. The door was unlocked, and he went silently in.

Julie, still gagged by the plaster, was pinned against the far wall by Tony Hawkins. Her eyes were wide with anger and fear. His fly was open, and he had torn her blouse open and was clawing at her breasts with one hand, while with the other he reached up under her skirt, hooked his finger into her panties and pulled them down to her knees. As he straightened up, she tried to head-butt him and knee him in the groin, all the time wrigging frantically to get away from him. He laughed off her attempts to hurt him. He was too tall, too strong. She was at his mercy. He had none. He was enjoying her fear. Raping her was going to be ecstasy.

Leaving his equipment in place, Phillip slipped out of the dug-out and set the rhododendron camouflage in place. He crawled until he was out of sight of the house, then ran the three miles to where he had parked the BMW. It took him seventeen minutes, across country.

Thirty-five minutes later he was queuing at the British Airways booking desk at Gatwick. He looked round the terminal with something close to hatred.

His mind filled with near-unbearable memories of the last time he'd been here, of how Julie had helped him, of how . . . He reached the head of the queue and forced his mind back to the task in hand.

'When's your next flight to Málaga?' he asked urgently.

He bit down hard on his impatience as the bookings clerk tapped a few computer keys and checked her screen. 'Well, there's one in forty minutes,' she said, 'and there are a couple of seats left. But you'll have to hurry.'

'I'll take it. Open return please.' Phillip wrenched a handful of fifty-pound notes from his wallet.

'Your name, sir?'

'Cole. Anthony Robert Cole.'

One eye constantly on the clock, Phillip made a lightning call to Peter Russell, explained the situation and asked him to send a couple of men to mount an unobtrusive guard on the Thompsons' house. Then he raced for the plane.

At five-fifteen p.m., British summertime, Anthony Robert Cole cleared Immigration and Customs at Málaga Airport. He changed sterling for pesetas at the *cambio* desk, raced out to the taxi rank, climbed into the battered old Renault at the head of the rank, and said, 'Puerto Banus. *Rápido – rapidísimo – por favor.*'

The taxi driver smiled blissfully. '*Sí, señor, claro, rapidísimo,*' he carrolled, and let out the clutch as the accelerator hit the floor. The car shot forwards as if starting a Formula One grand prix, flinging Phillip hard against the back of his seat. Less than twenty-five minutes later it screeched to a side-skidding halt at the security barrier of Puerto Banus.

The driver turned and grinned happily at him. '*Rapidísimo, no, señor?*'

'*Sí, de verdad,*' he agreed, smiling a little forcedly at the memory of the old car's headlong, lurching, zigzagging progress along the motorway. He paid the driver and added a generous tip as a thanks-offering for their survival.

'*Muchas gracias, señor, muchas gracias,*' said the driver cheerfully as he swung out into the road six inches in front of a container lorry.

Phillip paused for a moment to get his breath back, and looked around. He had stripped off his camouflage jacket and shirt on the plane, but still wore his camouflage trousers and combat jacket. Only his white T-shirt wasn't out of place in this setting. He checked his watch: quarter to five, British time. He walked quickly into the port, checking the shops until he found one that could sell him an eight-inch hunting knife. His next stop was a 'his and hers' boutique. He winced at the prices, but bought slacks and a pair of loafers. Then he set off in search of Robin Chalmers.

Not far along the quay he saw the area where the larger yachts were moored. Praying that the *Helena* would be tied up there and not out on a day trip or – he dared not think of it – a longer cruise, he set off towards them. He had to push through throngs of holidaymakers as he scanned the stern of each vessel for her name. After what seemed eons, he saw her: printed in bold letters on her stern was '*HELENA*', with the port of registration, Guernsey, underneath.

He wasted no time. On the after deck, ogling the scantily clad young women who wandered up and down the quay admiring the largest yachts, lounged two young men. He cast his mind back to the photos Hill had shown him, but recognized neither of them. A lucky break: they would be unlikely to know about him. He walked confidently up the gangway and asked, 'Is Robin here?'

The two men looked at him suspiciously as he went towards them, but their faces cleared at the mention of their boss's name. 'Yeah, but he's below, having his siesta,' said the taller of them.

Phillip smiled. 'Fine, I'll surprise him.'

'No, don't.' The tall man got to his feet and moved towards him. 'He's got his bird with him, and he won't want to be disturbed.'

Phillip wiped the smile off his face and let his voice harden to iron. 'Look, buddy, Frank Chalmers sent me, and I need to see Robin. Now!'

The deckhand still looked dubious, but the mention of Frank Chalmers's name brought instant obedience. He stepped back and said, 'Please yourself. But don't say I didn't warn you. You might tell him I did, by the way – stop him having my guts for garters.'

Phillip waved a hand in acknowledgement, crossed the deck to the rear saloon and went below. From his limited knowledge of big yachts, he guessed that the master cabin would be towards the stern of the yacht, and that that was where Robin Chalmers and his bird would be. He was right on both counts.

The bird was clearly the noisy type: from the closed door of the master cabin came sounds of a woman squealing and moaning as she neared orgasm. Pulling out his hunting knife, Phillip eased the door open, slipped through and shut it soundlessly behind him.

The cabin was in semi-darkness, the curtains drawn to shut out the brilliant Mediterranean sunlight. On the king-size bed were a man and a woman, their sweat-glistening bodies locked together, oblivious of everything but themselves. Robin Chalmers lay on his back, thrusting his hips up at the slender, fine-boned black girl who sat astride him, her head thrown back, grinding herself against him as she shrieked in pleasure. Her tongue flicked in and out over her full red lips, her eyes were shut tight, and she shrieked even more loudly as she climaxed. Phillip thought fleetingly of Julie's 'fairy story'; the thought fuelled his rage.

He cat-footed up to the bed and rabbit-punched the girl on the side of her head, just hard enough to put her out. She toppled sideways like a felled tree, slid off the man beneath her and crumpled on to the floor. Robin Chalmers opened his eyes and shouted

241

with pain and anger as the girl's fall twisted and wrenched at his erect penis. 'What the fuck are you doing, Shirl?'

He reached out a hand to drag her back on to him, and saw Phillip standing over him, the hunting knife glinting ominously in the half-light. Phillip leant over, slipped the blade between Chalmers's inner thigh and testicles, and turned the cutting edge inwards. Chalmers flinched, then froze, his mouth agape, his eyes appalled.

'If you think that hurts,' said Phillip coldly, 'you won't believe what happens next.' He sat down on the bed, pinning Chalmers's legs in place with his elbow. 'Phone your brother. He's at High Trees.'

'What the fuck is this all about?' asked Chalmers unsteadily.

Phillip twisted the knife slightly.

Chalmers whined with pain and fear. Not daring to do so much as turn his head, he reached out, groped around until he found the phone, dragged it across in front of him and dialled.

'Hold the receiver away from your ear a bit, so I can hear,' ordered Phillip.

He obeyed.

The cocky voice of Frank Chalmers reached Phillip clearly. 'You're late, Ross.'

West crossed the cellar in five long strides. He grabbed Hawkins by the collar and pulled him roughly away, priming him for the right hook that crashed to his jaw and sent him reeling against the opposite wall. Hawkins slid down to the floor, shaking his head muzzily.

West turned back to Julie. 'It's all right,' he said gently, 'I won't let him touch you again. I want to help you – I've got a daughter just about your age.' He buttoned up her blouse, reached down and pulled up her panties and smiled apologetically at her. 'This will hurt, I'm afraid, but there's no painless way to do it,' he said and in one move ripped the plaster off her mouth. 'No screaming now,' he said quietly, and put a reassuring arm round her shoulders.

He pulled out his knife and cut the cord round her wrists. She managed a shaky smile and a heartfelt 'Thank you' as she rubbed them. The cord had bitten deeply into her, leaving deep white marks surrounded by swollen red flesh.

West said, 'It's OK, miss. I've done a lot of bad things in my life, but rape – even standing by while it's done – isn't one of them.'

There was a swift sound behind him. West spun round, but too late. Tony Hawkins covered the space between them in one leap and smashed him across the back of the head with a piece of two-by-four timber. The knife went skittering across the floor and fetched up against the opposite wall. Dazed, West hit the floor and rolled. He tried to get to his feet, but a vicious kick from Hawkins caught him on the temple, sending him reeling again. Then Hawkins was on him, raining savage blows on his head. West caught him in the ribs with a short, sharp upper cut. Air hissed out of Hawkins's lungs, and he slumped forward on to West, as limp as a rag doll.

West was puzzled: he hadn't hit him that hard. He pushed Hawkins off him, and saw Julie standing over them, her face full of mingled horror, distress and resolution. From Hawkins's back protruded West's knife: she had driven it in up to the hilt.

Julie started to shake from head to foot as shock hit her. She sank to her knees, biting fiercely into the knuckle of her thumb, fighting off hysteria. West sat down beside her, put an arm round her and held her close.

'You saved my life, Miss Thompson,' he said quietly. 'Thank you.'

They sat in silence for a while. Julie leant gratefully against him, and gradually her trembling eased. It was strangely peaceful in the dimly lit cellar. Neither of them paid any heed to the body of Tony Hawkins, which lay crumpled where it had fallen.

The quiet was broken by Kenny Martin, who shouted down the stairs, 'Ron, are you there?'

They got to their feet. West pulled his gun from its holster and cocked the Uzi. 'You'd better come down here,' he shouted back.

Martin clattered down the stairs and came in. His jaw dropped as he took in the scene. He ran to

Hawkins and bent over him, then turned in disbelief to West. 'He's dead . . .'

'He was trying to rape the girl. I killed him.'

Martin was alarmed. 'Frank ain't going to like this – and nor's Tony's brother. John ain't going to like it one bit.'

'What's done is done,' said West flatly. 'Who likes it or doesn't like it is another matter. Miss Thompson, I've got to leave you now, but don't worry. Just sit tight here. You won't be bothered again.' He flexed his shoulders tiredly, and smiled down at her. 'I'm getting too old for this.'

He crossed to Hawkins's body, pulled out the knife, wiped it on Hawkins's shirt-front and slipped it back into its sheath. He slung the body over his shoulder and, urging Martin on in front of him, carried it up the stairs and into the sitting-room.

Martin was right: Frank Chalmers didn't like it one bit. 'Whose fucking side are you on?' he yelled. 'That's another man down, dead and gone, thanks to you. Why don't you tell Ross he needn't bother, you're doing his fucking killing for him!'

'He asked for it. I had to stop him raping the girl – and you can imagine Ross's reaction if he'd succeeded – and he tried to kill me.'

Chalmers looked sideways at the Uzi in West's right hand and moderated his voice. 'What the hell are we going to tell John?'

'Tell him the truth,' said West unemotionally. 'He

245

can make up his own mind what he wants to do about it.'

'Fuck me!' said Chalmers bitterly. 'He wants to kill another one of us. For Chrissake, Ron, we've got to play this thing down or it'll all get right out of hand. Can't we dump him in the woods and make out that Ross got him?'

West shrugged. 'It's up to you. You're the boss.'

'That's it, then. John'll believe it OK. Just because Ross ain't phoned, it don't mean he ain't fucking well creeping about out there. Could you get Tony out there without John seeing anything?'

West nodded.

'Then do it. With luck John'll never know the difference and this thing'll blow over.'

West reached for his radio and pressed the transmit button. 'Digger, this is Ron. Return to the house, and don't let anyone see you. Over'

The radio crackled back, 'On my way. Out.'

Five minutes later Johnson came into the sitting-room. 'Looking for me, guv?' he asked cheerfully.

West nodded in the direction of Tony Hawkins's body. 'I want you to take him into the woods. No one must see you – that's important. Plant a gun on him, then in an hour or so make a bit of a fuss, fire a few rounds and so on. Make out that someone came into the grounds and killed him.'

Johnson picked Hawkins up and slung him effortlessly over his shoulder. He grinned at West. 'No problem, guv. Anything else while I'm about it? Need any shopping done? Fetch you an Indian take-away? Anything like that?'

West grinned back. 'No, Digger, just what I told you.'

As Johnson went out with his grisly load, Chalmers said calmly, 'Well, that's that sorted out. One down, seven to go.'

West stared at him and thought incredulously, 'He simply doesn't give a shit about anyone except himself. How the hell has he kept his men's loyalty all this time?'

The next hour passed uneventfully until Johnson went into action and made his bit of a fuss. Two blasts from a twelve-bore were followed by a burst of pistol fire, and there was an artistic scream of agony, which trailed away into silence.

West hurried outside where he could be seen and overheard and spoke into his radio. 'What's up, Digger? Everything OK? Over.'

'It's OK, boss,' crackled back Johnson. 'I thought I saw a scuffle between two blokes. I just saw someone going over the wall. I took a couple of shots at him, but he got away. Over.'

'OK, Digger, carry on as usual. Out.'

Warren and Goddard appeared round the corner of the house, and John Hawkins came running out of the woods at the far side of the house.

'What's up?' demanded Goddard anxiously.

'I'm not sure, but Digger saw a man going over the wall. He threw a few shots after him but he got away. Digger thought the bloke was having a fight with someone.' West looked around. 'Where's Tony?'

The three men looked questioningly at each other. 'Ain't seen him,' said Warren.

'Ain't he down in the cellar with the bird?' asked Hawkins.

'No,' said West. 'I caught him trying it on and sent him out to join you about an hour ago.'

Hawkins cupped his hands to his mouth and shouted towards the woods, 'Tony! Tony! Get back here.' He shouted again and again, each time waiting for the reply that would never come. He turned on West. 'He could be lying out there wounded. You've got to find him, make sure he's OK.'

'Get back to your positions,' ordered West. 'I'll go and take a look.'

'I'll come with you,' offered Hawkins.

'No, if Ross is still out there I'll be better off on my own. Two of us would be spotted more easily than one. I'll get Digger to circle round.'

Hawkins nodded reluctant agreement. He wasn't trained for that sort of work and knew the mercenary was right.

West made his way to the garage block, where it adjoined the bushes. As he went, he said softly into his radio, 'Digger, I'm coming out. Where do I find the corpse?'

'Are you coming via the garage block?'

'Yes.'

Johnson gave him instructions, laughing as he described how he'd leapt around in the woods firing at twigs. 'Did you like my scream, boss? Good enough for a Hammer horror film, wasn't it?'

Half an hour later West returned to the house and called to John Hawkins to join him. Hawkins ran up, frowning in anxiety, his face full of concern.

'I found him,' West said bluntly. 'Dead, I'm afraid.'

'No–o–o–o–o–o!' howled Hawkins. 'He can't be! I don't believe it!' He started towards the woods. 'Where is he? I must go to him.'

West laid a hand on his arm and stopped him. 'I've laid him out in the garage. With Lofty.'

Hawkins threw his shotgun aside and ran to the garage. West grimaced in distaste as he watched him go. He didn't like what he'd had to do, but needs must when the devil – or Frank Chalmers – drives. He had quite enough on his plate without John Hawkins trying to kill him. He went inside and told Chalmers and Martin what had happened, then went down to the cellar to check that Julie was all right.

It was over an hour before John Hawkins came back to the house. His eyes were red and swollen with crying, and he looked lost, still unable to believe his brother was dead. He sat silently in a corner of the sitting-room, staring down at the floor, merely nodding acknowledgement when Chalmers and Martin offered their condolences and patted him sympathetically on the shoulder.

'I know how you feel,' said Chalmers emotionally. 'We'll get the bastard, I promise you.'

At quarter to six Chalmers said to Martin, 'Bring the bird up here. I want her here when Ross phones.'

West intercepted Martin before he reached the door. 'You stay here, Kenny. I'll get her.'

Martin sat down again. He watched through narrowed eyes as West went out. I wonder . . . ? he thought.

Julie's nerves jumped wildly as she heard someone start down the cellar stairs. She gave a little sob of relief when a soft voice called, 'Don't worry, Miss Thompson, it's Ron West.'

He briefed her rapidly on what he had done with Tony Hawkins. 'Just keep quiet. Don't say anything about anything unless you have to. If John Hawkins gets the slightest clue as to what happened he'll try to kill both of us. You've already shown you can keep your head under pressure. Just carry on like that and everything'll be all right.'

She took a couple of deep, calming breaths before following him up the stairs and into the sitting-room. He sat her down on the settee and they waited tensely for Phillip to ring.

Chalmers couldn't handle the tension. He fidgeted round the room, constantly checking his watch, demanding to know why Ross hadn't rung yet, and cracking his pudgy knuckles. The others watched

him warily, so intent on him that they jumped when
the phone finally rang.

Chalmers picked it up, and said cockily, 'You're
late, Ross.'

10

Robin Chalmers said in a hoarse, cracking whisper, 'It's me, Frank. Robin.'

'Robin? What's up?'

Robin swallowed hard and cleared his throat. His voice came more strongly. 'Yes, Frank, it's me.' He looked helplessly at Phillip.

Frank was irritated. 'Look, Robin, I'm expecting an important call. Unless this is urgent get off the fucking line and I'll ring you back later.'

'No, Frank, don't hang up. There's someone here. I think he wants to talk to you.'

'I've told you, I'm busy,' snapped his brother.

Phillip reached over and took the receiver.

'Chalmers, it's Ross.'

'Wha . . .? Where the fuck are you?'

'I'm having a little chat with Robin. On your yacht.'

There was a pause while the news sank in. When Frank spoke again, his voice was high and panicky.

'Don't hurt him, Ross. For Chrissake don't kill him. He hasn't done anything, he doesn't even know anything.'

'I've got a knife on your brother. Let the girl go,' said Phillip icily, 'or I'll cut off his prick and balls and suffocate him with them.'

'And what about the fucking Thompson bird?' Chalmers yelled. 'If you don't leave my brother alone and get the fuck back here and give yourself up, she's fucking dead meat.'

Phillip felt sick to his stomach. But he'd come this far, and there was no going back. He held the phone in front of Robin Chalmers. 'Say goodbye to Frank. He doesn't care whether you live or die. Tell him about the knife, tell him how much your death is going to hurt.'

'Frank!' said Chalmers hoarsely. 'Frank, it's true, he's got a knife. He's . . . Oh Christ!' he howled as the knife twisted again.

Phillip took the phone from his nerveless hand. 'If I ring off, Frank, it means that your little brother is about to die. Slowly. And very . . . very . . . painfully.' He waited for precisely two seconds. 'Goodbye, Frank.'

'No! No, Ross! We can make a deal, the girl can go, we'll take her home, we haven't hurt her, you can speak to her, Ross, she'll tell you she's OK.' Frank Chalmers was babbling. 'Just don't hurt Robin, don't kill him, I'll do whatever you say.'

'Put Miss Thompson on the line.'

'Yeah, yeah, Ross, right away.' Phillip heard him scream at someone, 'Bring her over here, now!'

Then Julie's voice came faintly to him. It was strained and shaky, but she was in command of herself – he felt a fierce glow of admiration and pride in her courage. 'Phillip, is that really you?'

'Yes, love. Are you OK? Have they hurt you at all?'

'No,' she said, her voice more confident now. 'I'm all right, really I am.'

'They're going to take you home. You won't be hurt in any way. They won't lay a finger on you. Do you understand?'

'Yes. Yes, I understand.'

'I'll ring you at your parents' home in two hours. Peter Russell's sent men there to protect them and you. You'll all be safe, absolutely safe, I promise you.'

For the first time Julie's self-control nearly cracked. 'Oh thank God, thank God! I've been so afraid you might have been taken too, and hurt – or worse.'

'You needn't be afraid any more, sweetheart. Everything'll be OK. I love you.'

'I love you too, Phillip.'

'Now put Frank Chalmers back on, and don't worry. I'll see you soon.'

Chalmers had had time to think. He decided to try again, a double bluff. 'You ain't gonna let us kill the girl, are you Ross? You're bluffing. You lay a finger on Robin and—'

'It's your call, Frank,' Phillip cut in. 'They both live or they both die. You decide which.'

There was a short but pregnant silence.

'You didn't think,' Phillip continued derisively, 'I'd leave you all alone and unguarded, did you? Your house is surrounded by two squads of heavily armed SAS men, just waiting for a word from me. Think about it, Frank, think about it. You have five seconds to give me your answer. Five . . . four . . . three . . . two . . . one . . . Now! It's your call, Frank, and you'll call it now. Which is it to be? A life for a life? Or a death for a death? It's your choice. Make it now and make it fast. Otherwise I'll kill your brother and then I'll come straight at you.'

He heard Chalmers yell, 'Get her back where she came from. Fast! And don't crash the fucking car on the way.' Then, to Phillip, 'OK, Ross, you win. A life for a life. But don't kill him. This is nothing to do with him, I swear it on my mother's grave.'

'If Miss Thompson's safely back in Dover when I ring my men there in two hours, I'll leave your brother unharmed. You have my word on it.'

All the fight had gone out of Frank Chalmers, and his voice was weary as he said, 'Can I talk to him? I don't want him to do anything stupid.'

Phillip passed the phone to Robin, whose fear had abated as he listened, though he was clearly still bewildered. 'Frank, what the fuck is going on? What's all this life-and-death stuff?'

'I'll tell you later. Just do exactly as Ross says.

Don't on any account try anything. He's a trained killer, Robin, far too good for you. He's fucking SAS. You wouldn't stand a cat's chance in hell. Got it?'

'Yeah, got it.'

Phillip took the phone back. 'All right, Chalmers, we have a deal. You stick to your side of it and I'll stick to mine. I've got SAS men guarding Miss Thompson's parents' house, so don't try anything bloody stupid.' He rang off.

He studied Robin Chalmers for a moment. The family resemblance was plain, but Robin was taller and a good deal slimmer than his brother. He looked like a swimmer, both well-muscled and supple. His voice was lighter and less coarse, and he sounded better-educated. Phillip eased the knife away from Robin's groin and slipped it into its sheath. Robin exhaled deeply with relief, and relaxed.

'Don't do anything silly. We've got two hours to spend together, and you'd better believe that I'll kill you if I have to,' Phillip warned him.

Robin blew out his cheeks and shook his head. 'Frank just told me about you, Mr Ross. I'm not fool enough to try anything.' He looked down at the unconscious girl, who was beginning to stir. 'Can I see to her? She's going to be all right, isn't she? You haven't done her any harm have you?' His concern was evident.

'She'll be fine – nothing more than a bit of head-ache, and it won't last long. Get your clothes on. Tell her you must have kicked her by accident. Tell her I'm a business associate, tell her what you like, but don't give her even a hint of what's going on.'

Robin pulled on a pair of Bermuda shorts. He lifted the girl gently on to the bed, sat down beside her and smoothed her tousled hair back from her face. Her eyelids flickered, then opened. He picked up her hand and kissed it. 'I'm sorry, Shirl,' he said. 'I must have caught you with my knee. Are you all right?'

She rubbed the side of her head, wincing as she touched the place where Phillip had hit her, and smiled up at him. 'You silly bugger, I was enjoying that!'

Her eyes widened as she caught sight of Phillip, and she grabbed for the silk sheet and pulled it hastily up to cover herself. 'Who the hell's that?'

'It's a friend of mine, love.' He turned to Phillip. 'This is my fiancée, Shirley, Mr Ross. Shirl, Mr Ross's a business associate of mine.'

'Hello, Shirley. Nice to meet you,' said Phillip, smiling. 'Sorry to barge in on you, but it was urgent.'

She smiled back. 'Well, I can't in all honesty say the way we met was nice. Perhaps interesting would be a better word, Mr Ross.' She laughed and said, 'I can't call you Mr Ross. What's your first name?'

'Call me Phillip.'

Robin got up. 'Do you mind if we go upstairs while Shirley gets showered and changed, Mr Ross? All her stuff's in here.' He gestured to the built-in wardrobe.

Phillip went over to the cabin door and opened it. 'After you.' He smiled at Shirley again, stepped aside to let Robin pass, and followed him up the companionway to the main saloon.

'See you guys in ten minutes,' she called after them.

Robin poured two beers and set one down in front of Phillip, who watched him closely. The man was back on balance, calm and fully in control of himself, and Phillip was reluctantly impressed by his courage. 'You don't seem very concerned, Chalmers,' he said.

'When you gave Frank your word, I believed you. I don't think you're going to hurt me, Mr Ross.'

'Aren't you curious about all this?'

'Well, yes, in a way, but I can't say I'm all that surprised.' Chalmers was obviously choosing his words carefully. 'My brother's often been involved in aggro, but he's always kept me well clear. I suppose I've been lucky. It had to catch up with me sooner or later.'

'I thought you were part of the gang,' said Phillip, surprised.

Robin shrugged. 'Well, sort of. Frank pays my wages and expenses and everything, but I stay out of it all, as much as I can.'

'Why?' asked Phillip bluntly.

Robin looked him in the eyes. 'I don't like the business my brother's in, Mr Ross. It's not the way I want to spend my life, and, like I said, I do my best to keep out of it.' He dropped his gaze and said painfully, 'I know Frank doesn't tell me about a lot of what he does – the rackets, the violence, the killing. I hide my head in the sand, pretend to myself that if I don't know about it it can't touch me. But I'm not so stupid that I don't know what sort of money pays for me to spend time out here. And I'm ashamed of it. I'm ashamed sometimes . . . to be Frank's brother . . .'

That statement, though he didn't know it, saved Robin Chalmers's life. Phillip mentally crossed him off his list.

Curious about the difference in the brothers' characters, and to confirm his snap judgement of Robin's, he asked, 'Have you really never found yourself involved in the rough side of the business?'

'No, never,' said Robin firmly. 'I do a bit of book work now and then, run errands – and look after the boat. But that's the strength of it. To be fair, Frank's never asked me to do any more than that.'

Phillip changed tack. 'Shirley – I'm sorry I had to hit her. She seems a nice girl.'

There was glowing affection in Robin's smile. 'She's the tops, Mr Ross, as bright as she is beautiful. We're getting married in a couple of months. I get quite a bit of stick about her back home – you know, about her colour. But she's worth it, and worth a helluva lot more besides, so I don't take any notice. As for the thump, I suppose we've to blame Frank for that. But she seems OK and you did say, didn't you, that she wouldn't have anything worse than a headache? I have to believe you.' His eyes clouded, and he said hesitantly, 'I heard you mention a Miss Thompson on the phone. Was Frank holding her hostage?'

Phillip nodded.

'And that's why you came for me?'

Phillip nodded again.

'You made the right move. Frank'll let her go. I know he can be a right shit at times, but for some reason he worships the ground I walk on. He's a lot older than I am, and when we were kids he always took care of me, saw I got a decent schooling, and all that. And since I grew up he's been good to me, given me everything I wanted, let me stay away from the business and do my own thing. He wouldn't risk anything happening to me, not Frank.'

Phillip sincerely hoped Robin was right. He'd lost his ace in the hole: even if the worst happened to Julie, no way could he kill this man now. His only hope was that Frank Chalmers would judge by his own vicious standards and believe the threat held good.

Shirley came into the saloon, bringing laughter and gaiety with her. She wore a golden-yellow sarong, which brought out the warm tints of her skin, highlighting her elegant bone structure, and her hair was damp and riotously curly from her shower. She perched on Robin's knee, kissed him soundly and said, 'You silly sod! Fancy knocking me out just when I was enjoying myself. I'll sort you out later, my love.' She grinned across at Phillip. 'Can you believe this bloke?'

Phillip couldn't help grinning back. 'No, I don't believe him. And he's a very lucky man – in more ways than one.'

'Yeah, he's lucky all right. He's got me,' and she began to talk of their life together and their hopes for the future. Soon the conversation became general, and Shirley let the two men take the lead. Once or twice she looked very shrewdly at Phillip; but she said nothing out of place.

Robin's right, he thought. She's as bright as she is beautiful.

The time passed quickly. Even before Phillip checked his watch, Robin knew the two hours were up. 'Give us five minutes, will you, Shirl? Phillip and I've got an important call to make.'

Shirley stood up. 'Men!' she said in mock exasperation. 'OK, you can have your five minutes. Will you stay for dinner afterwards, Phillip?'

'No, I'm afraid I can't. I'll have to be off as soon as this call's done, so I'll say goodbye now.'

He held out his hand, but Shirley swept it aside and kissed him warmly on both cheeks. 'That's how we say goodbye to friends in Spain. Drop in and see us again – but knock next time!' Laughing, she went down the companionway to the master cabin.

As soon as she was out of earshot, Robin said, 'Phillip, I know things are bad between you and

Frank, as bad as anything could be between two men.' His face was sad and deeply troubled. 'I don't know how to say this . . . I've always known Frank would come unstuck one day . . . the way he carries on . . . the things he's done. And, though he'd never admit it, I think he knows it too, has done for some time.' He drew a deep, difficult breath. 'What I'm trying to say is that I'm surprised someone hasn't killed him by now. God knows there are enough people with reason. And now there's you, and you have reason. Are you the one who'll do it? No, don't answer that. I always knew there'd be someone. And I always knew he had it coming.'

Phillip said nothing.

'Don't get me wrong. I'll be broken up if it happens – when it happens. I can't forget what my brother's done for me, and I still love him in a funny sort of way. But if ever a man asked for it, it's Frank Chalmers.'

Phillip gave him his most piercing, merciless stare; Chalmers looked away.

'Keep well out of this, Robin,' he said evenly, his quietness more menacing than any threat. 'Your brother's in a no-win situation. If I get him, I get him. If he's lucky and gets me, my SAS friends will step in and finish the job. And if you interfere, if you so much show too much interest in Frank's health, you'll become part of the job. Do I make myself clear?'

Without waiting for an answer, he picked up the

phone and dialled the Thompsons' number in Dover. Peter Russell answered at the first ring. He confirmed that Julie was shaken but physically unharmed. Julie snatched the phone from Russell, confirmed that she was well and sent him her love. Reassured that all was indeed well there, Phillip rang off. He said a brief, unrevealing goodbye to Robin Chalmers, walked off the yacht and was swallowed up in the crowd.

As soon as Warren and Goddard left for Dover, taking Julie back to her parents and safety, the tension started to build again. Chalmers's temper became increasingly uncertain as he counted the minutes until he could ring his brother and check he was safe. The instant that two hours and fifteen minutes were up, he grabbed for the phone and dialled frantically. His relief when Robin answered was palpable.

The brothers spoke for five minutes. When Chalmers hung up, much of the strain had left his face. 'He's gone,' he said in a half-sigh. 'He left the boat five minutes ago. Robin's OK. Fucking Ross kept his word.'

John Hawkins sat forward abruptly. 'If Ross is in Spain, who the fuck killed my brother?' he demanded.

West answered him. 'If Ross has got men at Dover, he'll have men here too, covering the house while he's away.'

Chalmers had an idea. 'Perhaps we could piss off out of it, while Ross is a thousand miles away. It'll take him time to get back. We could disappear.'

'No,' said West. 'It's certain Ross has got men out there – one of them killed Tony. But maybe, just maybe, we could give them the slip.'

Chalmers thought aloud. 'It's an hour to the airport, minimum thirty minutes to check in, two and a half hours' flight, and he's still got to get through Immigration and Customs. Then half an hour back here. That's . . . four and a half, five hours, if he's lucky and don't have to wait for a flight.'

'Where would we hide?' asked West quietly. 'And for how long? Ross isn't going to go away and forget the whole thing just because we all go missing for a couple of weeks. He'll keep looking, keep waiting, till we stick our heads back up over the parapet and then he'll start shooting again. We can't hide from him for ever.'

Chalmers's shoulders slumped. 'Yeah, you're right. We've got to see this bleeding thing through, finish him somehow.' He looked round at his men; they looked back resignedly. 'But what if we piss off before Ross gets back? We could rent a house or a farm in Scotland or Ireland or somewhere – anywhere. We could use false names. How would Ross know where to start looking? How would he find us? But if he did . . . it'd all start up again, wouldn't it?

'No,' Chalmers continued with feverish determination, 'we don't fucking run, we stay and fight.

We'll finish it here, kill fucking Ross here, at High Trees, where we know he'll come looking for us. And we know roughly when.'

'In that case,' said West calmly, 'I'll need to go out for more supplies. And we'll have to make up a burial detail. Grant and White will start to stink if they aren't buried soon, and there's Lofty and Tony Hawkins as well.'

He called Digger Johnson into the house and told him that when Warren and Goddard got back from Dover they were to bury the four men in the kitchen garden while he, Johnson, guarded them. John Hawkins didn't seem to register what was happening, but sat in his corner staring vacantly at the floor.

Having prised more cash out of Chalmers, West set off for London in the Range Rover to fetch the anti-personnel mines and listening devices he'd already told Chalmers he needed.

Phillip arrived back at Gatwick at two-thirty-five a.m., the journey having taken him just over seven hours. He booked into the Gatwick Hilton, fell into bed and slept soundly through what remained of the night.

In the morning he phoned Julie in Dover, checked that she hadn't mentioned the Biggin Hill cottage to anyone, and arranged for Peter Russell to take her there and stay with her until Phillip arrived. From Russell he learnt that Mary Thompson had cracked up badly when she discovered the truth of what had happened, so she and Victor had been taken to Yorkshire to stay with Russell's parents until it was safe for them to return home. Russell knew a good doctor in the area who'd be able to help Mary.

Once assured of all three Thompsons' safety, Phillip drove straight back to High Trees, concealed the car in woods about a mile from the house, and made his way back to his dug-out. Careful examination of the area showed that his hide-out was undetected, its rhododendron camouflage undisturbed. He slid inside, switched on his receiver and listened. To his relief he immediately picked up murmurs of conversation and sounds of men moving about. The birds were still in the nest; and if they hadn't flown by now it was more than likely that they intended to stay put. Satisfied, Phillip made his way quickly back to the car and set off for Biggin Hill.

Peter Russell came out of the cottage to meet him. 'Go a bit carefully with Julie, Phil,' he said when they had exchanged greetings and the essentials of their news. 'She had a worse time than she let on to you over the phone. Physically she's unharmed, but it's going to take her a bit of time to get over the mental and emotional side of things. But go on in. She's waiting for you in the lounge. I'll just take a quick look around to check everything's still secure.'

When he went in Julie flung herself into his arms and clung to him fiercely. It was some time before he could get her to let him go and sit down beside him on the settee. Gently and patiently he got the full story out of her.

'I killed him, Phillip,' she said, her face white and hollow-eyed and haunted. 'I've killed a man. I keep thinking that perhaps I needn't have done, that I could have knocked him out or disabled him somehow. I keep hearing the sound of the knife going into him, over and over again. I couldn't sleep last night, because every time I went to sleep I dreamt the whole thing again. How am I going to live with it? How am I going to live with myself?'

He held her close. 'Darling, you couldn't have done anything but what you did. The man was a street fighter from way back. If you'd tried to knock him out or something, he'd have known exactly how to react. And then he'd have killed West and raped and killed you – he'd have had to kill you to stop Chalmers learning the truth. So it wasn't a case of whether you could have done something else. It was a case of the life of one murdering scumbag against your life and West's. What you did wasn't just the right thing to do, it was the *only* thing. If you weren't still suffering from shock and exhaustion you'd see that. Give yourself a bit of time, love. You can and will live with yourself, I promise you.'

'I feel so dirty, Phillip. I keep bathing and showering and scrubbing myself to wash away the feel of his hands on me, but it doesn't seem to help much. I still feel . . . soiled.'

Phillip kissed her almost roughly. 'Don't be a damned little fool. He may have put his filthy hands on your body, but there's no way he could even come close to touching your spirit. And that's what matters, that and the courage you showed. You were alone and afraid, and yet you kept your head and did what was needed when it was needed. Nothing that bastard Hawkins did can change that. You're not soiled, love, you're a damn' great heroine.' He kissed her again.

Slowly she grew calmer. Weariness overcame her, and she went to lie down for a while. Phillip called Russell back in, and they talked for a while about the next step.

'I think you've done enough on your own, Phil,' said Russell. 'It's time you called on me and some of your other friends to come in and help clear this whole thing up.'

Phillip shook his head. 'No, not yet, Peter. I can still handle it. If I slip up in any way it's all down to me – the police can't say anyone else was involved. But if the worst happens, look after Julie and finish the job for me, won't you? That's all I ask.'

'No need to ask, mate,' said Russell. 'Goes without saying.'

They talked a little longer, and then Russell left to get back to Yorkshire, where he was due to relieve one of the men guarding the Thompsons.

Phillip and Julie were both quiet that evening. Julie was still wrestling with her personal demons, and Phillip was careful to provide reassurance when she needed it, but not to intrude too much. He knew she had to work things out for herself, come to terms in her own way with the near-rape and with the fact that she had killed a man.

He was worried about leaving her on her own in the cottage, even for a short time, when he went back to High Trees, and offered to take her up to Yorkshire to join her parents. 'Peter says there's plenty of room, darling, and you might find it a help to have your parents with you.'

But she flatly refused to go. 'I'm staying here with you, Phillip. Whatever happens, I'm staying with you.'

They went to bed early. For a long time they lay quietly in each other's arms, seeking and giving warmth and security. Phillip stroked Julie's hair and comforted her with gentle caresses whenever the horror of the last few days threatened to shatter her fragile calm. Gradually their embrace changed and became one of desire. But when Phillip entered her he could feel her flinch.

He kissed her gently. 'What is it, sweetheart?'

'I . . . I can't help thinking of that man. He came so close to . . . And if he had raped me, every time you came into me so would he. I can't explain, but it . . .'

Phillip held her close and, without withdrawing, rolled them both over on to their sides. He tucked Julie's legs round his waist, then leant back a little and looked into her distraught face.

He kissed her again and said, 'Earlier, I told you to give yourself a bit of time, love. It's not yet twenty-four hours since it happened. It'll take longer than that to get over the sort of terror and shock you felt. You'll never completely forget it, but I promise you that time *will* heal you, just as it'll heal these' – he stroked her breast, where the bruises left by Hawkins's fingers had turned purple – 'and these' – he ran a hand softly over the scratches left on her thighs by Hawkins's bitten fingernails. 'You have the basic strength and courage to defeat him. I know that as certainly as I know that I love you.'

'Defeat him?'

'Yes, defeat him. You've done it once, and you'll do it again – this time for keeps – by not letting him wreck the rest of your life.'

She was silent for a long time. He wondered anxiously if he'd misjudged how best to comfort her. Then, suddenly, she gave him a vivid smile. 'Damn it, you're right. I won the battle against him – well, with help from Ron West – and now I've got to win the war. It's a challenge I've got to meet. And I *will* meet it, darling, I swear I will. Now, make love to me, nice and slowly and gently. I want you, Philip, I want you more than anything else in the world.'

Phillip was more than happy to oblige.

Ron West and Digger Johnson had spent the morning of Phillip's return from Spain busy in the woods, setting anti-personnel mines, booby traps and electronic listening devices that could pick up even the faintest footfall. They mapped as they worked; it took them several hours.

When at last they had finished, Johnson straightened his back and eased his shoulders. 'If Ross gets through that lot,' he said, 'we'd better piss off out of it fast.' And he grinned his tiger shark's grin.

West nodded and grinned back at him. He knew very well that Johnson never had and never would run from a fight. Come to that, he'd never run from a fight himself, and he didn't intend to start now.

He went back to the house, leaving Johnson on guard, and in the sitting-room set up the radio receiver to scan the six listening devices in the grounds. Satisfied it was working properly, he set about sweeping for the bugs Ross had planted in the house. The sweeper was a small hand-held receiver, which picked up any signal being transmitted in a given area. When the antenna was pointed in the direction of an active bug a red light came on and the sweeper bleeped a warning. Before long West had amassed quite a collection of thirteen-amp plugs and light bulbs, which he piled up in front of Frank Chalmers.

'Ross can't listen in any more,' he told him.

Chalmers picked up an ordinary-looking light bulb and examined it closely. 'It don't look any different from the ones you buy in bleeding Woollies,' he said in astonishment.

'That's why there's no point in looking for them unless you've got one of these little jokers.' West held the sweeper out to him and Chalmers peered vaguely at it.

'What do we do now?'

'We wait for Ross to show up,' said West flippantly, 'and hope he steps on a mine.'

Chalmers smiled slowly. 'I'd like that,' he said. 'I'd like that a lot.'

11

In the morning, having collected what he needed from the crates of supplies at the cottage, Phillip loaded the BMW and made his way back to High Trees. As soon as he arrived he switched on the receiver and listened. Nothing. He flicked through the channels. Still nothing, not even a crackle.

The silence was ominous. If the gang now had an anti-bug sweeper, someone must have been out for supplies, which meant they would now also have the anti-personnel mines and listening devices West had told Chalmers he needed.

Phillip scanned the grounds through his binoculars. There was no movement, not even a sign of guards patrolling round the house. He picked up his mobile phone and dialled. Kenny Martin answered.

'Put Chalmers on the line,' Phillip ordered.

Chalmers's voice was flat and unconcerned. 'What do you want?'

'I want the name of the man who killed Gary Thompson.'

'Well you ain't getting it.'

'Anti-personnel mines won't stop me,' said Phillip, and switched the mobile off.

He had achieved two things: he had checked the gang were still in the house, and he had served notice on them that he was back. He intended to give them no respite, no rest, no peace of mind. He would wear them down and then, one at a time, kill them.

In the sitting-room at High Trees, Chalmers looked uneasily at West and said, 'He knows the place is mined.'

West shrugged. 'It'll make him more careful about footsying around in the grounds, that's all.'

'But it ain't likely he'll just step on one, like we hoped.'

'Look, Frank, I've set fifteen mines, some on the tracks, some off. I can't predict what Ross will do or whether he'll trigger one. Who knows? He might get unlucky.'

John Hawkins hauled himself up out of his chair. He was drawn and haggard, and his eyes were shadowed and empty, as though his spirit had died with his brother.

'I'm not waiting any longer,' he said. He pulled an automatic pistol from his shoulder holster, checked it was fully loaded, and hefted it in his hand. 'I'm going out there and I'm going to find Ross and kill him.' Chalmers, Martin and West watched in silence as he crossed the room, picked up a pump-action shotgun and walked to the door.

'I've had enough,' he said tonelessly. 'I'm going up the hill. You can follow me or not, as you like.'

West turned to Chalmers. 'Are you just going to let him go out there and commit suicide?' he demanded. 'You know bloody well he doesn't stand a chance against Ross.'

Chalmers smiled. 'This could be our chance, here. You and Digger follow him. You never know, he might flush Ross out into the open and give you a clear shot at him.'

West shook his head disgustedly and followed Hawkins out of the room. He called Johnson on the walky-talky. 'Meet me at the gate right away, and make sure you aren't seen.'

'Roger, wilco,' Johnson's voice crackled back.

Phillip saw Hawkins coming. It would have been hard to miss him. He strode purposefully down the drive and climbed over the wrought-iron gates. He crossed the road, staring fixedly up at the hill, and bawled, 'Ross! Ross! I'm coming to get you.'

Once across the road, Hawkins started firing the twelve-bore wildly into the undergrowth. As he shot, he screamed, 'Come out, you yellow bastard! Come out and fight. But you haven't got the guts to fight face to face, have you, you cunt? Too cowardly, aren't you? Come out here, you fucking murderer.'

The firing pin fell on an empty chamber. Panting

with rage, Hawkins paused to reload, then continued up the hill, firing and yelling as he went.

Phillip ignored him, and focused his binoculars on the perimeter wall and the gates. He spotted West in the woods near the gates, studying the hill through his own binoculars. To the right of him, Phillip saw movement. He adjusted the zoom on the binoculars and made out the form of a man in full camouflage dress, his face blackened and the shape of his head and shoulders disguised by twigs and leaves tucked into his gear. Digger Johnson.

Hawkins was getting closer. He was angling up the hill no more than sixty yards away, still firing the twelve-bore; the shot ripped through the bushes and smacked into the trees. He was getting close enough to do real damage with that heavy-gauge shot. He stopped to reload again.

Phillip cocked his small crossbow and slid a bolt into position. Hawkins came closer still and aimed the shotgun straight at the rhododendron bush concealing Phillip's dug-out. Phillip crouched down in the hole and ducked his head and shoulders as low as possible. Hawkins fired. The explosion was followed by a tearing sound as the leaves of the rhododendron were shredded. Then there was silence. Phillip risked a cautious look out. Sobbing with rage and grief, Hawkins had thrown down the empty shotgun and was dragging out his pistol. As soon as it was clear of the holster, he fired again – and again and again, until the pistol was empty. He flung it away into the bushes behind the dug-out and sank to his knees, almost sobbing, 'Come on, you bastard, come out and fight. See if you can kill me too.'

Phillip obliged. The crossbow bolt struck Hawkins in the temple. He toppled over on to his side, an expression of total astonishment on his face, and died quickly and silently.

Phillip swung his attention and the binoculars back to West and Johnson. They were still in position, watching and listening intently. They had seen Hawkins throw away his pistol, drop to his knees and then topple sideways.

'He's down,' West called softly to Johnson.

Johnson scowled. 'Nah, he's just stopped for a little cry.'

'I think he's down. Ross got him with a knife, or maybe with that crossbow of his.'

'If he has, we know his position to within a few feet.'

West nodded. 'Yeah, but we still can't bloody see him, can we?'

They watched and waited for over half an hour. Finally Johnson said, 'I reckon you're right, Ron. He must be down.'

'Yeah. So there's no point hanging around down here any longer. Let's get back to the house.' West stepped into the open and started walking back up the drive.

Johnson fell into step beside him. 'Ain't this a bit

fucking daring?' He glanced back over his shoulder at the hill: they were well within range for a good rifleman.

'Don't worry, Digger,' said West amusedly. 'That isn't Ross's style.'

Johnson laughed. 'Well, we'll know that for sure if we reach the house without a sodding great hole in the back, won't we?'

'Ross will kill us only if and when we're a threat to him, in a combat situation. As for Chalmers and his men, they could die at any time.'

'How do you know that?' Johnson was puzzled.

'I'm getting to know the man, how he thinks, why he acts. Ross is a total professional. He'll kill only if he has to. He has to kill Chalmers and every last member of his gang, because he's sworn to do it, and because they killed his friend and kidnapped his girl and nearly raped her. He'll kill us, too, because we're here and trying to stop him. But only when we try to stop him.'

Johnson eyed him sceptically. 'Oh yeah? Then what about Lofty? And Luke and John?'

They had reached the shelter of the house, and West stopped and turned to him. 'Lofty must have put up some kind of a fight. Luke . . . well, I don't know about him. My bet is that if Ross had killed him he'd have done it in the grounds and left his body where we'd be sure to find him. But we didn't find him, did we? Just a blood trail leaving the grounds. We just don't know if he's dead or if he's alive and being held prisoner. And John? He was just unlucky. Ross didn't know exactly where he was. He sent over a couple of mortar rounds to shake us all up, to rattle Chalmers. John just happened to be in the wrong place at the wrong time and one dropped into his lap.'

Johnson thought it over for a minute, then gave his shark-grin. 'I could do with the bonus for killing Ross.'

West looked at him steadily. 'It could be the hardest bonus you ever tried to earn, Digger. I hope you live to spend it. Well, while you think of all the things you'd like to do with it, I'd better go and tell Chalmers he's probably lost another of his men.' He turned on his heel and went inside.

Goddard and Warren had been woken by the firing and had come downstairs to find out what the hell was going on. They were sitting uneasily in one corner of the sitting-room while Chalmers and Martin talked in undertones in another. All heads turned West's way as he went in.

'Well?' demanded Chalmers.

'He just walked up the hill, firing at every bush and tree in sight,' said West. 'And just in case Ross couldn't hear that little lot, he was yelling and screaming as well. He emptied the shotgun and threw it away. Then he fired off the full magazine of his pistol and threw that away too. Then he knelt down and cried. Then he fell over. I think he'd been hit. I think he's dead.'

'What about Ross? Did you spot him?'

West shook his head. 'No, but we know pretty well where his hideout is. There was no sound of a shot, so he must be close to where Hawkins was when he fell over.'

'Aren't you going up after him?'

'Not in daylight. We'd never get near him. And I doubt if it'd be a good idea in the dark, either. Ross isn't going to stay in one position now he knows we've got a fix on him. He's going to move about, camouflage his hideout and cover his tracks, just in case we try to jump him.' West studied the four faces in front of him and asked, 'Any of you lot fancy trying to jump him?' He listened sardonically to the ensuing silence, then went on, 'I suggest we wait for Ross to come to us. This time he'll have an obstacle course to negotiate. It won't be so easy.'

Chalmers wasn't reassured. 'We're down to six men. Just six of us left.' His voice rose almost to a whine. 'Can't you get any more experienced men? Soldiers, mercenaries, blokes who know how to do this sort of thing?'

West shook his head decisively. 'I'd have to tell them what they're up against, and I doubt if many guys'd fancy it. And what would it achieve? Nothing would change. We'd still have to kill that one man. Besides, Ross threatened to bring in his SAS mates if we got reinforcements. If he brought in, say, five of them, how many men would we need? Thirty? Forty? No, the whole thing would get right out of hand. Those SAS blokes wouldn't fuck about. They'd drop on us like a ton of shit. It'd all be over in less than five minutes, and' – he smiled coldly – 'I know what the result would be.'

Chalmers glared up at him. 'So we just wait for Ross to come in here and kill us? Fuck that for a lark!'

'That's right,' said West, 'we wait. We wait for Ross to make a mistake.'

Goddard and Warren exchanged meaningful looks. They had discussed the situation at great length before going to sleep. They knew Ross wanted a name from Chalmers. They also knew Ross intended to kill the whole gang, one at a time, to put pressure on Chalmers. They'd been loyal to Frank Chalmers for many years, but they reckoned that loyalty should work both ways, whereas Chalmers seemed to think it was a one-way street. They reckoned that his attitude meant their loyalty went only so far, and that it had already gone quite far enough. They'd done their bit, and were ready to leave while they still could. West and Johnson, plus the prospect of getting to Chalmers, would keep Ross busy while they made their break. Once they were away free, they intended to get out of Britain fast. And stay out. Ross would never find them, they reckoned.

Goddard eyed West nervously and asked, 'What do you want us to do, Ron?'

'You and Bert, come over here.' West crossed to the desk, which he had set out as a makeshift operations table with the radio receiver and six speakers set along the rear edge. In the centre of the desk was a hand-drawn map of the grounds and house, and West drew it towards him. 'Those circles with a cross inside are anti-personnel mines. There are fifteen of them, buried just below the surface. They make a little clicking noise when you step on them, and then, as you step off' – he grinned at them – 'they blow your legs off.' He traced his finger along a series of dotted lines. 'These are the only safe footpaths, so make sure you don't use any of the others.' He pointed to a single cross. 'Digger is here. But he moves about, so be careful. These squares numbered from one to six are battery-operated microphone transmitters. They'll pick up the slightest sound and send it to these speakers. It's up to me to distinguish between birds or small animals and Ross. Or between you and Ross.'

He stared hard at the two men, trying to gauge their reactions, and went on, 'I'd like you both to patrol the paths that are clear of mines.' He pointed them out again on the map. 'As you see, they've got listening devices along them, so I'll be able to hear you as you go. If Ross is watching you, he'll think your route is clear. He'll take the same route as you to the house. I'll hear him coming, and Digger and I will get him in a crossfire.'

'How will you know it's us passing the bugs?' asked Warren.

West opened the middle drawer of the desk and took out a walky-talky. 'As you pass each transmitter, press this button here twice, like that.' As he suited action to words, the radio on his belt buzzed and howled in protest at the closeness of the signal. 'Don't speak unless you have to, or unless I call you to warn you someone else is nearby.' He consulted the map and pointed out speaker number six. 'If I hear anyone at one of the other transmitters, I'll simply call out that number. I'll repeat it once. Then you press the button and repeat it back to me, and tell me what you're going to do. That'll be one of three things. "We're standing by" means you're going to stay where you are. "We're returning to base" means you're coming back to the house. And the third is self-explanatory: "We're going to investigate".'

West sat down behind the desk. He was far from happy at having to use Goddard and Warren for this job, but there was no one else: he needed Digger for when Ross arrived. 'Those are also the only three instructions I'm likely to give you over the air. Do you think you can handle it?'

Warren and Goddard looked at each other, then slowly back at West. It was the chance they were looking for, the chance to get the hell out of here.

Goddard spoke for both of them. 'Yeah, we can handle it.'

'Good. Start your patrol at dusk. Make sure you've got good torches, but don't use them unless you have to – Ross would spot them a mile away.'

Goddard checked his watch. 'OK. We'll go and get something to eat, then.'

They went out. As they went down the passage to the kitchen, they grinned at each other in silent accord, happy in the knowledge that they'd soon be getting their chance of freedom.

West looked after them thoughtfully. 'How far do you trust those two, Frank?' he asked.

Chalmers spread his hands. 'They've been with me for nearly fifteen years. They've never let me down.'

'Do you think they're prepared to die for you?' West pressed.

Chalmers grinned nervously and shot a glance at Kenny Martin. 'Well, the others all have.'

'They know we're using them as bait. If Ross keeps up his MO, he'll kill them both. What I mean is that if they intend to desert this'll be their chance.'

'No, they wouldn't do that. They'd be too fucking afraid of what I'd do to them if they pissed off out of it. No, I've been good to them. They wouldn't do that to me. Besides, I've got a little bit of, er, what you might call insurance. My hitman. Anybody crosses me up and he goes after them. So yeah, they'll stay.'

Kenny Martin kept his thoughts to himself, but he wasn't so sure. He was the closest to Chalmers, Chalmers's number-one man, but he didn't fancy dying for him. Besides, he reckoned Warren and Goddard had agreed a bit too readily to patrol the woods. They'd been too willing. They hadn't squirmed at the thought of Ross out there waiting for them.

He thought back to the Friday night it had all begun, when Bobby Wilks, Mickey Steele, Chris Goddard and he had gone to the Starlight Club and demanded the night's takings as protection money. 'Must be good for a monkey a week at least, maybe more,' Chalmers had told them. 'And it'll be easy money. They're just a couple of soldier boys. They won't know what's hit them.'

Martin grimaced at the memory. He knew that even if he managed to get away from High Trees Ross would hunt him down remorselessly. And if West and Digger killed Ross and Chalmers was left alive, Chalmers would send his hitman after him. No, he'd stick it out to the end. After all, he was an East End boy. The East End was his home, and all his family and friends were there. He had nowhere else to go, nowhere else to hide. Besides, he hadn't any money. Chalmers had always been generous to his men with money. At times it seemed to flow fast and furious from his pockets to theirs. It had been easy money, too, for little work. And membership of the Chalmers gang gave a man prestige, brought him the respect and fear of even the toughest of London's hard men – not to mention plenty of free drinks at any pub or nightclub in Frank's manor.

But for all of them it had been easy come, easy go. The only one to save his money was Frank Chalmers, who'd invested it in property. The whole gang lived in houses and flats he'd provided. It dawned on Martin how tightly Chalmers controlled his men's lives. He gave them everything: homes, work, cars, food, entertainment and spending money. Without him they'd have nothing and no way of making lives for themselves. He pulled their strings, kept them wholly dependent on him. And then there was his hitman, whose identity only Chalmers knew . . .

Martin smiled sourly to himself, as he thought, 'Easy money? It ain't easy now, is it, Frank? Ross changed all that. Here we are, what's left of us, up shit creek without a paddle. And the tide's going out fucking fast.'

Chalmers nudged him out of his reverie. 'You ain't going to leave old Frank, are you, Kenny boy?' He smiled encouragingly.

Martin returned his smile and said wearily, 'No, Frank, I ain't going nowhere.'

Chalmers lumbered to his feet. 'See?' he said triumphantly to West. 'That's the loyalty I get from my boys. They'll stick with Frank Chalmers right to the bitter end. That's why we're winners. Ross'll never beat us while we stick together.'

The light began to fail as the sun dropped below the horizon. Goddard and Warren reported to Ron West. 'We're ready to start the patrol,' said Goddard, his face and voice expressionless.

West nodded. 'Good. Come and check the map

again. I don't want any slip-ups.' He crossed to the operations table and waited until he had both men's full attention. 'You'll start here, by the garage block.' He pointed it out on the map, then swept his hand right-handed over the paper. 'Go clockwise on your first round. When you get back to the house, here – and not before – do an about-turn and go round in the opposite direction for your second tour.' He glanced up to make sure they understood. They both nodded.

'On your third tour, keep on going in the same direction until you reach the halfway point, here. Then turn and go back the way you came. Got it?'

They nodded again.

'Keep up that pattern until I give you further instructions. Ross won't work the pattern out for quite a while. Each full tour, if you take it easy, will take you about . . . say an hour. I'll know to the minute after your first tour.'

West followed Warren and Goddard to the door. 'I'll see you off from the garage block,' he said encouragingly. 'Don't forget Digger's out there. You won't know he's there, but he'll be following you and covering you all the way. He'll see you come to no harm. If Ross turns up, Digger will get him.'

The two men gave him slightly forced smiles, and set off on their first, clockwise, patrol. West waved them good luck, then went back to the house. Once inside the hall, he said quietly into his walky-talky, 'Digger, Goddard and Warren will pass you in about twenty minutes, on the clearway. Once they're away and clear, return to base. Over.'

'Roger. In twenty minutes.' West could picture the grin on Johnson's face. 'ETA base twenty-five minutes. Out.'

West checked his watch, grunted to himself in satisfaction, and went back into the sitting-room. He found Chalmers and Martin deep in discussion, but they fell silent when they saw him. He went over to the desk, sat down, slipped the earphones on and listened intently. As he tuned from speaker to speaker lights flashed, informing him of transmitted sound and density. He heard Goddard and Warren pass the first transmitter and bleep twice as instructed. He kept an eye on the second hand of his watch, mentally ticking off the minutes as they dragged by.

Chalmers and Martin jumped and reached for their guns as, right on schedule, the door crashed open and Digger Johnson appeared.

'What the fuck is he doing here?' asked Chalmers in astonishment. 'I thought he was going to follow Chris and Bert.'

'That's what I told them,' said West, 'but I need Digger here. When Ross shows up, we both go out there together.'

'I like your style, Ron, I like your style,' said Chalmers appreciatively. He relaxed, sat back in his chair, and grinned across at Martin.

Relaxation was the last thing on Warren's and

Goddard's minds. As they passed the first transmitter, Goddard dutifully pressed the transmit button twice. He looked sideways at Warren and said, low-voiced, 'I don't fucking well like all this. Not one little bit I don't.'

Warren peered uneasily into the shadows and shook his head. 'Me neither, Chris.' His deep voice was tight with strain.

A woodmouse rustled past them through the undergrowth. Both men jumped violently and swung their shotguns towards the sound. There was a long, sweating pause until they realized it was a false alarm.

Warren wiped his forehead with his sleeve and forced a pale grin at Goddard. 'That was probably Ross, disguised as a bleeding rabbit.'

Goddard grinned shakily back. 'Not Ross. He'd be a fucking werewolf or something.' He screwed up his face in anxiety and beckoned Warren closer. 'If West's told Digger to follow us,' he murmured, 'how the bleeding hell are we gonna piss off?'

'I don't know. Us Londoners ain't cut out for this sort of thing,' said Warren helplessly. 'Christ, Digger or Ross – I don't know which one I'd least want to meet in the dark.' He shivered.

'Well, come on, let's get moving. If we hang around here gassing, West's likely to send Digger after us and then you'll get a chance to find out.'

They moved off and quickened their pace until they reached the second checkpoint. Again Goddard pressed the transmit button twice. He glanced behind them. 'Digger must be with us now,' he said.

A shrill squeak had them both clutching their shotguns more tightly.

'Christ,' said Warren in horror, 'the whole bleeding place is alive with rats and things. How the fuck are we going to know what's an animal and what's Ross?'

The twilight darkened into near-total blackness. It became difficult to follow the track. Occasionally a break in the cloud cover would send shafts of moonlight through the overhead branches. Slivers of mottled light were reflected off the leaves; it seemed to the two jittery men that the bushes were alive and moving. Then the light would die, and again there was stillness.

The two men passed within three feet of Phillip. If Warren had leant over and stretched out a hand, he could have patted him on the head.

Phillip strained to see them as they moved off. He smelt their sweat and cigarette smoke. He moved not a muscle. He waited, every sense fully alert, until the darkness had swallowed them up. When he was certain no one was following them, he set off silently after them.

West pressed the earphones to his head, concentrated as hard as he knew how, and strained to hear. His walky-talky bleeped loudly twice. He could easily make out the footfalls of the two men as they stumbled, out of step, along the path. But there was something else . . . Or was there?

He passed the cans over to Johnson. 'Have a listen, Digger. I might have been listening too hard, but there could be something. Just could be.'

Johnson put them on and listened hard. West turned up the volume on speaker number six. The sound of Warren and Goddard approaching came through loud and clear. West was almost certain that after they'd passed speaker five he'd heard something else, only the merest whisper of sound, but something . . .

Warren and Goddard passed speaker six, the final checkpoint before reaching the house. West's walky-talky bleeped again.

He nudged Johnson. 'Now listen,' he said urgently.

Johnson nodded, frowning in concentration as he strained to make out the sound. After two minutes, he removed the cans and grinned up at West. 'I heard something, but it didn't sound human.'

Chalmers and Martin, who had been listening in puzzlement to the proceedings, came over to the desk.

'What the fuck's going on?' said Chalmers.

West stood up and stretched. He drew the Uzi from its holster and cocked it. 'I don't know,' he said calmly, 'but we're going to take a look. Come on, Digger.'

The two men went out.

'Lock that fucking door,' yelled Chalmers as soon as they had gone, 'and put a chair under the handle.' He snatched up a shotgun, pumped a shell into the chamber, and retreated to the far corner of the room, where he propped his back against the wall, the gun pointed unwaveringly at the door.

Kenny Martin rammed the back of a chair under the door-handle, turned the key in the lock, and followed his example.

Goddard and Warren walked into the light. They reached the corner of the house, about-turned and walked back the way they had come, totally oblivious of the presence of West and Johnson, who watched them from the bushes, only feet away, at the corner of the house.

Johnson started forward, but West put a restraining hand on his shoulder. He pointed down at the ground, mouthed 'Give it five', walked his index and middle fingers in the direction of the track and gave a thumbs-up sign. Johnson nodded and settled back, his eyes fixed on the path along which Goddard and Warren had disappeared.

West kept one eye on his watch, counting the minutes. When five minutes were up, he nudged Johnson and mouthed, 'Let's go.'

Guns at the ready, they covered each other as they sped silently forward. West dropped to a crouch in the cover of a bushy shrub beside the track and waved Johnson past. Bent low, Johnson zigzagged past him for about ten yards, took cover and waved West on. As he ran forward, West felt a wire snag on his foot, heard the dreaded snap and ping. He flung himself to the ground, yelling, 'Trip-wire! Get down!'

The two men were only five yards apart, both hugging the ground closely, when the flash-stun grenades exploded around them. The air was filled with deafening sound and blinding light as the blasts tore at them, searing their eyes, numbing their brains, beating against their ears until they huddled helplessly where they lay.

It was some time before their minds began to clear. Johnson came round first, coughing and choking on the blood that ran from his nose down the back of his throat and filled his mouth. He could barely see. His head was still filled with the coruscating flash that had blinded him though his closed eyelids. His ears sang and buzzed as though angry hornets were attacking his eardrums mercilessly. The back of his throat felt as though some great claw had forced its way in and ripped part of it away.

Crawling unsteadily, he dragged himself over to where he judged West to be. He felt West's body and shook him. Pain lanced through his skull, as he croaked, 'Ron? Ron, are you all right?'

West stirred and groaned. He rolled over, holding his head. Blood ran freely from a gash on his forehead. He sat up, coughed, and spat out blood and dirt. 'Ross suckered us,' he growled bitterly.

The two men helped each other up, and, feeling their way, stumbled back to the house.

It took them a while to convince Kenny Martin it was they, not Ross, outside, and that he could safely open the sitting-room door. Chalmers whitened with shock when he saw them. They staggered in and half fell into chairs.

'Lock the door,' Chalmers snapped at Martin. Then he turned on West. 'What the fuck happened out there? I thought you'd got him when I heard the explosions. I thought that bastard Ross had stepped on a mine.'

West started to shake his head, but winced and changed his mind. 'No, he got us with flash-stun grenades.'

'What about Chris and Bert?'

'I don't know. We were taken out of it just after they'd passed us. They were OK up to then.' He squinted at Chalmers and shaded his eyes from the lights. 'The grenades blew all sight and sense out of us. What happened next is anybody's guess.'

Chalmers sat forward, elbows on knees, and dropped his head into his hands. 'Bert and Chris,' he said sickly. 'The bastard's getting closer.'

Less than half an hour before, Phillip had followed a few yards behind Goddard and Warren, his bare feet whispering along the hard trail as he picked and felt his way among the fallen leaves and twigs that littered the track. Once he stopped to set a series of four more flash-stun grenades. He pulled the thin trip-wire taut across the path, before hurrying on again. He had covered his rear.

He caught them up as they approached the last leg of the track, leading back to the house. He set four more grenades, but let the wire lie loosely across the track. Playing out more wire, he backed into the undergrowth and crouched in its cover to wait.

As he worked, he calculated. If the two men about-turned at the house they would pass this way again in about fifteen minutes, twenty at the outside. He'd let them pass, then set the wire. They'd be caught between the two trip-wires. If West and Johnson came to their aid from either direction, they'd spring one of the traps and catch the blast.

If, on the other hand, Goddard and Warren didn't about-turn but kept on going in the same direction, he'd have time to set the wire that lay across the track in front of him, then get back to the first one and release it until such time as Goddard and Warren crossed it and were caught in his box.

There was a risk that West might pick up his footfalls as he sped along the track, but it was a risk he had to take. He'd had plenty of practice at walking silently in bare feet during his karate training, and with that and his skill in jungle warfare he was confident that he could run rings round any of his opponents.

Phillip estimated that from the house to the point where he'd chosen to attack Warren and Goddard it would take a running man three minutes, possibly four. And if they came running, which he rather doubted, they couldn't possibly miss the trip-wire. He had plenty of time to do the job and then to retreat by the route by which he'd entered the grounds, over the entrance gates, along the grass at the edge of the drive, then into the woods behind the garage block – the last route Chalmers or West would think him foolhardy enough to take.

Sixteen minutes ticked past before Phillip heard Warren and Goddard returning. Only his eyes moved, following the two men as they stumped nervously along the path. As soon as they had passed he pulled the trip-wire taut and tied the trailing end firmly round the trunk of a sapling. He waited a few minutes to ensure no one was covering them from behind, then, cocking and loading the crossbow, set off after them.

It took only a couple of minutes to catch them up. He fell into step close behind them and listened to their whispered conversation. Absorbed in planning their escape, they were totally unaware that the man who sought to kill them was almost treading on their heels. To Phillip's astonishment, neither so much as glanced back to see whether all was clear behind them. What, he wondered, had become of their survival instinct?

He judged that they would soon be at the halfway point between the two trip-wires. His baser self took over. He moved to within a few feet of them, and said quietly, 'Excuse me.'

'What did you say, Chris?'

'I didn't say anything. I thought you did.'

They looked at each other in bewilderment.

Phillip moved still closer. 'Excuse me,' he said again.

Two heads turned as one. A shaft of moonlight broke through, and Phillip's smile, very white in his blackened face, met their stricken gaze.

'Drop the guns and raise your hands in the air, please,' he said, still smiling.

Warren and Goddard dropped their shotguns as though they were red-hot.

'Now turn round.' Phillip stepped back and covered them with the crossbow.

Hands raised high, the two men turned to face their captor. Goddard gaped when he saw that Ross was armed only with a small crossbow. What he could not see was the double-edged hunting knife strapped across Phillip's back, its handle within easy reach of his right hand, or the Browning High Power nine-millimetre pistol holstered in the small of his back.

Hanging from Phillip's shoulder was the bag that had contained the grenades. Goddard eyed it speculatively. He figured there was no way Phillip could reach into that bag for a weapon before he, Goddard, could draw his pistol from his shoulder holster and fire.

'You can't get us both with that little toy,' Goddard sneered. He tried desperately to think of a way of getting Bert Warren to move and take the first crossbow bolt.

Noise and flaring white light exploded around them as the grenades back along the track were set off. Warren and Goddard jumped out of their skins; Phillip didn't move a muscle.

Goddard was quick to recover. Seeing his chance, he dodged behind Bert Warren, pulling him across as cover. He grabbed for his pistol, but Warren stumbled backwards with a gasp as a crossbow bolt thudded into him. He fell against Goddard, wedging his arm to his side. Goddard pushed the dying man forward and away from him. He cleared his pistol from its holster and was swinging it on to target when Phillip's knife flashed through the air and embedded itself in his chest.

He stood for a moment, staring in disbelief at the knife handle. He took an unsteady step backwards and raised his pistol. It felt like a ton weight. His arm was starting to go numb, his eyes wouldn't focus, his legs were weak and trembling. He could see three Rosses, all smiling mockingly at him. Which one should he aim at? He jerked at the trigger and the pistol kicked and roared, then fell from his shaking hand. He bent to retrieve it, but the ground rushed up and smacked him in the face. He felt no pain. He clutched at the pistol, but it was kicked away from him. He heard a voice echoing from far away: 'You have something of mine. I want it back.' The knife was wrenched from his chest. It felt as though it pulled his heart and lungs with it. 'Fuck you, Ross,' he whispered, as blood gushed into his mouth. Then he died.

Phillip wiped the blade clean on the dead man's shirt and slipped it back into its sheath. He crossed to Bert Warren and felt for a pulse at the side of his neck. Warren was dead, too. He pulled the crossbow bolt free, cleaned it and slotted it into the bow, before moving back up the trail to his sprung trap.

He arrived just in time to see the two mercenaries lurch and stagger back to the house. Phillip reckoned they'd each have a nasty headache for quite a while. He watched until they had gone inside, then loped back to where the two dead men lay. One at a time, he carried them to a massive oak tree that stood alone on the lawn at the side of the house, visible from both the sitting-room and the kitchen, and strung them up by the neck. They swung gently in the slight breeze. He smiled grimly at the thought of Frank Chalmers's reaction when he saw them in the morning.

Skirting the garage block, he walked soundlessly down the edge of the drive and climbed back over the gates. By one-thirty he was back at the cottage. Julie smiled in her sleep as he climbed into bed beside her. Careful not to wake her, he took her in his arms and held her close as he waited for sleep to come.

12

No one at High Trees slept much that night. West and Johnson took several strong pain-killers and announced that they were going to get some sleep. Chalmers protested but West turned fiercely on him.

'Do you want to live, Frank? Because if you do you'll need us in good shape to protect you. And we are not' – he gestured to the blood and dirt that covered himself and Johnson – 'in good shape. If we have to sit up all night soothing your fevered fucking brow, come morning we won't be able to protect you from a goddamned teddy bear let alone Phillip SAS Ross.'

Johnson's shark-grin gleamed through the blood that masked his face. 'Come on, Ron,' he said. 'Let's get a couple of beautiful blondes to tuck us up for the night.'

'Make mine a redhead, will you?' said West.

'What about Chris and Bert? You ain't gonna

leave them out there on their fucking own, are you?' asked Kenny Martin in astonishment.

Johnson's menacing grin turned in his direction. 'They don't need our help where they are, son.' He looked up at the ceiling and chuckled. 'They're up there rattling the goddamned pearly gates, wondering why no one opens up.'

He and West rolled themselves in blankets in a corner of the room and instantly fell deeply, heavily asleep.

Chalmers and Martin sat cradling their shotguns in their arms, listening fearfully as the night creatures hooted, whistled and croaked the night away. The house contributed its own squeaks and creaks as it cooled from the heat of the day. Each creak convinced Chalmers that Ross was outside the door, about to burst in and kill him. He took panicky refuge in a bottle of Scotch and drank himself into a fitful, fuddled sleep.

Dawn seemed a long time a-coming. Martin greeted it with silent but passionate relief as streaks of light began filtering through the clouds and dispersing the darkness. As the light grew it roused West and Johnson. Johnson climbed groaning from his blankets, stretched and yawned, then went over to one of the boarded-up windows and peered out through a crack between the boards. The first thing he saw was Goddard and Warren hanging from the oak tree like two sacks of rotten fruit. He grinned and turned back into the room.

'I'm starving,' he announced. 'Anyone fancy a fry-up?'

'Coffee, strong and black, is what I need,' said West, hauling himself to his feet.

Their voices woke Chalmers. 'Wha ... what's happening?' he stuttered, clutching wildly for his gun.

West removed the chair from under the door-handle and unlocked the door. 'We're going to get something to eat and drink,' he said. 'If you want something come and get it.' Johnson followed him out.

Chalmers and Martin, guns in hand, went hastily after them.

Johnson took command in the kitchen, and soon the air was full of the smell of frying bacon and eggs and the fizz and crackle of spitting fat. Martin made coffee and set four steaming mugs down on the pine table.

'I want my eggs turned over,' ordered Chalmers.

'Then turn them yourself, or take them as they come,' said Johnson. 'I'm not the cook here, I'm doing you all a favour.'

Chalmers looked furious at this disobedience from a man whose wages he was paying. But he made no move to turn his eggs and, with Johnson's malevolent gaze full on him, didn't dare protest.

Johnson dished up the eggs, sunny side up and snotty. He loaded the plates with bacon, done well, the way he liked it, and heaped baked beans on top. He forked beans into his open mouth as he carried his plate to the table, sat down and scooped up a handful of French bread. 'Breakfast is served, gentlemen,' he said through his mouthful. 'Help yourselves.'

Careful not to catch Chalmers's eye, Martin fetched the remaining three plates to the table and set them down.

'You'd make a good waiter, Kenny,' said Johnson. 'I don't mind doing the odd bit of cooking, but I never could serve.'

Martin ignored him and looked steadfastly down at his plate. There was silence, broken only by the clack of knifes and forks on plates and the slurp of Johnson drinking his coffee. Chalmers closed his eyes as he forked half-raw egg white into his mouth, his hunger overcoming his loathing of snotty eggs.

'Enjoying that, are you?' asked Johnson solicitously.

Chalmers nodded, his mouth full of bacon and eggs.

'I bet they'd like some,' said Johnson, nodding in the direction of the window.

Puzzled, Chalmers turned and looked out. He saw Goddard and Warren hanging from the huge oak, their chests drenched in blood, their eyes half open, and their tongues lolling from their mouths like panting dogs'. He threw up.

Johnson roared with laughter and shovelled more

food into his mouth, egg white dribbling down his chin.

Martin gagged and pushed his plate away, fighting down the nausea that filled him.

'What's the matter, Kenny, not hungry?' said Johnson cheerfully. 'Give it here, then. It'd be a crime to waste it.' He pulled Martin's plate over, tipped the food on to his own plate and carried on eating.

West had seen too many dead men to let two more put him off his much-needed breakfast. He cleared his plate and wiped it clean with bread, which he stuffed into his mouth and washed down with coffee.

Chalmers stared in horrified disbelief at the two mercenaries. 'How the fuck can you two keep eating while you're looking at Bert and Chris swinging from that fucking tree?' He wiped a trickle of vomit from his mouth with the back of his hand.

Johnson smiled. 'Eat, drink and be merry, for tomorrow we die,' he said lightly.

Chalmers looked out again. 'They were my mates,' he said.

'Go and cut them down, then,' said Johnson.

Chalmers recoiled. 'Er . . . I . . . they're dead, right? So it won't hurt them to wait a bit.'

Martin had won his battle against nausea. He went over to the window and gazed out. 'They're right out in the open,' he said hesitantly. 'Ross could be waiting to pick us off as we cut them down. I don't fancy it.' He went back to his seat.

'Christ, you're right,' said Chalmers. 'Let 'em wait. They won't know no different.' He turned to West. 'So what do we do now? I mean, you're the fucking expert. I'm paying you a small fucking fortune to protect us. You cut them two down.'

West kept his voice rigidly under control. 'I'll cut them down when I'm good and ready.' He stared unflinchingly at Chalmers. 'I'm here to try to protect you from Ross. I don't know if I can do it. So' – he smiled – 'if you want to break off the contract, be my guest.'

It took a moment for the implications of what he'd said to sink in. Then Chalmers glued a wide smile to his face, lumbered to his feet and held out his hand. 'Now, Ron,' he said soothingly, 'don't be like that. We're all in this together. Ross is the enemy, so don't let's start playing silly buggers with each other. There's still four of us, ain't there? We can handle Ross, no problem.' He studiously avoided looking out of the window.

Johnson stood up. 'Anyone fancy seconds? I'm still hungry.'

No one took up his offer. He laughed and headed for the cooker.

Before Digger Johnson had finished his breakfast, Phillip Ross was back in the woods. He'd walked brazenly up the edge of the drive and settled in position. He could see the two dead men in the oak, the kitchen side of the house and part of the front.

Apart from the windows, which he had taken into account, the only exits were the front and kitchen doors. Through his binoculars he studied the four men in the kitchen. The only one still eating was Johnson. First Martin and then West came to the window and peered out. Chalmers stayed put in his chair.

Phillip checked the Mannlicher rifle, zeroing in on Chalmers as he adjusted the telescopic sights. The cross-hair settled on Chalmers's forehead. The urge to pull the trigger was powerful: he could end it all now and get the hell out of here, go back to Julie. But he resisted. He had to know the name of the man who'd killed Gary. Then, and only then, would he deal with Chalmers.

He waited patiently. No one ventured out of the house. He turned his attention to the dead men in the oak. The distance, he reckoned, was something like two hundred yards. He tossed some dead grass in the air to judge the wind. It had picked up to about fifteen knots, and was gusting from the west. He sighted in and squeezed the trigger.

At the rifle's sharp crack, the four men in the kitchen dived for cover.

'What the fuck's he shooting at now?' screeched Chalmers.

Johnson got cautiously to his feet, edged over to the window and looked warily out. There was a second shot and the corpse of Bert Warren crashed to the ground. Johnson gave a yelp of laughter. 'That's nice of him, very helpful, very cooperative. He's cutting them down for us. Save us the trouble.'

The others got up and, bent double, hurried to the back of the room, where they could see out of the window but couldn't be seen from outside.

'Where is he?' asked West urgently. 'Can you get a fix on him?'

Johnson peered out again. 'I can't see him, but then I wouldn't expect to.'

Another shot cracked out, and Goddard's body jumped on its rope as the bullet cut halfway through the rope, the remaining strands of which stretched taut.

'Wow,' said Johnson, impressed. 'He must be shooting from a least two hundred yards, and there's a good wind blowing out there. Now that is what I call shooting. One more shot should do it.'

He was right. The next shot severed all but a few strands of the rope, and the weight of Goddard's body did the rest. Jerking and bouncing under the impact of the bullet, the rope snapped, and Goddard crashed to earth in a sprawl, arms and legs splayed at awkward angles. His face, a macabre, half-blind mask, stared at the window as though pleading for help.

Chalmers looked as though he was about to throw up again. 'Christ, Ron, why don't you go out there and get the bastard?'

'You're kidding! That's a high-powered hunting rifle he's got out there, and I'd bet he's using a telescopic sight. He'd pick us off like fish in a sodding barrel before we got anywhere near him with this' – he held up the Uzi – 'or the shotguns. They're no good until you get in close. We need Ross to come to us, preferably under cover of darkness.'

'Why did he shoot them down?'

'Could be several reasons,' said West. 'To let us know he's there, to put more pressure on us, maybe to tempt us to go out after him. But it's not going to work.'

Digger Johnson's face lit up as a thought struck him. He looked out of the window again. 'The wind's blowing from the west,' he said. 'If I can sneak round to the far edge of the woods and get upwind of Ross I could fire the woods. It's tinder-dry out there. The wind would blow the flames down towards him like a fireball, drive him out this way towards the house.'

West spoke sharply to Chalmers. 'Have you got any cans of petrol?'

Chalmers looked questioningly at Martin, who said, 'Yeah, there's four or five one-gallon cans in the first garage. We always keep a bit for emergencies and for the lawnmowers.'

'Come on, then, let's take another look at the map,' said West and led them at a run to the sitting-room. There he and Johnson leant over the map together.

'Make a wide detour – here, and then round here – around the perimeter wall,' said West. 'Set a trail of petrol, starting here, and run it along the wall, about ten feet inside so the wind can get under the flames and blow them towards Ross. I'll be waiting in the brush here' – he stabbed a finger down at the corner of the house nearest the woods – 'and with any luck the fire will drive Ross straight into a burst from the Uzi. It should cut him in half.'

'Now you're fucking talking,' said Chalmers with relief. 'What about me and Kenny? What do we do?'

West studied him for a moment. 'Get to a bedroom window at the front of the house, one that's been blown out. And if Ross shows his face keep pumping lead at him with those shotguns. You won't kill him from that distance, but it'll take his attention off me.'

'What if he starts shooting back?' Chalmers didn't look too keen on the idea.

'Duck.'

Chalmers reluctantly picked up one of the shotguns. 'Come on, Kenny. Let's see if this works.'

Johnson watched them leave, stuck his bottom lip out and shook his head. 'What a pair of wankers,' he said unemotionally.

'Got your radio?' asked West.

Johnson slapped his pocket and nodded.

'Right, get to it then, Digger, before Ross has a chance to get organized and change his position.' West raised a singed eyebrow quizzically. 'And keep your head down.'

312

Johnson raised his gun in mock salute and left. West checked the Uzi and picked up one of the shotguns, then went out into the hall.

Johnson made his way rapidly to the dining-room at the other side of the house. He figured, correctly, that Ross wouldn't have had time to circle round and cover that part of the house since firing his last shot. Slipping out of a window, he looked warily around. All was quiet. He ran across to the garage block and collected a full can of petrol, then moved cautiously to the point West had indicated on the map. Once in place he paused to listen, but was sure he was undetected. He unscrewed the cap, bent low and began pouring a trail of petrol along the ground beneath the undergrowth.

From upwind of him, Phillip watched sardonically as Johnson worked his way through the woods. The wind carried the smell of petrol away from him, but he was in no doubt about what Johnson intended. He checked the direction of the wind and quickly worked out his escape route. Then he moved silently forward until he hit the petrol trail, took out a Zippo lighter and flicked its flame alive. He lit some dry leaves and tossed them on to the ground.

The petrol ignited with a whoomph. Flames licked along the trail at terrifying speed. Johnson heard a crackling behind him and glanced round. The fire was almost on him. He flung the petrol can at the approaching flames and dived for cover. No sooner had he hit the ground than the flames reached the can and it exploded in a roar of energy. A fireball shot into the air and spread out. Burning petrol fell on and all around him, searing his skin and scorching the undergrowth. Thick black smoke rose and hung for a split second before being shredded and whirled away by the wind.

It was some minutes before Johnson dared raise his head. He looked at the backs of his hands. The skin had blistered into large bubbles which were rapidly filling with blood. He touched the left side of his face, the side that had been uppermost when he hit the ground. The skin felt wet and sticky. He pulled his hand away and stared at it. It was covered in a thin film of bloodied skin. He pulled the skin off and flicked it away. It caught on a low branch nearby and swung in the wind.

Scooping up the shotgun, he pumped a shell into the breech and leapt to his feet. He fired wildly into the surrounding bushes and roared out his rage and pain.

He was too late. Phillip had already moved on. Hit hard and run, he'd been taught. It seemed like good advice just now.

Back at the house Chalmers and Martin saw the fireball hurtle into the air and heard the harsh smack of the shotgun firing.

'Something's gone wrong,' said Chalmers, his voice full of foreboding. 'That's not what Ron said would happen. Ross was supposed to be driven down here, to the house.'

Martin could offer him no reassurance. 'I don't know what the fuck we have to do to kill that bastard. It's like he's got nine lives or something. Everything we think of, he's got the fucking answer.'

West, too, knew instantly that something was wrong. Concern for Johnson overrode concern for himself. He launched himself out of cover, crossed the lawn at full stretch, and dived headlong into the bushes. He lay still for a moment, forcing himself to breathe silently while he took stock of his surroundings. He could hear nothing but the crackle of the flames as they devoured the undergrowth in their path.

The sound of the shotgun pierced the din of the fire and echoed through the woods. West edged cautiously towards it. He reached a gap in the trees and saw Johnson firing blindly around him. The left side of his face was raw and ugly and streaming with blood. His lips had been partially burnt away, exposing his teeth and gums. His left eye was invisible behind the blood that poured from his head; his right eye was wide, the white showing all round, and there was madness in it.

West waited until the shotgun was empty. Then he stood up, slipped the Uzi into its holster, raised his hands above his head and walked out into the open.

Johnson saw a blurred figure coming towards him and pulled frantically at the shotgun trigger. He screamed with rage as the firing pin clicked on to an empty chamber, and flung the gun at the approaching figure.

'Digger, it's OK, mate. It's me, Ron.' West kept on walking. 'I'm coming to get you and take you in.'

Johnson froze at the sound of his voice. 'Ron?' he said uncertainly. 'Is that you? Where are you? I can't see properly.'

'Yes it's me. Hang in there, Digger. I'll get you out of here.'

Johnson fell to his knees. The pain began to pierce though his adrenalin defences and he keened aloud. West could see him start to shake as he went into shock, then, to West's relief, he fell forward, unconscious.

West rolled him over and patted out the sparks that still smouldered on his clothing. Grimacing at the sight of his injuries, he picked him up and slung him over one shoulder, then set out, openly and with defiant disregard of danger, back to the house.

The Mannlicher cradled in his arms, Phillip watched him go.

From their window Chalmers and Martin saw West trudging across the grass towards the house, carrying Johnson across his shoulder like a sack of vegetables. The unconscious man's arms swung limply in time with West's heavy steps.

'Christ All-bleeding-mighty!' exclaimed Martin. 'He's got Digger.'

They hurried downstairs and met West as he came through the shattered front door.

'Is he dead?' asked Chalmers.

West ignored him and went into the sitting-room. He lowered Johnson carefully on to the settee and bent over him to inspect his injuries. Chalmers and Martin craned their necks to see; Martin hastily looked away, his gorge rising, as he saw the burnt and bloodied flesh.

'Get me lots of cold water and ice,' ordered West. 'Also clean towels and plastic freezer bags.' He reached over for his first-aid kit.

Chalmers and Martin hesitated, afraid to leave the room in case Ross was loose in the house and stalking them.

West turned on them. 'Get that stuff and get it now,' he said, his voice icy with contempt.

The two men fled to the kitchen without a word. Hastily they filled two buckets with cold water, grabbed handfuls of freezer bags, emptied the contents of the ice-maker into a towel and hurried back to the sitting-room. When they went in West was withdrawing a syringe from Johnson's arm.

'What's that?' asked Chalmers.

'Morphine. I don't know when he's likely to come round, but it's going to hurt like hell when he does.' West splashed cold water on to the blistered flesh, then tipped ice into freezer bags and packed them round Johnson's burns. 'That's the best I can do for him. He ought to be in intensive care.'

'But if you take him to hospital, we'll be all alone here,' said Chalmers in quick alarm.

'We'll wait till he wakes up. See how he feels and what he wants to do. If Digger woke up in hospital he'd probably get out of bed and come straight back here.'

Chalmers sighed with relief. 'Thank fuck for that.'

West looked at him contemptuously. It took much effort to control his anger. He felt like shooting the worthless, selfish little bastard on the spot. Then he thought, No, let Ross take care of him. Let him live in fear a little longer. His time will come, and when it does Ross will do a good job on him.

It was three hours before Johnson came to. He rolled over and groaned, 'Ooh . . . shit. What the fuck happened?' He dragged himself up until he was sitting, his back supported by the arm of the settee, threw aside the ice-packs and inspected his hands. West, Chalmers and Martin winced in sympathy as he felt the burnt side of his face and his charred mouth.

'I can't see out of my left eye,' he slurred through his ruined lips. He turned his head until he could see them with his good eye. 'The right one's OK, though.'

West went over to him. 'You should be in hospital, Digger. Want me to take you?'

The good side of Johnson's face creased into a

grotesque caricature of his shark-grin. 'Don't be bloody daft, Ron.' He hauled himself to his feet, went over to the hearth and inspected himself in the mirror over the mantelpiece. 'Well, there's a thing. The bastard's spoilt my looks. And there was I all ready to sign a Hollywood film contract.' Spittle oozed from where his lips had been and ran down his chin. He wiped it away with his sleeve and turned back to West. 'You know what I have to do, Ron.'

West nodded. 'I'll help you get ready. The morphine will start wearing off soon, and you'll need to take more as the pain increases.' He went to his first-aid kit and fished around inside. While he did so Johnson picked up a shotgun and checked it. He was as calm as if nothing had happened, as if this were a training exercise.

'This is all you'll need,' said West, handing him a small package. 'Good luck, Digger. I'll be listening on the radio. If you need help just give me the word.' He clapped Johnson gently on the shoulder.

'See you around, Ron.' Johnson's face twisted again into that horrific grin. Without so much as a look at Chalmers and Martin he turned and walked out.

There was a long, numb silence. It was shattered by Johnson's slurred voice shouting from the front of the house, 'Ross! Ross, can you hear me? I'm coming out to finish it.'

Chalmers crossed to the window, peered out

through a crack and watched him. 'Is he off his head, Ron, or what?' he asked bemusedly.

'A man like you couldn't begin to understand, Frank.'

'No, and I wouldn't want to, either. It's fucking madness.' Chalmers gave a high-pitched, neurotic giggle and turned to look out again.

Johnson walked straight across the lawn towards the woods. The wind had dropped. Smoke rose in palls from the burnt and blackened stems of bushes stripped of their foliage by the fireball that had raced through them. Small flames still danced and flickered over patches of grass that had been green enough to survive the first blaze.

Phillip heard Johnson yelling. He circled round until he could see him thrashing his way through the smouldering undergrowth.

Johnson shouted again. 'Come on, Ross, you bastard. Come out and fight. See what you can do against a real man.'

Phillip studied him through the Mannlicher's telescopic sight. He grimaced at the sight of the charred and ruined face. The left eye-socket was an empty hole filled with blood and torn tissue, and beneath it the cheekbone jutted, red-smeared white, through the burnt flesh. And yet the man came on, and there was no doubt that, appallingly injured as he was, his invitation to fight was in deadly earnest.

When he was only a hundred yards away, he suddenly veered off to his left.

Phillip called out, 'I'm over here.'

Johnson stopped and turned in the direction of the voice. His head was angled to the left so that he could see out of his good eye. His face twisted into a hideous grimace of satisfaction as he thrashed forwards.

Phillip panned the house and grounds through the telescopic sight, checking that it wasn't a trap and that Johnson was alone. Satisfied, he laid the Mannlicher carefully on the ground and stepped out into the open.

Johnson saw him and stopped in his tracks. They stared measuringly at each other for several seconds. Abruptly, Johnson threw down his shotgun, then drew his pistol and flung it down beside the shotgun.

Phillip understood instantly. He dragged the Browning High Power from its holster in the small of his back and tossed it aside.

The two men drew their knives and advanced slowly towards each other until only six feet separated them.

Cocking his head to the left, Johnson looked at Phillip out of his right eye. 'Good to meet you, Ross,' he said without rancour. 'You're a good soldier, the best I've ever come across. But then I always knew you SAS bastards were good.' He gave a pain-racked laugh. 'I admit, though, I didn't know just how good until recently.'

'Too bad,' said Phillip quietly.

Johnson dropped his gaze to the knife in Phillip's hand. 'I know you're good at throwing that thing, but can you fight with it?'

'You won't find out if you just stand there talking.' He glanced quickly around, his attention never leaving his opponent.

Johnson's wrecked mouth contorted in a grin. 'Don't worry about Ron,' he slurred. 'He understands. He won't interfere.'

'Let's get to it, then.'

They crouched and began to circle. Despite his injuries, Johnson was surprisingly fast and accurate with his thrust. Phillip parried and side-stepped, narrowly avoiding the eight-inch blade as it slashed through the air only inches from him.

Johnson's macabre shark-grin grew wider. 'To the death, Ross, to the death.'

'I wouldn't want it any other way.'

Johnson flicked his knife expertly to his left hand and lunged again, changing hands in a split second in mid-lunge. His move was so quick and skilful that Phillip at first swerved the wrong way, almost spitting himself on the blade. At the last instant he twisted and spun away, leaving a smear of blood from his arm on Johnson's blade.

There was battle-madness now in Johnson's one good eye. He attacked again, swinging his blade in a vicious upward arc across Phillip's body. Phillip leapt back and the knife hissed past, missing him by the breadth of two hairs. His foot caught on a root and he fell backwards. With a snarl, Johnson hurled himself forward in a flying leap, diving in for the kill. His knife was drawn back for the strike, his face triumphant. Phillip kicked upwards and, using Johnson's own momentum, flung him past to crash headlong into a smoking tangle of brambles.

Phillip leapt to his feet and spun to face his opponent. Johnson was up and coming straight at him. The two men locked together, grasping each other's wrists. Phillip could feel his hand slipping as skin from Johnson's wrist came loose and peeled away. Johnson twisted and brought his knee up hard into Phillip's groin. Phillip turned, taking the blow on his thigh. Pain lanced up his thigh and into his stomach. He turned again, bent and threw Johnson over his hip, but Johnson kept his hold on Phillip's wrist and the two men crashed down to the ground. Locked together they rolled over several times. Sparks and soot flew up in clouds around them. Johnson had the strength of a much taller man. He fought fearlessly and with tigerish ferocity. It took all Phillip's strength and skill to contain him. Another roll brought Johnson uppermost. He used every ounce of his weight to press his knife down towards Phillip's throat. The needle-like point and scalpel-sharp blade inched down as Phillip strained every muscle to keep it away. At the last second, the knife-point almost piercing his skin, Phillip released his pressure and wrenched his head and neck aside so that the blade crunched into the fire-hardened earth. He tore his wrist free and plunged his blade to the hilt into Johnson's armpit. Johnson screamed in pain and shock as the knife sank into him. Phillip yanked the knife free, turned Johnson on to his back and plunged the knife into his chest. He stood up, panting, gasping for breath, and looked quickly around. Nothing stirred. He looked back down at Johnson, who lay still on his back, his face a hideous, grinning mask.

Johnson coughed feebly and spat blood. 'Thanks, Ross,' he whispered. 'I enjoyed that.' The whisper faded, then strengthened again. 'I nearly got you a couple of times, didn't I?'

Phillip nodded. 'Yes, Digger, you nearly got me.'

'Good fight, good fight . . .' Phillip had to strain to make out the words.

The breath rattled hoarsely in Johnson's throat. His limbs relaxed, his face rolled to the left so that the ruined side was hidden, and his one good eye stared fixedly up at the sun.

Phillip bent to retrieve his knife. He drew it out as gently as possible, wiped it clean on his torn sleeve and slotted it back into its sheath.

He straightened Johnson's legs and crossed his arms over his chest. He felt in Johnson's pocket for his walky-talky and took it out. Straightening up, he stared down at the dead man for a long minute. 'Wasted talent,' he said quietly. He turned and walked soundlessly away, back to his dug-out.

It was intact. He slipped inside, picked up his

mobile phone and dialled High Trees. When Martin answered he said, 'Message for West. Tell him Digger Johnson is in the woods. He can go and get him.' Then he rang off before Martin could answer. He packed more flash-stun grenades into his knapsack and set off down the hill towards the house.

Martin turned to West. 'That was Ross,' he said nervously. 'He says Digger's in the woods, and you can go and get him.'

Chalmers looked away disgustedly and muttered, 'Another hundred grand down the fucking drain.'

West clamped his mouth into a hard line and left the room without a word.

He found Johnson without difficulty, and noted with gratitude that the body had been laid out with respect. He pulled Johnson's knife from the ground and knelt down to return it to its sheath. 'Well, Digger,' he said aloud, 'peace at last. I don't suppose there's much need for soldiers where you are.' He studied the trampled ground. 'I can see you put up a good fight. I always thought that in hand-to-hand combat you'd be a match for Ross. Without your wounds, who knows? And now it's just him and me.'

He looked back towards High Trees and scowled. 'And those two useless bastards. Not that they'll be any trouble to a man like Ross.' He stood up and hauled the dead man up over his shoulder. 'I'm getting tired of lugging you about, mate. But I reckon I can do it this one last time.' He trudged wearily down the hill to the rose garden in front of the house.

He fetched a shovel from the garage. He dug a deep grave, lowered Johnson carefully into it, shovelled the earth back until it was piled high, and firmed it down. He stood back and tried to think of a suitable prayer for a man like Digger, but no prayer seemed appropriate – ribald songs were more Digger's line. He grinned wearily as he envisaged a po-faced vicar solemnly intoning 'Eskimo Nell' over the grave, and leant on his shovel. 'That'll have to do for now, Digger,' he said. 'No doubt someone else will come along and dig you up again, cut you about like the carcass of an old bull, state officially that you died of knife wounds. Killed by a person or persons unknown. And that will be that.' He coughed and cleared his throat. 'Till we meet again,' he said tiredly. He turned and tramped back to the house.

Chalmers was almost frantic with relief when he saw West. He put down the shotgun he'd been clutching and heaved himself out of his chair. His greeting was characteristic. 'Where the fuck have you been, Ron? We thought you'd pissed off and left us. And' – an obvious afterthought – 'what happened to Digger?'

West ignored him and slumped down on the settee where Johnson had lain not long before.

'Is Digger dead?' pursued Chalmers.

'Yes, dead and buried.'

Chalmers glanced fearfully across at Martin. 'That leaves just the three of us,' he said shakily.

Slowly West turned his head and looked at Chalmers. His voice thick with loathing and contempt, he said, 'What you really mean, you yellow-bellied scum, you worthless son of a bitch, is that Ross has got only two more of us to kill before he gets to you.' He spat on the carpet. 'I hope he takes his time with you. I hope he kills you v–e–e–r–y slowly.'

Beads of sweat pimpled Chalmers's forehead and upper lip and he wiped them away, gazing at West in mingled fear and hatred. He forced a smile on to his face. 'Don't be like that, Ron. We're all in this together.' He looked at Martin for support; Martin looked away. 'I'm the guv'nor here. I pay the wages. And I say we're all in it together and we're all mates.'

'Like you said,' snapped West, 'you pay the wages. But that's as far as it goes.'

Chalmers managed to look aggrieved. 'That's gratitude for you, I don't think,' he said sourly.

The three of them lapsed into morose silence.

Phillip watched as West set off in search of Johnson. Once satisfied that West was out of the way, he ran across the lawn, shinned up a corner drainpipe and cut the telephone wires. Dropping down to the ground again, he ran to the garage block. The garage doors were unlocked and he slipped silently inside.

His knife cut easily into the tyres of West's Range Rover and Land Rover, slashing them beyond repair. Chalmers's four cars received the same treatment. He worked quickly, wasting no time or effort, and set flash-stun grenades attached to trip-wires around the garage block. In minutes he had done and was back in the woods, circling through them along the paths West had left unmined. He set another ring of grenade booby-traps on all the likely avenues of escape from the house. He connected a master wire to all the trip-wires and trailed it some distance from the garage block towards the gates, so that he could explode all the grenades with one good pull. Then, satisfied that no one could leave the house without setting off one of the grenades, he settled himself under cover and watched West bury Digger Johnson.

Chalmers was close to panic. He paced restlessly round the sitting-room, neat whisky spilling from the glass in his hand.

'We can't stay here any longer,' he flung at West, his voice high with strain. 'I should never have fucking well listened to you in the first place. It was a mistake to stay here. We've got to get out, go somewhere safe.' He looked across at the windows. Sunlight streamed through the cracks in the boarding, at an angle that showed that dusk was not far off. 'As soon as it's dark we make a run for it.'

'You're the boss,' grunted West. He smiled maliciously and added, 'Provided Ross doesn't object.'

Chalmers gnawed at a fingernail as he tried to think of a safe refuge. 'We'll stop off in London for a couple of nights, stay at a hotel while we phone round and book a place. A hunting lodge in Scotland or Wales for a couple of months. It won't look funny there if we're seen carrying guns.'

'Do we go in one car or two?' asked Martin.

Chalmers looked enquiringly at West.

'One of us will have to open the gates,' said West. 'I think we should go in one vehicle, the Range Rover. I can cover the rear from that, if Kenny'll drive.'

Martin was past caring. He raised his hands in surrender. 'I'll drive. Anything to get away from this bleeding place.'

'Right.' The prospect of escape seemed to give Chalmers new energy and confidence. 'Ron, you get the gates open. We'll drive down, give you time to jump in the back of the wagon. It's as simple as that. We'll leave Ross sitting here all on his fucking own.' The rolls of fat over his belly jounced around as he laughed. But his laughter trailed away as he saw the dubious looks West and Martin exchanged. 'Well, what's wrong with that?' he said petulantly.

West was blunt. 'Ross isn't going to let us leave.'

'But . . . but . . . he let *you* leave, he let you drive out – twice. Once when you took John to hospital and then when you went for the mines and all that electronic shit.'

'Ah yes, true, but then he isn't after me, is he, Frank? It's you he wants, and he isn't going to let you slip through his fingers, or Kenny either.'

But Chalmers refused to let his idea drop. 'Well, we're fucking well gonna try it. Ron, go and bring the Range Rover round the front of the house. We'll load it up and get ready to make a run for it.'

'Anything you say, Frank,' said West, rising wearily from his chair.

While West went out to the garage, Chalmers and Martin collected all the remaining guns and ammunition and stacked them in the hall, ready for loading into the vehicle. The activity made them feel better, and they were almost cheerful by the time West returned.

'All the cars and both four-wheel-drives are out of commission,' he said. 'The tyres have been slashed, the spares too.'

The smiles died on their faces.

'And that isn't all,' West went on. 'I nearly caught another headache. Ross has booby-trapped the grounds.'

'What do you mean?' asked Chalmers.

'I snagged my foot on a trip-wire. Fortunately I felt it and scotched it at the same time. This little joker' – he held up a grenade – 'was attached to the end of it.'

Chalmers went over to him and peered at the grenade. 'Is it safe?' he asked doubtfully.

West nodded and shoved it into his pocket. 'If I found one, there are bound to be more. Ross wouldn't piss about with just one, so from now on it's dangerous to walk about outside the house.'

'Do you mean we're trapped here? Like in a fucking rat-hole?' demanded Chalmers.

'Unless you can get someone to come in and get us out, yes, Frank, we're trapped.'

Chalmers thought rapidly. 'Jimmy Simpson,' he said. 'He'll come and take us out of here if I offer him enough dosh.' He snatched up the phone and waited for the dialling tone. Nothing. He rattled the cut-off buttons angrily, the receiver almost slipping from his hand. 'It's dead,' he moaned. 'The bastard's cut us off.' The colour faded from his fat cheeks; he looked pasty and mean.

Martin took the receiver from his limp hand and listened. 'Dead as a bleeding dodo,' he said, and dropped the handset back on to its rest.

'We've only one chance left,' said West, 'and that is to walk – if we can slip past Ross without him seeing us.' He pulled thoughtfully at his lower lip. 'But if he catches us in the open with that hunting rifle, we're all dead.'

'I don't fancy walking for miles across country in the dark,' said Chalmers, 'with that bastard creeping about. Besides, you said he's booby-trapped the fucking place.'

331

'I'd have to find a way through the traps, and hope I don't set any of them off.' West pulled the flash-stun grenade out of his pocket and weighed it in his hand. 'Of course, just because I found this one before I set it off doesn't mean I'll find the others in time. And he could have set a few shrapnel grenades – they'd be a very different proposition.'

Martin said diffidently, 'What I can't make out is why Ross left the phone working until now. Why wait till now to cut us off? He can't contact us now, even if he wants to put the frighteners on us again.'

'Oh yes, he can,' said West. 'I didn't think of it before, but Digger didn't have his walky-talky on him when I buried him.' He took his own from his belt and set it down on the table in front of him. 'Kenny, Ross didn't cut the phone wires before for two reasons. One, he could check from anywhere in the world if we were still here, just by ringing in and getting an answer. And two, it made us all feel safer. The fact that we could contact people if we needed something. He knew it was unlikely we'd call in more troops while there were four or five of us, and he didn't care because he'd have done the same. Now he knows we'll be getting a bit panicky and we'd ring out for help if we could. So he's cut the wires. And he guessed we'd try to make a run for it, so he fucked up the cars at the same time. Ross has been two steps ahead of us all the time. He knows we'll try to get the hell out of here, and he's out there waiting for us to try it.'

Chalmers said, 'Well, that's blown that idea right out the fucking window. I ain't going out there now, no way.'

'But Frank,' appealed Martin, 'we can't stay here for ever, just waiting for him to come in and kill us. It's me or Ron next in line, and then he'll come and torture you until you give him the fucking name he wants. We've got to do something, anything.'

'Shut it, Kenny,' snapped Chalmers.

For the first time in his life, Martin lost his temper with his boss. He leapt to his feet and shouted, 'No, fuck it! My fucking life has been on the line for too long now. The only reason I'm still alive is because I've been stuck in this bleeding house guarding you. I've had enough, Frank, I'm not taking any more of this shit!' Panting, he stared across at Chalmers. He waited for a reply . . . and waited . . . His anger drained away into the silence, and a pleading note came into his voice. 'Talk to the bastard, Frank, offer him more money. Give him the name he wants. Perhaps then he'll leave us alone and go after the hitman. It could give us a chance to make a break for it.'

Chalmers stayed stubbornly silent. He refused to meet Martin's eyes. He knew that, as soon as Ross learnt the identity of his hitman, he himself was dead.

13

Darkness fell. The cracks in the window, which had been slivers of light, were now black slits. The air was still and humid. Chalmers switched on a small reading lamp on the desk and angled it to illuminate the locked and chair-jammed door. Outside the circle of light around the doorway, the shadows were deep and eerie. The three men sat in silence. They had nothing more to say to each other. They simply waited for Phillip Ross to make his next move.

Finally, Ron West stirred in his chair and said, 'Well, I never did believe in dying on an empty stomach.' He felt the saliva start to come into his mouth as he went on, 'There are four T-bone steaks in the fridge. Digger took them out of the freezer this morning. I intend to eat one of them. Anyone care to join me?' He rose to his feet.

'I'm not going out there,' snapped Chalmers.

West shrugged and said, 'I'll cook it and bring it to you if you'll eat it.'

Chalmers nodded and grunted something unintelligible.

'Thanks, Ron,' said Martin. 'I could murder a steak.'

'All medium?' enquired West. Both men nodded.

West unlocked the door and removed the chair. Cautiously, he opened the door a fraction and peered out into the hall. It was empty. As he crossed the hall, he heard the sitting-room door being locked behind him. He made his way down the passage to the kitchen, turning on lights as he went.

While the fat in the chip pan was heating, he turned on the grill, took a large packet of frozen peas from the freezer, and set water to boil in a saucepan. From the fridge he took three steaks. He brushed them with oil and rubbed in garlic salt and black pepper. Engrossed in his task, he didn't notice he was no longer alone. Not, that is, until a quiet voice behind him said, 'Do the fourth steak as well, Ron. I'll eat it.'

West froze. Without turning round, he asked, 'OK to get it out of the fridge?'

'Yes, but do it nice and slowly, from one side, and keep your hands where I can see them.'

West nodded and obeyed. 'Four steaks coming up,' he said, and began to oil and season the fourth. When he had finished, he wiped his hands on kitchen paper and turned round.

A tall, dark-haired man in camouflage combat gear was sitting at the pine table, his hands out of sight beneath it. The two men regarded each other with interest.

Careful to keep his hands in sight, West crossed to the table and sat down. He raised one eyebrow and said, 'Mr Ross, I presume.'

Phillip nodded.

'Why aren't I dead?' West enquired.

'Because I haven't bothered to kill you . . . yet.'

West smiled grimly. 'You've had more than one opportunity. I know that very well.'

'I haven't tried to kill you, Ron. I used flash-stun grenades instead of the real thing last night because I want to say something to you.'

'About the girl? I'd have done that for any woman.'

'You saved her from being raped, and put your own life on the line. I owe you for that, Ron West.' He cracked a half-smile. 'You get the chance to walk away, if you're prepared to take it.'

West looked at him unflinchingly and said, 'Tell me something, Mr Ross—'

'Call me Phillip, Ron.'

'Phillip. What happened to Luke? Is he dead?'

'No. I gave him a choice between walking and dying.' Phillip smiled. 'He chose to walk.'

West let out a sigh of profound relief. 'Thank God for that,' he said quietly. 'And Lofty? Why? Why Lofty?'

Phillip shrugged. 'He made the mistake of struggling. He would have had the same chance, but he swung the barrel of his gun at me.'

West nodded his understanding. 'All's fair in love and war,' he said, then, more sombrely: 'And Digger? Did he give you a good fight?'

Phillip turned slightly so that West could see the slash in the arm of his combat jacket. The blood had dried and crusted to dark brown; the stain ran down to his wrist. 'He cut me. That was good enough.'

'He was very good at hand-to-hand. A bad bastard if you were on the wrong side, but a good man to have around.'

'I thought that when I first saw him, when you and your men arrived. Why "Digger", by the way? Was he originally a miner or something?'

West laughed. 'Not bloody likely! You a boxer? No? Dig's boxing slang for an upper cut. When Digger was in the US Marines he did a bit of boxing, and his dig was famous. He won seven fights with it – each time by breaking his opponent's ribs.'

The fat in the chip pan began to sputter as it boiled. West went over to the cooker and lowered the frozen chips in their wire basket into the pan. Steam hissed into the air as the hot fat bubbled in protest and rose, threatening to overflow the pan. West lifted the basket to let the fat settle, then lowered it in again. He put the four steaks under the grill and sat down. Phillip kept the Browning High Power trained on him from under the table all the time.

'What are you going to do, Ron? Walk or die? You get' – Phillip chuckled – 'to eat the steak either way.'

'It's not easy,' said West uncomfortably. 'I took the contract, and I've never yet broken a contract, or my word once I've given it.' His eyes were deeply troubled.

'Those two murdering scumbags aren't worth it, Ron. I don't want to have to kill you, but I will if you leave me no choice. And you know very well that I can do it.'

Frowning heavily, West got up and turned the steaks. He lifted the chips clear of the fat and shook them, before dropping them back in. The water for the peas had come to the boil and he emptied the packet into the saucepan. He stood for a long time looking down at the pans. Phillip could see the tension in his shoulders and neck muscles, saw relaxation come as he reached his decision.

He turned and looked Phillip full in the face. 'You're right. They aren't worth a shit. I've regretted accepting the bloody contract since the first day. Needless to say, Chalmers didn't tell me the full story until it was too late.'

'Well?'

West grinned broadly. For the first time in days he felt happy, almost light-hearted. 'I am, with your permission, going to eat my steak, drink a cup of strong coffee, and then go for a very long walk.'

'Do I have your word that you'll keep going?

And that you'll keep your mouth shut about all this?'

'For what it's worth, you have my word.'

'I think your word's worth quite a lot, Ron West, quite a lot. And you haven't really broken your word to Chalmers. After all, you wouldn't have been in a position to fulfil the contract. A dead man can't protect anyone, can he?'

West laughed outright. 'I don't think the logic of that would stand up to close examination, but I'm not going to argue. Now, those steaks should be ready. I'd better dish up.'

He dished the food out on to four plates, carefully ensuring that all shares were equal. When he'd finished he looked enquiringly at Phillip. 'Do I take this through to them and come back, or what?'

'Why not? Tell them you couldn't carry it all and that you'll join them later. Oh, and leave them a radio. I'll want to talk to them later.'

West loaded plates and cutlery on to a tray. 'I hope they bloody well choke on it,' he said acidly. 'Don't worry about them coming out here, by the way. They're too scared even to go for a piss.' Chuckling, he went out towards the hall.

When he got back, Phillip Ross had gone, and so had one plate of steak. He nodded approvingly. Careful man, he thought. I like his style. He sat down, shook tomato ketchup on to his chips and set to with an appetite and enjoyment he had not felt for some time. For him the battle was over.

He was still alive. And his leave had just started. He'd go and visit his daughter, he thought; Julie Thompson had reminded him strongly of her. When he'd finished his steak, he wiped his plate clean with a slice of brown bread, made himself a cup of coffee and drank it slowly, savouring every mouthful.

He set down the empty cup, stood up, and took the Uzi from its holster. When he had wiped it clean of fingerprints, he laid it down on the kitchen table and walked down the passage to the hall. He took a long farewell look around, then went out through the wrecked front door. He strode down the middle of the drive, keeping his chin in, his chest out and his shoulders back. His boots crunched loudly on the gravel. He felt eyes on him as he went, as he had done so often over the past few days. But this time he felt no uneasiness: Phillip Ross had given him free passage. He did not look back.

Phillip watched Ron West climb over the entrance gates and set off in the direction of civilization and a new campaign. Once West was clear, he returned to the house, went in through the kitchen and soft-footed down the passage to the hall. The sitting-room door was firmly shut.

Inside the room Chalmers and Martin had finished eating. Chalmers had only picked at his food. Martin had cleared his plate.

'Ron's taking his time,' said Martin uneasily.

'Perhaps he's taking a look around,' said Chalmers, but there was an edge of alarm in his voice, and he reached for the shotgun that leant against his chair and pointed it at the door.

Martin picked up his own gun and, for the umpteenth time, checked that it was loaded. The minutes ticked by as they waited for West to return. Two minutes, five, ten . . .

Chalmers grabbed a bottle of whisky from the table beside him, unscrewed the cap and took a long swig from the neck. The spirit burnt in his throat and warmed its way down to his stomach. He took another swig, then recapped the bottle. He offered it to Martin, who shook his head and continued to gaze at the door.

A crackle and buzz from the radio West had left on the table startled them. Instinctively they swung their shotguns towards the sound. A metallic voice came from the speaker: 'Kenny, come in. Over.'

Martin looked doubtfully at Chalmers. 'That didn't sound like Ron,' he said. He went over to the desk, hesitated for a moment, then reached out a reluctant hand to pick up the radio.

'Kenny, come in' – he snatched his hand away – 'over.'

He swung round to face Chalmers and there was dread in his eyes. 'That's Ross,' he said. 'That's fucking Ross's voice!'

Chalmers got slowly to his feet and came reluctantly over to join him. He stared down at the radio, then looked fearfully up at Martin. 'What does he want?' he whispered.

'He wants to fucking well kill us,' snapped Martin. 'That's what he wants. What the fuck do you think he's been doing all this time, playing fucking boy scouts?' He snatched up the radio and, his brain whirling, tried to decide whether to answer or to ignore it. He almost dropped it as it buzzed again and Phillip's voice came clearly through: 'Come in, Kenny. I know you can hear me.'

Swallowing hard, Martin took a firmer grip on the radio, pressed the transmit button and said, 'I hear you, Ross. Speak your piece. Over.'

'You're next, Kenny. West's out of it. You're the next one on my list. I just wanted you to know. Over.'

Martin avoided Chalmers's eye. The palms of his hands were greasy with sweat, and he had to grip the radio tightly to keep hold of it. He pressed the transmit button again. 'Fuck you, Ross!' he screamed defiantly. 'Come and get me!'

'I will,' came the mocking reply. 'See you soon. I'm nearer than you think. Out.'

The radio went dead. Martin slammed it down on to the table. He was very pale and his hands were unsteady. He clutched his shotgun tightly and swung round to face Chalmers, baring his teeth in a snarl of fear and rage. 'This is all your fucking fault. You had his mate murdered and now all of us fucking well have to die.' He flung the shotgun the length of the room. It thumped against the far wall, shattering an ornate mirror, spun down and clattered to the floor behind an armchair. He dragged his pistol from its shoulder holster and hurled it after the shotgun. 'I'm finished, Frank, out of it. You started it and you can finish it. On your fucking own.' He half ran to the door and reached out to turn the key.

The roar of Chalmers's shotgun filled the room. The heavy shot smashed Martin against the door and spun him round, a huge hole in his side. Blood gushed out down him and streamed on to the carpet.

Martin rammed his hand into the hole to try to staunch the blood and stared disbelievingly at Chalmers, who stood in front of him, smoke wisping from the hot barrel of the shotgun.

'No one walks out on Frank Chalmers, do you hear me? No one.' He pumped another shell into the chamber.

Martin staggered a step forward, his free hand held out in front of him as if to ward off the next shot. Pain and terror drained all colour from his face. 'No, Frank,' he begged. 'No—'

The shotgun roared again. The blast took Martin full in the face, blowing off the top of his head and splattering bone, blood and brain tissue over the door and walls behind him. He was slammed back against the door. Then he crumpled slowly, almost lazily, to the floor. His right hand twitched once, then relaxed.

For several minutes Chalmers stared down at the mess of blood, bone and guts that had once been his closest friend. The blood pumped a couple of times from the gory hole where the top of Martin's head had been, then slowed to a trickle. Chalmers shuddered violently and looked away. The shotgun slipped from his hand and thudded to the floor. He kicked it angrily away, turned and went back to his chair. He slumped into it and closed his eyes.

Half an hour passed. Chalmers sat motionless, his eyes still closed.

The thunder of machine-pistol fire shattered the silence. Splinters slashed through the air as the nine-millimetre slugs ripped through the wood round the lock and hinges of the door. Chalmers started and opened his eyes, but made no other move. He stared dully at the door.

Something thudded against it, and it fell into the room, toppling on to the mangled body of Kenny Martin. It rocked a couple of times, then was still.

A tall, dark-haired man filled the doorway. Blue eyes blazed in his blackened face; his clothing was that of a soldier on combat duty. The Uzi machine-pistol in his right hand swept the room and settled on Frank Chalmers, who sat motionless, staring at him.

Phillip flicked the light switches, flooding the dim room with light. Chalmers winced and screwed up his eyes. Phillip crossed the room with long, lithe strides. He removed the pistol from its holster under Chalmers's left arm and tossed it aside.

'So we meet at last,' said Phillip evenly. His face

creased with disgust as he studied the slumped and broken man in front of him. 'The big man. Frank Chalmers.'

Chalmers opened his eyes wide and stared up at him. 'I'm not armed,' he said. 'You can't kill an unarmed man.'

'Can't I?' Phillip was implacable. 'My friend Gary Thompson wasn't armed when you had him murdered.' He shoved the barrel of the Uzi hard against Chalmers's nostrils, forcing his head against the back of the chair. Blood started to trickle down his face.

'I want the name of the man who murdered him. And you, Frank, are going to give it to me. Now.'

Chalmers nodded, trying to press his head deeper into the chair-back.

Phillip pulled the gun away sharply. Its foresight snagged on Chalmers's nostril and tore it open. Chalmers yelped in pain and clutched his nose. Bright blood oozed though his fingers, and tears flooded his eyes.

Phillip produced a pencil and small notepad and threw them into Chalmers's lap. 'Write down his name, address and phone number. It will be incredibly painful . . . if you get it wrong.'

Chalmers scribbled shakily on the pad and passed it back to Phillip. 'That's the man you want. He's the one that killed your mate.'

Phillip glanced quickly down at the pad. 'Who ordered him to do it?' he asked icily.

Chalmers glanced over to the ~~wreckage~~ of the door. 'He did. Kenny Martin.'

'I expected as much from a shitheap like you,' said Phillip with icy contempt. He took his mobile phone from his pocket and threw it to Chalmers. 'Ring him. Get him out here. Tell him you want him to finish the job, that he's to come and kill Phillip Ross.'

'What if he won't come?'

'Persuade him. Offer him anything you like. He'll accept a tempting enough offer.' His eyes glittered wickedly as he said, 'If he doesn't, you will die . . . very slowly . . . and very . . . very . . . painfully . . .'

Chalmers fumbled with the buttons on the mobile. Phillip leant closer. 'Keep it away from your ear,' he ordered. 'I want to listen.' He pressed the barrel of the Uzi against the side of Chalmers's throat.

The phone rang several times before it was answered. 'Hello,' said a deep voice with a strong south London accent, 'Alex Gómez here.'

'Alex, this is Frank, Frank Chalmers.'

'Hello, Frank. Been expecting you to call. Where've you been hiding?'

Chalmers gulped. 'I've . . . er . . . I've had a sore throat, Alex. Been staying in the country for a bit.'

Gómez chuckled. 'Keeping your head down, eh, Frank?'

'Yeah, sort of. Look, Alex, I need to see you. Got a little job for you.'

There was a brief pause before Gómez said, 'If it's

the continuation of the last one, Frank, the price is going to be high, very high.'

'I'll pay you twenty-five grand to finish the job. I know where Ross is going to be tomorrow, so we can plan it tonight.' There was silence at the other end of the line. 'Alex? Can you hear me, Alex?'

'Yeah, I heard. I'm thinking on it.'

'Well make your fucking mind up. It could be your only chance to get him on his own.'

'On his own?'

'Yeah, on his own. I can't say more on the phone. If you're going to do it, say so now,' Chalmers demanded. 'I'll fill you in on the details when you get here.'

Phillip pressed the barrel of the Uzi harder against Chalmers's fat neck and whispered, 'Tell him you've got the money here. In cash.'

'I've got the cash here, ready, Alex.'

Gómez must have been able to hear the desperation in Chalmers's voice, because he decided to push a bit. 'If you make it fifty, Frank, I come straight away.'

'You got it,' rasped Chalmers. 'I'm at High Trees, my place in Sussex. It's just over an hour from Streatham.'

'Give me the address. I'll be right over.'

Chalmers slowly and clearly told him the address and gave him directions.

'Bit out of the way,' complained Gómez.

'Nice and peaceful.' Chalmers winced as the Uzi dug harder into his neck.

'OK, Frank, expect me in about . . . let's say an hour and a half.' A note of wariness crept into Gómez's voice. 'There's no one there, is there, Frank? Nothing out of order?'

'No, I'm on my own. I've sent the boys back to London, told them I'd follow later. I'll be waiting for you, Alex.'

'Good. I'm on my way.'

Phillip leant over and took the phone out of Chalmers's hand. 'For that you get to live a little longer, Frank.'

He produced lengths of nylon cord from his pocket, ordered Chalmers to stand up, and tied his hands behind his back. Then he shoved the fat man back into his chair and bound his ankles and knees. Satisfied that Chalmers was totally immobilized, he left the room. He had to open the gates to let Gómez's car in. And there were a few preparations to be made for when he arrived.

14

Alex Gómez smiled happily as he opened his garage door, switched on the light, and removed the dust-sheet from his six-year-old Mercedes 300D. It was his only luxury, his pride and joy. He stood back to admire the gleaming white coachwork, then glanced inside to savour the black leather upholstery. He patted the roof of the car, and spoke out loud to it: 'One last job, my beauty, and we're off home to Spain.' He had worked out that, with his savings, the sale of the café and the fifty grand he was about to collect, he would have enough to buy a small *tapas* bar, with enough left over not to have to worry too much about making a profit. He'd spend the rest of his life in his homeland drinking the local wine in his own establishment and chatting to his friends in the shade of a palm tree as he ate the locally caught seafood, peeled a locally grown orange and ate a few locally grown grapes.

Except for the occasional holiday, he'd not been

back for any length of time to the small village near Cádiz where he'd been born. He'd left as a child, with his parents, for his father had had to find work in England. Now he was ready to return, a rich and successful man, to be looked up to and respected by the villagers; the poor boy who'd gone to England with his parents to make his fortune – and succeeded.

Gómez walked to the rear of the garage, stepped up on to a packing case and reached into an air vent near the ceiling. He withdrew a parcel wrapped in oil-soaked cloth. Carefully he unwound the cloth and produced a Walther P38. From a small, rusty tin, he took two full clips of ammunition. He slid one into the butt of the pistol and slipped the other into the pocket of his long, dark overcoat. Even though it was hot, he wore his overcoat, a habit picked up from his long-dead father. It was a kind of uniform: it marked his station in life.

He sang happily as he drove across Purley Way, then along the Godstone road. He'd contact an estate agent first thing in the morning, he decided, and put the café on the market. It didn't occur to him to wonder how his wife would react to being uprooted from her home and asked to start all over again in a strange village. She would do as she was told. She always had and she always would. But perhaps, once he was well-established in Spain, he'd allow himself the pleasure of a discreet liaison with a younger, more beautiful and, above all, close-mouthed woman. Money might not be able to buy happiness, but it could certainly buy some of the trappings that went with it.

Fifty grand, to kill one man, he thought, and laughed out loud. This particular man, though, had been a member of the SAS, hadn't he? For a moment Gómez felt a cold uneasiness, but he shrugged it off. He'd just creep up behind him and blow his fucking brains out. It'd be a piece of cake, he assured himself. He pressed harder on the accelerator, and the Mercedes responded with a surge of speed.

The entrance gates of High Trees loomed up in the beam of the car's headlights, and Gómez swung the car in through them. He could see the distant glow of lights from the house as the car crunched up the gravel drive.

He braked to a halt outside the front door. The door was wide open and the porch and hall lights were on. Otherwise the house was in darkness.

Gómez climbed out of the car and slammed the door. He looked at the front of the house, and noticed that all the windows had been smashed. The curtains fluttered in the night breeze. Alarm bells rang in his head. He called out, 'Frank, it's me, Alex,' and drew his gun. He pulled the slide back and checked as a bullet nosed its way into the breech, then let the slide move forward with a metallic click.

'Frank,' he called again. 'It's Alex. Where are you?' He backed towards the car.

'Gómez' – the harsh voice seemed to echo in the darkness – 'drop the pistol and put your hands in the air.'

Gómez swung in the direction of the voice. Fingers of fear clawed at his stomach. He peered into the gloom, and fired three quick, spaced shots into the thick bushes from where he thought the voice had come.

'Drop the gun,' the voice commanded again. It came from a different direction, this time, from his left. Gómez spun round, his feet swirling and kicking up gravel, and fired again. Two quick shots. The Walther bucked in his hand.

'Gómez, drop the gun,' this time from behind him.

He swung round in panic. His hands were shaking and wet with the sweat of fear. 'Come out where I can see you,' he yelled.

A footstep crunched in the gravel behind him. A cold, hard voice said, 'Drop it.'

Gómez turned his head and looked back fearfully over his shoulder. He saw a tall, dark figure, blackened face, combat camouflage. The barrel of a pump-action shotgun, a gaping black hole.

Life went into slow motion for Gómez as he spun, bringing the Walther to bear on the soldier. He saw the flash from the barrel of the shotgun, flame licking out into the night air, saw in his mind's eye his dream of a *tapas* bar shatter, as the heavy shot ripped into his shoulder, tearing flesh and splintering bone.

The force of the blow knocked the Walther from his grasp and spun him against the Mercedes. He sprawled across the bonnet, and saw streaks of red splash over his cherished white coachwork.

Rough hands pulled him upright and turned him round. He cradled his useless left arm in his right hand. Staggering, he was pushed towards the door of the house. As he neared it he could see that what he had taken for the front door was in fact a makeshift. What the fuck had been going on here? He was shoved rapidly through the hall and into a darkened room – he tripped and fell headlong, screaming as the fall jolted his shattered shoulder.

The lights flicked on. Gómez stared around. He had tripped over a door that had been smashed off its hinges and fallen into the room to rest on . . . His stomach heaved and bile flooded into his mouth as he saw a man's head, the top half of the skull blown away to expose sticky grey brain tissue streaked with blood. He looked hastily away; and saw Frank Chalmers sitting in an armchair, his hands behind his back, his ankles and knees tied together.

Gómez looked up at the soldier. Merciless blue eyes stared back. The man was holding his, Gómez's, own Walther P38, as well as the shotgun.

An eight-inch hunting knife thudded to the floor. 'Pick it up and cut Chalmers free,' ordered Phillip Ross.

Gómez staggered to his feet, cradling his left arm, and crossed the room. He cut the cords binding

Chalmers's legs, then, as Chalmers leant forwards, sliced through the ties round his wrists. Chalmers stood up, rubbing his wrists.

'You knew this bastard was here when you rang me,' said Gómez venomously, 'didn't you? I tell you, Frank, you're a dead man.'

Chalmers didn't answer. He gave Gómez a sour, 'fuck you' look, which froze on his face as Gómez, smiling wickedly, plunged the knife into his stomach and then staggered back, his eyes half crazed with pain and satisfaction.

Chalmers shrieked. He grasped the knife in both hands and pulled it out, releasing a flow of blood that ran down his belly and legs to the floor. Dropping the knife, he clutched at the wound and collapsed back into his chair, keening with pain and shock.

The two wounded men stared at Phillip Ross, who reached into his kitbag and produced two bottles of clear pinkish fluid. A cotton wick protruded from the neck of each bottle and hung down the neck.

Phillip looked at Gómez and said, 'No need to tell you what these are.' He smiled grimly. 'And there are no prizes for guessing what happens next.'

Clutching his belly, Chalmers struggled out of his chair in terror. 'You ain't going to burn us alive?'

Phillip raised the shotgun and squeezed the trigger. The shot tore a hole in Chalmers's left shoulder and flung him back into the chair.

'My friend Gary Thompson was shot like that, in the shoulder, with a shotgun.' Phillip flicked his

Zippo lighter and lit the fuse of one of the petrol bombs. He hurled it against the far wall of the room, and it exploded in a sheet of orange flame. Searing heat blasted through the room.

Gómez backed away, his good hand shielding his face. Chalmers, screaming as his face and hands were scorched, fought his way up from his chair, his right hand pressed hard against the knife wound. He lurched away from the fire, which had taken hold strongly. The curtains were ragged banners of flame, and tongues of flame were licking out across the ceiling.

Phillip lit the second fuse. 'This is the only way out, gentlemen,' he said as he backed out of the room, and he threw the petrol bomb hard against the door-jamb so that it smashed and bounced back into the sitting-room, filling the doorway with fire.

Gómez was first through the flaming doorway. He was screaming as he stumbled blindly though into the hall, his hair and clothing beginning to catch alight. He felt heavy-calibre slugs thud into his body. He staggered for a moment as he remembered, tottered as he stared at the man who had killed him . . . Then his legs failed him, and he collapsed. The shock of his fall extinguished the flames in his clothes; smoke rose gently from his body.

Squealing like a stuck pig, Chalmers lurched though the flames. His bulk and forward thrust absorbed the impact of the steel-jacketed nine-millimetre slugs that tore into his chest, tumbled through his body and exited in a spray of red, leaving holes the size and colour of ripe plums in his back. As his legs started to fail him, he tripped over Gómez and slid along the polished floor. He rolled over in agony and stared up into the implacable face of Phillip Ross. 'Help me!' he implored, his face a red, swollen mass of bubbling, blistering flesh. A blackened, blistered, swollen hand reached out in entreaty.

'Yes, I'll help you,' said Phillip flatly. He raised the pistol.

Chalmers turned his head away from the black barrel that promised death. He tried to move his arms and legs, to crawl away. They didn't respond. He was paralysed. He coughed, and tasted blood. He felt the cold steel of the pistol barrel touch the soft skin behind his right ear. He heard, like an echo from a vast distance, Phillip Ross say, 'I'll help you, Chalmers. This is how Gary Thompson died.'

Chalmers tried to shake his head in protest. A great roar came from his throat: 'No-o-o! It isn't fair!' His shout was drowned by a massive boom as his head exploded into a rainbow of brilliant colour, which turned instantly to dead black.

In two long, quick strides, Phillip was standing over Gómez. He pressed the pistol barrel behind Gómez's right ear. Gómez's eyes flickered open and turned to look up at Phillip.

Phillip smiled like iron. 'I'm glad you waited for the *coup de grâce*, Gómez.'

'Fuck you, Ross.'
'This is from Gary.' And he pulled the trigger.

Phillip retreated fast from the scorching heat of the flames. The sitting-room was now an inferno and it would not take long for the fire to spread to the rest of the house. He went out on to the driveway and crossed to Gómez's Mercedes. The splash of blood that streaked the car's bonnet was still wet and tacky. He dipped his gloved forefinger into it and drew a skull and crossbones, then wrote on the gleaming white paint,

DANGER! THE GROUNDS OF THIS HOUSE ARE MINED WITH HIGH EXPLOSIVES. CALL BOMB SQUAD!

He made his way down the drive to the point where he'd laid his master wire to the grenades and gave it a sharp tug. Instantly, there was a massive explosion and a blinding flash of light as the whole string of grenades detonated in unison.

Phillip grinned. If that doesn't attract attention, nothing will, he thought. He turned and climbed up to the hillside beside his dug-out. He sat there and watched the house burn until he was satisfied that the fire brigade would have no chance of saving it, that it would be totally destroyed. Then he slung his pack on his back and walked wearily back to the BMW.

He stopped at the first phone box he found and,

having dialled 999, in an Irish accent informed an astonished operator that High Trees was burning and that the grounds of the house were liberally sown with anti-personnel mines. He gave a codeword used by the IRA in their bomb warnings. That done, he got back into the car and drove fast back to the cottage.

He let himself in silently and cat-footed through to the kitchen, where he stripped off his smoke-stinking clothes, scrubbed the blacking off his face and washed and washed until he felt clean inside and out. Only then did he go through to the bedroom.

Julie was deeply asleep. She stirred when he slipped in beside her, and came slowly to the surface when he took her gently in his arms and held her close against his heart.

'Phillip, is it over?' she asked, her voice still soft with sleep. 'Is it finished?'

'Yes, sweetheart, it's over. The murderers are all dead. Go back to sleep now. I'll tell you about it in the morning.'

She switched on the bedside light and gave him a long, assessing look. 'All right, darling,' she said. 'In the morning will do fine.' She switched the light out and nestled closer in his arms. Phillip, exhausted, was soon asleep, but Julie lay for a long time listening to the sound of his deep, even breathing as she stared into the darkness.

* * *

In the morning Phillip was awoken by the aroma of freshly ground coffee. He opened his eyes to see Julie waving a steaming mug six inches from his nose.

'It's nearly noon,' she said. 'How does the thought of coffee and breakfast in bed grab you?'

'Like a crocodile.'

She laughed, turned round and lifted from the chest of drawers a tray which bore a plate of bacon, eggs, fried bread, mushrooms, sausage and tomatoes; orange juice, the coffee pot, milk jug, toast, butter, Cooper's marmalade; even a single carnation, of a red so deep as to be almost black, tucked into his napkin ring.

Phillip blinked.

'Now tell me, while you eat,' she said.

She was very quiet as he talked. Much of what he said seemed to trouble her. But she smiled her pleasure when Phillip told her how Ron West had taken his chance and walked away from the fight.

'I'm so glad,' she said. 'He saved me from that man, and he was kind to me after . . . after . . .' She couldn't finish the sentence. 'And he said he's got a daughter about my age.'

They spent a quiet day, packing their belongings and cleaning the cottage. Phillip phoned Peter Russell, brought him up to date, in carefully worded sentences, and told him they'd soon be leaving the cottage.

'Leave it to me, Phil. I'll see that the place is cleared up, and get Julie's parents back home to

Dover. See you when you get back from France.'
Clearly Russell was taking no chances. 'We'll have a
couple of drinks and you can fill me in on the details
of your holiday then.'

Phillip promised that indeed they would, then
thanked him and rang off.

Julie dropped him off at Gatwick Airport and
drove straight down to Dover to get her parents'
house ready for their return. She planned to cook
them a very special welcome-home dinner, with
wine, flowers and candles, and she wanted the house
to be fresh and clean for them.

Meanwhile, a certain Anthony Robert Cole flew
on a one-way ticket to Charles de Gaulle Airport in
Paris. He took a taxi into the centre of Paris, booked
into a small private hotel and went out for a meal.

The following morning he went by taxi to the
garage to collect his Range Rover.

The proprietor was surprised and pleased to see
him. 'Ah, monsieur, I was not expecting you for a
week or two. But do not worry. Your Range Rover
is ready and waiting for you.' He explained that the
timing had been out and the new exhaust box had
been fitted only two days previously.

Phillip was pleased to see that the vehicle was
tucked away in a corner of the big workshop and
covered by dust-sheets.

The proprietor was pleased to see a large wad of
francs emerge from Phillip's wallet as he said he'd
like to pay the bill. He was even more pleased when

Phillip said he wouldn't be needing a receipt; the francs vanished instantly into the hip pocket of his overalls.

The Range Rover was divested of its dust-sheets and brought out to the forecourt. Phillip thanked the proprietor again and drove off. He picked up the Paris ring-road and circled round to the south, fighting his way across three lanes as the sign for Le Mans and Rennes came into view. He'd decided to spend a few days camping and fishing in Brittany to unwind and to establish some sort of alibi.

Six days later he arrived at Dover docks, after a calm crossing from Calais. He made a point of dropping his passport and having to climb out of the Range Rover to retrieve it. The immigration officer was irritated at the hold-up and showed it. Phillip smiled: the officer would remember him.

He was delayed a little at Customs. An officer who had clearly got out of the wrong side of bed that morning poked at Phillip's luggage, tapped the Range Rover's door panels and looked suspiciously at the bumpers, spare wheel, tool kit and anything else that took his notice. Finally, though, he waved the vehicle officiously through and Phillip drove out of the docks and straight to the Thompsons' house.

Mary and Victor Thompson greeted him like a returning hero. Mary fussed around him and insisted on bringing out tea and cakes, despite his assurances that he'd had a proper meal on the boat.

Julie's joy at seeing him back, looking relaxed

and at peace with himself, shone in her eyes, but after the first hug and kiss, she hung back and let her parents make much of him. They were full of questions about his future plans, but shied away from asking about the Chalmers gang and Julie's kidnap, of which they knew little.

Not until Julie and Mary had taken the tea things out into the kitchen, and then gone for a walk round the garden, did Victor raise the subject.

'So it's all over,' he said. 'My son has been avenged, and we have nothing to fear for the future.'

Phillip smiled and nodded. 'It's all over. Finished and done with. We can all get on with our lives in peace.'

Victor muttered thickly, 'Thank you, Phillip. Let's say no more about the matter.' He gazed for a moment at the photograph of his dead son, then fished for a handkerchief and blew his nose hard.

Phillip waited until he had regained his composure, then asked diffidently, 'Would you approve, sir, if I asked Julie to marry me?'

Victor's face was transformed. He leapt to his feet, beaming with happiness, shook Phillip's hand vigorously and clapped him on the shoulder. 'Approve? I'd be delighted – more than delighted – and so would Mary. You know we've always looked on you' – his voice faltered for a second – 'as our second son.'

Phillip smiled. 'Of course, I haven't asked her yet.' He became serious. 'She may say no.'

'Nonsense, my boy. Mary and I know how much

she thinks of you. She'll accept, I know she will. In fact I shouldn't be at all surprised if she and Mary are talking about it at this very moment.'

Phillip proposed to Julie at the end of the breakwater of the eastern harbour of Dover Docks. She flung herself into his arms, gave him a smacking kiss, and said, 'Yes, darling, oh yes, oh yes, oh yes.' He lifted her off her feet and swung her round in circles, both of them laughing with joy.

'Put me down, darling,' said Julie, suddenly serious. She pulled slightly away from him, leant back against his arms and looked up at him shyly. 'Would . . . Do you . . . When would you want to start a family, Phillip?'

Phillip was startled for a moment. 'I don't know.' He smiled down into her eyes. 'I'll leave that up to you. Straight away if you like.'

She hid her face against his shoulder and said, her voice muffled by his coat, 'That's fortunate. You see, I've missed my period. I've never been late before.'

Phillip gaped. Then his face lit up and he took her face between his hands and kissed her forehead, her eyelids, the tip of her nose, and lastly her lips. 'In that case,' he said joyfully, 'we'd better get married as soon as possible.' He turned on his heel, pulling her by the hand, and let out a whoop of happiness. 'Come on. Let's go and tell your parents the good news.'

'Not about the maybe-baby,' cautioned Julie. 'It

may not be true. It could be just the stress of these last weeks. Let's not count our chickens just yet. But about us getting married, you bet. I happen to know that Dad's got two bottles of champagne stashed away – and he's been refusing to say what they're for.'

Hand in hand and laughing like teenagers, they ran back up the breakwater towards the town.

Epilogue

Phillip and Julie were married at Dover register office three weeks later. Mary and Victor Thompson had wanted them to take their time and have a proper church wedding, but they were adamant that they would get married as soon as possible. Mary, being no one's fool, and noticing how radiant her daughter had begun to look, stopped protesting and talked her husband into accepting his daughter's wishes.

The following months passed quickly. Phillip sold his flat and, after a long search, the couple found a semi-detached three-bedroom house in a quiet road in Farleigh in Surrey. The house had a large garden, and the countryside was within easy reach, something they agreed was essential. They were determined their children wouldn't grow up thinking milk came from a bottle, not a cow, or never seeing wild flowers and animals.

As he signed the cheque for the house, Phillip

couldn't help but be ironically aware that it was Frank Chalmers's hundred grand that made the purchase possible. He pushed the thought hastily away: that was all behind him now; this was a new life, a fresh start.

Having found a home, the next thing they had to decide was what sort of work Phillip was going to do.

'I must do something, love,' he insisted. 'I can't sit around here all day, just watching you get bigger and fatter.'

Julie aimed a mock blow at him. 'There won't be much sitting done. The windows in the kitchen still need painting, and the cellar could do with another coat of whitewash, and the loft isn't insulated yet, and when you've done that you can start digging where I want the vegetable garden. And then, of course—'

Phillip put his hand over her mouth. 'Peace, woman,' he said sternly. 'I'm beginning to think you only married me for my skill with a paintbrush and a screwdriver.'

She tickled him until he yelped and let her go.

'All right,' she said, 'let's be serious for a moment. Can you honestly see yourself as a wage-slave for the rest of your life? Battling with the rush-hour every day, and going to boring meetings about meetings week in, week out?'

'God no!' said Phillip, appalled. 'Eventually I'll want my own business again. Of course I will. But

368

we haven't got a lot of money left, what with buying the house and doing it up, so I'll have to get some kind of job to keep us going until I find the right opening, won't I?'

Julie thought for a minute. 'It would be nice if you could find something fairly close by,' she said diffidently, 'so that you're around while I'm pregnant. Something that doesn't involve you travelling for hours a day, or even having to be away for days on end. It's not that I'm scared of having the baby, it's just that I'd like you around so that we can share things.'

Phillip kissed her. 'My lady's wish is my command.'

He found work with a Croydon-based electrical-appliance company, as the manager of one of their branches. Julie giggled like a schoolgirl when he told her.

'Oh Phillip, I wish I could see you in action, telling Mrs Smith all about the merits of this washing machine or that cooker.'

He gave her a gentle clip round the ear.

The job was as boring as he'd feared it would be, but he gave it his best. He pressed his staff constantly to improve sales, and because he involved them in discussions on how this could be achieved, and because they saw how hard he worked himself, they responded enthusiastically, and worked well and willingly for him. Turnover increased, and the company directors were well pleased. They even gave everyone a small bonus.

The months passed peacefully. Julie's pregnancy was trouble-free, and she took much pleasure in the garden as spring came in and her seedlings flourished. At Easter she gave birth to a healthy boy. He weighed in at eight pounds, three ounces, had all his fingers and toes in the right places, a shock of black hair and blue-green eyes. They named him Gary.

When Gary was a little over two months old, his mother decided it was time he came on his first shopping expedition. At ten o'clock on a bright, sunny morning, she parked her Volkswagen Golf in the multi-storey car park off Park Lane, Croydon. She hoisted the baby out of the back seat, sat him in the baby buggy her parents had bought him, tucked his rug round him, and set off for the shops. She reckoned she had plenty of time to get everything she needed before meeting Phillip for lunch at noon.

Phillip spotted Julie as she waited to cross the busy street at the traffic lights, her blonde hair dancing in the wind. She waved to him, then bent over Gary, pointed to Phillip, laughed and whispered something in the baby's ear. The traffic lights turned red and the waiting pedestrians began to cross.

Tyres shrieking, a Jaguar with five men inside swung broadside into the street from the main road. At the last minute the driver saw the people crossing the road and leant on his horn as he accelerated away. Pedestrians scattered in all directions. In the distance a police car's siren could be heard. Phillip ran frantically forward.

Julie was caught by the Jaguar's nearside wing and flung fifteen feet into the air. She landed as limply as a rag doll, her head on the edge of the pavement, her body sprawled in the road. The baby buggy spun wildly, tipped over and came to rest in the gutter.

He knew as soon as he reached her that she was dead. There was no trace of a pulse, and the wounds where the car had hit her bled hardly at all. Her green eyes were half open, unblinking. Phillip caught her in his arms, screaming over and over again inside his head, 'No! No! No-o-o!' It wasn't real, it couldn't be happening, not this, not Julie, not Julie as well as Gary. A woman passer-by who had seen her pushing the buggy picked up the screaming baby and brought him over, but Phillip had thoughts only for Julie. The woman cradled Gary in her arms, rocked him and hushed him until he cried himself into an exhausted sleep.

Ambulances soon arrived. One of the paramedics came straight over to Phillip, and gently persuaded him to let Julie go. After examining her, he shook his head sadly and rested a hand on Phillip's shoulder. 'I'm sorry, sir,' he said, 'very sorry. There's nothing we can do for her.' He paused for a moment, then went on, 'We'll have to take her to hospital now. Would you like to come with her in the ambulance?'

Phillip nodded numbly. He took Gary in his arms,

somehow regaining enough self-control to thank the woman who'd cared for him, and climbed into the ambulance.

He had no idea how long he waited at the hospital before a tired-eyed young doctor came out and told him Julie had been pronounced dead on arrival. Time had no meaning. Over and over again, there flashed before his eyes that split-second glimpse of the Jaguar, the driver's stocking-masked face as he gunned the car away, three masked faces looking out of the rear window, the letter and first digit of the number plate. He knew that image would remain with him for as long as he lived.

Three weeks later a pale, drawn Phillip Ross was shown into the office of Chief Inspector George Hill of the murder squad at New Scotland Yard. They exchanged the usual civilities, while Sergeant Thorpe went to fetch some coffee.

Hill waited for Thorpe to close the door behind him, then said gruffly, 'I was terribly sorry to hear about your wife, Mr Ross. It was a dreadful thing, tragic.'

Phillip raised a hand. 'Thank you, Mr Hill, I appreciate your sympathy. But sympathy isn't what I need. What I need is to know that you've caught the men who killed her.'

Hill dropped his eyes to the blotter on his desk. 'I can't give you that comfort, Mr Ross, because we haven't caught them. They got away. They were being chased by one of our cars, but when it reached the scene of the accident it couldn't get through after them, not without hitting people who were already injured, some of them seriously. The car was stolen, of course. We recovered it later that day, abandoned a few miles away. But the thieves had worn gloves the whole time they were in it. We haven't so much as a single fingerprint by way of evidence.'

Phillip digested this for a minute, then tossed a manila envelope on to Hill's desk and said, with an edge to his voice, 'Well, here are some crimes you *can* solve.'

Hill gave him a long, measuring look before opening the envelope and taking out two typewritten sheets of paper. The first was headed 'The Signed Confession of Phillip Ross'. He raised his eyebrows and began to read; Phillip watched him in silence.

When he had finished, Hill grunted to himself, and ran his hands over the bald dome of his head, ruffling his horseshoe of grey hair. He put the confession back in its envelope, dropped the envelope into the right-hand drawer of his desk, and stared blandly at Phillip.

'Well,' demanded Phillip after a long pause, 'aren't you going to arrest me?'

Hill smiled kindly. 'I know you're still deeply distressed over the death of your wife, Mr Ross.' He shrugged. 'We get all sorts of people, mostly cranks, coming in here to confess to crimes they haven't committed. If I locked them all up . . .'

Phillip started to protest, but Hill waved him to silence. He got up from his desk, went over to the window and looked out over the traffic below.

'We have a very good idea who killed your wife, Mr Ross.' He turned to face Phillip. 'They are at this moment sunning themselves in Spain, spending the proceeds of the bank robbery they'd just carried out. Now, if you go to prison for a crime or crimes that you may or may not have committed, and we can't prove a case against these men, so can't get them extradited' – he grinned evilly, crossed back to his desk, took a folder from one of the drawers, and tossed it down in front of Phillip – 'who, Mr Ross, who, I ask you, is going to nail these bastards?'